The Professor Woos The Witch
Nocturne Falls, Book Four

Kristen Painter

THE PROFESSOR WOOS THE WITCH:
Nocturne Falls, Book Four

Copyright © 2015 Kristen Painter

All rights reserved. No part of this book may be reproduced in any form or by any electronic or mechanical means, including information storage and retrieval systems—except in the case of brief quotations embodied in critical articles or reviews—without permission in writing from the author.

This book is a work of fiction. The characters, events, and places portrayed in this book are products of the author's imagination and are either fictitious or are used fictitiously. Any similarity to real person, living or dead, is purely coincidental and not intended by the author.

ISBN-13: 978-1-941695-14-2
ISBN-10: 1-941695-14-0

Published in the United States of America.

Welcome to Nocturne Falls, the town that celebrates Halloween 365 days a year. The tourists think it's all a show: the vampires, the werewolves, the witches, the occasional gargoyle flying through the sky. But the supernaturals populating the town know better.

Living in Nocturne Falls means being yourself. Fangs, fur, and all.

Pandora Williams is Nocturne Falls' most successful real estate agent. And least successful witch. Her magic never has the intended outcome, but she's learned to live with that. Mostly. Yes, it sucks, but what can she do? Then a hot new neighbor shows up and suddenly her magic works. Very cool, but very suspect. Especially since he's a total non-believer.

Cole Van Zant likes practicality and absolutes. Things he can see and touch. So not magic. But when his teenage daughter insists she's a witch—and they're now living in a town that celebrates Halloween every day—he needs help. Of the witchy variety. Thankfully, his sexy neighbor buys into all that hocus pocus.

Enlisting her help seems like a great idea until spending time together reveals a supernatural surprise about who Cole really is. A secret even he didn't know. Could Pandora and Cole really be meant for one another or is their attraction too much to believe?

*Dedicated to all my readers
with endless thanks for being so awesome
and keeping me going.*

1

Cole Van Zant's running shoes pounded the well-maintained sidewalks of his Nocturne Falls neighborhood. Restoring the house he'd just inherited usually gave him plenty of exercise, but tonight, after the blowout with Kaley, he'd needed to run. And think. Things had changed so much so fast.

This was the first September in many years that he wasn't standing in front of a classroom full of freshmen explaining the intricacies of higher math. Teaching math in some form had been Cole's life until he'd taken a sabbatical from East State University, but if he was going to restore this house to its maximum resale potential, taking a year off was the only way to do it.

And really, the sale of the house would yield more money than he could ever hope to make teaching for the next few years.

The money that had come with the inheritance of the house was making everything possible, including the temporary move to Nocturne Falls. He'd known he had family in Georgia, but until he'd gotten the news that Ulysses Pilcher, his great-uncle on his mother's side, had passed and left Cole everything (everything meaning a three-story Victorian-style mansion and a nice chunk of change) Cole hadn't known this crazy town existed.

The downside was that the chunk of change from the inheritance was probably going to get eaten up making the house saleable.

The upside was that selling the house should net him a decent-size nest egg that'd grow into a huge nest egg for Kaley's college fund and his retirement years. And seeing as how working construction had been his summer job for more years than he'd been teaching, he could do most of the repairs and restoration himself.

He took the next left, intent on making a wide square around the neighborhood.

Kaley hadn't wanted to leave North Carolina to come to Georgia, and frankly, Cole hadn't wanted to bring her with him. He'd already talked to his dad about Kaley staying with him until Cole finished the house, but then she'd Googled the town of Nocturne Falls. After that, her attitude had done a one-eighty, and she'd pitched a bloody fit until he'd agreed to let her come.

He understood that a town where Halloween was celebrated every day must seem like a fun way to live to a kid of thirteen.

He'd explained that moving meant leaving her friends and going to a new school for a year, but she hadn't cared. Instead, she'd clung to the fact that it was the perfect town for a witch-in-training like herself.

Which was what had started the current and ongoing round of arguments. Cole had stopped trying to explain to his daughter that there were no such things as witches. Sure, there were Wiccans, but *not* the kinds of witches she was talking about, the kind she saw in movies and on TV, the ones who waved their hands and wiggled their noses and made magic happen. Those did not exist.

Kaley insisted. Cole rebutted her. And so on and so on.

He blamed Lila for that particular issue.

Lila. Just thinking her name made his vision go red around the edges. She was reason enough for a man to never want to be involved with a woman again. Cole concentrated on breathing out when his left foot struck the ground, a technique he'd read about that was supposed to prevent cramping up, and tried to keep his stride easy despite the charge of anger in his system.

Lila hadn't been in Kaley's life in a meaningful way for a long time. A once-a-month phone call and the rare, maybe yearly visit didn't constitute active parenting. But then, Lila wasn't legally Kaley's parent anymore. Lila and Cole had been divorced since Kaley was nine, which was when he'd gotten full custody too.

For Lila to just out of the blue drop the kid a letter when she turned thirteen and announce, *You're a witch now!*—that was so...Lila.

Sweat trickled down his back. It was one thing for Lila to live under the crazy delusion that she was a master of all things hocus-pocus (which she wasn't), but to make Kaley think it was somehow her birthright? To tell the kid she'd so casually left behind that any day now Kaley should be coming into her powers was just cruel. Especially when she hadn't bothered to be in Kaley's life with any kind of consistency for the last six years.

Cole swore between measured breaths. Maybe his ex-wife *was* a witch. Once upon a time, she'd certainly charmed him into thinking she was sweet and wonderful. That hadn't lasted long, though. He'd stayed for Kaley.

The same moody, eye-rolling teen who was currently not speaking to him.

He turned the corner and headed home, slowing down to cool off. The house loomed ahead as twilight fell. Even in this light, the paint looked sad through the wrought-iron fence that surrounded the once impressive property. One more thing to add to his list of jobs.

He jogged through the open gate, past the dumpster in the driveway, already half-full with junk from the house, up the steps of the front porch and stopped for a stretch. He'd check in with Kaley, take a hot shower, heat up some leftovers for dinner and then hit the sack. Tomorrow he hoped to tackle the final cleanout of the first floor. Then maybe he could get started on demolishing the kitchen. It would mean they'd have to rely on takeout for a bit, but Kaley had yet to complain about pizza.

Actually, until Lila's letter, Kaley had never been much of a complainer. Of course, she was just now hitting the dreaded teen years, so maybe that was all about to change. He sighed and went inside. "Kaley? Sweetheart? I'm back."

No response. Not that he really expected one. She was probably in her room, earbuds firmly tucked in, tablet on her lap and open to yet another online witch wannabe forum. He sprinted up the steps and knocked at her door. It swung open.

He stuck his head in. "Kaley, I—" She wasn't in her room.

He walked into his room at the end of the hall and looked out the rear windows into the thicket that was the backyard. Not there either, that he could see. Maybe she was on the back porch. Downstairs he went. Back porch was empty.

A small thread of alarm unraveled in his brain. She had to be in the house. He opened the basement door. A wave of mustiness rose up to greet him. He wrinkled his nose. It was dark and damp and packed to the rafters with boxes of whatever his great-uncle had decided had value. No way she was down there. Not in the dark. "Kaley?"

He got the answer he'd been expecting. Silence.

He ran up the steps and checked all the rooms on the second floor. She was probably taking a shower. But the shower wasn't running. And she wasn't in any of the other rooms, which were as filled with stuff as the basement.

That left the attic. It was a big space. The whole third floor. They'd been up there once when they'd first arrived. It had junk in it too, but not nearly as much as the other floors, and unlike in the rest of the house, the junk up there was organized. Also slightly creepy. They'd found a box of animal bones on a shelf next to rows and rows of old glass jars, some empty, some not.

He took a breath. For a girl who fancied herself a witch-in-training, that would probably be the perfect place to retreat from her less-than-understanding father. He snorted softly and went up the last flight of steps.

But his search came to an end when he opened the attic door. The light was off. He highly doubted Kaley would be up here in the dark. He flipped the switch, and the bare overhead bulbs flickered on. The attic was empty.

Kaley was gone.

Pandora Williams dropped her purse and her briefcase on the table by the front door, kicked her shoes off, grabbed her chubby cat, Pumpkin, and headed for the bedroom to change. She gave Pumpkin's pudgy belly a squeeze. "How was your day, sweetums? A lot more relaxed than mine, I'm guessing."

She plopped the purring cat onto the bed and opened a drawer to retrieve her at-home clothes: gym shorts and a tank top. She had stacks of each because they were the best way she knew to stay comfy and beat the Georgia heat, which lingered, even in September.

She shucked her pantsuit and changed with a satisfied sigh. It had been a *long* day. Busy, which was good, always good, but she was beat. Two closings, a brand new listing and a showing. Being Nocturne Falls' most popular real estate agent had its perks, but kept her moving too. She grabbed the first ponytail elastic she saw and knotted her hair on top of her head. Being a witch? That just gave her a little edge. She understood her supernatural customers much better than any human realtor could.

Pumpkin waddled behind Pandora as she headed to the kitchen. She grabbed a bottle of pinot grigio from the wine fridge, set it on the counter, then spiraled her fingers around the top.

The foil unwound in a long strip, like an apple peeling. Then she curled her fingers upwards. The cork wiggled free with a soft pop, flew across the room and ricocheted off the sliding doors that led to the backyard. She sighed. Her magic had always been faulty at best which was why she only used it for very small things, if at all. At least she hadn't broken anything. This time.

She talked to Pumpkin, who was now winding around her legs meowing for a snack, as she reached for a glass. "I know you want treats, but a little running around in the yard would be a lot better for you."

Pumpkin meowed again and pawed at Pandora's leg.

"Yes, I know. You want food. But you're fat. And you're on a diet. If you'd just spend time on the treadmill every morning like I do, this wouldn't be a problem. Let's go outside, and maybe you can run off a few calories."

Pumpkin's diet had only started two days ago,

and it was already clear that the cat thought very little of it.

She pawed at Pandora in one more feeble attempt at treats.

"I'm sorry, but that's just how it is." Pandora poured a big glug of wine into a double-walled insulated cup (not the classiest thing to drink wine out of, but she was home, wearing ratty gym shorts and a bedazzled tank top missing half its rhinestones, and who cared anyway), then headed for the back porch. She flipped the switch for the ceiling fans but left the lights off. The sun had just started to set, and there was still plenty of light to see by.

Besides, this was her favorite time of day, that last hour or so before the world went completely dark but the air was still sweet with the scent of flowers and grass. Everything just seemed to quiet down and breathe easy as the day slipped into night. Twilight was enjoyed by a lot of supernaturals, not just witches, but her witchiness made her especially appreciative of nature.

She stood at the sliding door, waiting for Pumpkin. "C'mon, poky cat."

Pumpkin plodded out onto the patio, and Pandora shut the sliders. The orange butterball made it about three steps before she flopped down, rolled over and lay with all four paws in the air. The ceiling fans ruffled her tummy fur.

Pandora shook her head and snorted softly. "Pumpkin, you're a mess. That is no way to burn calories." She bent and scratched the cat's belly. "Mama loves you, baby. We can both be a mess together."

She sat down on the glider and kicked her feet up on the rattan coffee table. Her yard was looking good thanks to the nights of work she'd put in weeding the flower beds and adding a flat of yellow and purple petunias.

A long sip of wine and she settled a little deeper into the glider. Pumpkin hadn't moved. Pandora reached for the bag of treats she kept on the side table.

The first crinkle of foil and Pumpkin's head came up, eyes wide. It was the closest thing to a sit-up the cat was capable of.

Pandora laughed. "You're so predictable." She fished a treat out and tossed it into the stone path that led from the patio back to the shed, about five feet from where Pumpkin lay.

The cat watched it land, then stared wistfully after it, but didn't move.

Pandora's brows lifted in disbelief. "Seriously?" She tossed a second one. It landed close to the first.

Pumpkin took a moment to consider it, then finally rolled onto her feet and trotted after it.

Pandora tossed a third treat farther along the

path. "I hope you know food-induced exercise probably doesn't count."

Pumpkin didn't seem to care. Pandora sealed the bag of treats and went back to sipping her wine. Pumpkin found the third treat, then got distracted by a bug and gave chase. Pandora nodded in satisfaction. "My plan worked."

She watched her orange fluff ball traipse around the yard, sniffing flowers and batting at insects. It was the perfect entertainment for drinking wine and relaxing after a long day. She thought about dinner and was about to get up and make herself a sandwich, aka Easy Dinner For Single People, when Pumpkin started scratching at the shed door.

"Please don't tell me that squirrel is in there again." Pandora put her glass down then thought about just letting Pumpkin wear herself out. It *was* good exercise.

Then the caterwauling started. For an overweight cat, Pumpkin had a very healthy set of lungs. Pandora jumped up. "Stop that before the neighbors think I'm killing you."

She ran out to where Pumpkin was and scooped her up. "Hush, you silly thing. Honestly, where are your hunter instincts? You have to be quiet to catch stuff. That squirrel is long gone by now."

But Pandora's witchy senses were twitching. For a moment, she contemplated getting her shovel to brandish as a weapon, but the shovel was in the shed. So was her rake and her pruning shears. Basically, all her best weapons. If there was a serial killer hiding in there, he was well armed.

"Bother." Well, everyone had to die sometime, right? She grabbed the handle of the shed and yanked it open.

The transom windows on the side walls let in just enough light for her to see there was no squirrel.

There was, however, a young girl sitting on Pandora's gardening stool. She had a backpack at her feet, a bag of beef jerky on her lap and a smartphone in her hands. The screen was illuminated, lighting up her face. She stared at Pandora. "Hey."

"Hey." Pandora stared back. Then put Pumpkin on the ground. "Um, your beef jerky is making my cat crazy. Also, what are you doing in my shed?"

The girl sealed up the bag of dried meat and tucked it in her backpack. "Hanging out."

A real conversationalist. "I can see that. Can I ask why you're hanging out in my shed?"

Sensing the jerky was no longer in play, but also realizing there was potentially a new source of tummy rubs, Pumpkin plopped down on the kid's flip-flops and rolled over, exposing herself like the shameless hussy she was.

"Nowhere else to go." The girl shrugged, then reached down and scratched Pumpkin's belly. "Hi, kitty. You want some jerky?"

"No jerky for the cat. And what do you mean nowhere else to go? You don't have a home?" A homeless teenager? In Nocturne Falls? Wearing really nice clothes and in possession of an iPhone? Pandora's witchy senses were picking up the distinct aroma of manure. And that wasn't just because the shed held all her gardening stuff.

"I have a home." The girl sighed. "I got kicked out."

Pandora dropped her snark for a second. "Why?"

The girl stopped scratching Pumpkin to pick at the seam of her jeans. "Because…I'm a witch."

Pandora blinked. And an odd protective instinct kicked in. "Your parents kicked you out because you're a witch?"

That really didn't happen in Nocturne Falls.

The kid continued to stare at her jeans. "Yeah. Well, really just my dad. My mom's dead."

Cue guilty feelings. "Oh, kiddo, I'm so sorry."

The girl shrugged. "I'm not even a good witch. Well, I don't mean I'm a bad witch. Like, I'm not putting curses on people or anything. I just turned thirteen, so I don't really know how to do any of that stuff yet. I just know that I'm a witch."

"Thirteen." Pandora nodded. And spoke without thinking. "That's about when we get our powers."

The girl looked up. "We?"

"Um...is that what I said?" Fiddlesticks. "So what's your name?"

"Starla." The girl squinted at Pandora. "You definitely said *we*. Are you a witch? I know there's a coven in town."

Pumpkin stared longingly at Starla and made Puss In Boots eyes in a last ditch effort at scoring some jerky.

"You do? How do you know that?" Pandora was genuinely interested. She wasn't aware that that info was public knowledge. It wasn't a secret, but it wasn't printed in the paper. Or was it? She might need to check on that. Or maybe the kid's mentor had told her. Every fledging witch was assigned one. It was how you learned. And hopefully avoided making big mistakes. Like giving yourself a tail.

Not that Pandora knew anyone personally who'd done that.

Starla gave Pandora a look like the answer was *so* obvious. "I read about it on the Cauldron. What's your name?"

"Pandora. What's the Cauldron?"

"You know, Cauldron.com? The online forum. Pandora? Like the girl who opens the box that lets all the trouble into the world? That's a cool witch name."

"Thanks. I guess." Pandora shook her head. "Sorry, Starla, never heard of the Cauldron."

Starla made a face. "How can you be a witch and not know about the forum?"

Because real witches didn't need a forum? Because adults with jobs didn't live their lives online? Or a thousand other reasons why. None of which Pandora was going to explain. Being a witch was...personal. "I was just kidding about being a witch."

The squint deepened. "No, you weren't. And you're fibbing now. I can see your aura. I might not know any spells or be able to do any magic, but I can see auras. And yours looks witchy."

"Fine, I'm a witch." Pandora crossed her arms. This ought to be good. "What exactly does my aura look like?"

"Purple and kinda sparkly."

Pandora did her best not to react. But, unfreaking-believable. The kid really was a witch. Pandora wished she'd brought her wine with her. She could drink about all of it right now.

"But it's also sort of...broken." Starla tipped her head. "Is there something wrong with your powers?"

If Pandora had been chewing gum, she would have choked on it. "My powers are just fine, thanks." If fine meant crap. Double bother. The kid wasn't just good at reading auras, she was spot-on. "Who's your mentor?"

Starla made a face. "My mentor?"

"Your witch mentor."

"I don't have one." Her face brightened. "That would be hella cool, though."

Pandora's head was starting to hurt. "Look, it's getting late. You can't sleep in the shed."

"I'm good."

"You might be, but I'm not. In the house. I have a guest room. Also, there are spiders in here." That ought to do it. "We'll call your dad, tell him you're okay, and tomorrow morning I'll take you home."

"I hate spiders, but I'm not going home."

"Yes, you are. I'll talk to your father." What she was going to say, Pandora had no idea, but the kid couldn't sleep in the shed. She also couldn't live with Pandora. "Actually, don't you have school tomorrow?"

That earned Pandora a big sigh, but at least Starla stood and picked up her backpack. "Yes."

"You don't like school?"

"No, I like it. But nobody loves it. It's *school*."

"Where do you go?"

"NFH."

Nocturne Falls High. Pandora nodded. "Now that your powers are starting to develop, you really ought to be at Harmswood Academy."

"Sounds snooty."

Pandora rolled her eyes. "It's not. It's for those who are…gifted."

Starla's eyes lit up. "You mean witches?"

"Yes." All the supernaturals sent their kids there.

Starla walked out of the shed, then stopped. "Can I get a mentor there? Will you talk to my dad about it?"

"No and sure." Pandora pointed toward the house. "Let's go inside and give him a call, okay?"

A long huffy breath answered her, followed by a beleaguered, "Okay."

Pandora hefted Pumpkin into her arms as she looked at Starla. "You hungry?"

Pumpkin meowed.

Pandora got a whiff of cat breath. "Excuse me, I was talking to our guest."

Starla laughed. "Your cat's fat."

"Thank you, Princess Obvious." Pandora grinned. "She's on a diet, but she hates it. So? Are you hungry? I could make sandwiches." Pandora tried to think like a teenager. "Or mac-n-cheese."

Starla nodded. "That sounds cool."

They went inside, and Starla dropped her bag by the kitchen counter, then sat on one of the bar stools and leaned her elbows on the counter. "Can't I just call my dad in the morning?"

"And have him spend the night worrying about you? No, ma'am. Dial."

Starla heaved out a sigh (apparently sighing was another form of teenage communication) but grabbed her phone and tapped the screen a few times. After a brief pause, she shrugged and put the phone down. "Went to voicemail." She rolled her eyes. "Pretty sure he's not taking my calls."

Pandora's sympathies were shifting to Starla's side pretty hard. What kind of father was this guy to kick out his kid and then not take her calls? Crappy, that's what kind. Well, Pandora knew about crappy fathers. "I'm sorry, Starla. I can imagine how that feels. Look, I'll make you that mac-n-cheese and we can talk about something else."

Starla perked up. "Witchy things? Like how I can get a mentor to teach me stuff?"

"Sure." Why not? Pandora had grown up with the benefit of a mother and two sisters in the practice. This kid should have someone to talk with about all the stuff that was coming her way. Getting your powers was a pretty big time in a young witch's life. In comparison, Pandora's puberty had been a breeze.

"Cool." Starla smiled. "Hey, do you have a bathroom I could use? I didn't want to pee in your flowers."

"And I appreciate that. Down the hall and on the right."

She hopped off the stool and disappeared. Pandora got a pan out and was headed to the pantry for the box of mac-n-cheese when her doorbell rang. She opened it and found a tall, sweaty, scruffy stranger with the most piercing black eyes she'd ever seen. He was dressed almost exactly like her. Basketball shorts and a tank top.

Except his looked really, really good on him.

2

Cole wasn't one to be swayed by a woman's looks, but he hadn't expected Venus on the Half Shell to answer the door. It took an exceptional amount of fortitude not to stare directly at the prodigious cleavage on display. He said a quick prayer of thanks to whatever universal force had convinced the woman before him that her tank top wasn't a size too small.

He focused on the reason he was here. "I'm sorry to bother you, but I think my daughter's here."

Her pretty green eyes narrowed, and she crossed her arms beneath her breasts, turning the cleavage valley into a bona fide fault line. "And you are?"

"Sorry. Cole Van Zant. My daughter's name is Kaley." He stuck his hand out.

She stared at it, but didn't uncross her arms.

He pulled it back, realizing how sweaty he was

from his run. "Sorry. So is Kaley here?"

"There's no one here by that name. I'm Pandora."

Of course she was. He could imagine her being responsible for unleashing all kinds of trouble into the world with that wild red hair and those amazing—he cleared his throat and wiped his hand on his shorts. "Nice to meet you, Pandora. Any chance you've seen a teenage girl in the area?"

A fat orange cat sat by Pandora's feet. He'd never been a cat person. They always looked at you like you could be dinner. This one was no exception. "What makes you think she's here?"

He pulled his phone out of his pocket and held it up. "I have a tracking app installed on her phone. She wasn't home when I got back from my run, so I checked it and it directed me here."

"Hmph."

At that moment, a familiar voice reached his ears. "Hey, Pandora, do you need any help with..." Kaley strolled out from the hallway and came to a sudden stop behind Pandora.

He looked at her. Then back at Pandora. "Any reason why you didn't want to tell me my daughter was here?"

The cat had walked out onto the front porch and was now winding around his legs. He cut his eyes at it, just to make sure it wasn't doing anything nefarious.

"You said your daughter's name is Kaley." Pandora tipped her head back at Kaley. "Her name is Starla."

"She might have told you that, but her name is definitely Kaley." Cole frowned and looked at his daughter. "Get your backpack. We're going home."

"No." Kaley crossed her arms like Pandora.

"Kaley. This isn't your house." He looked at Pandora. "I'm sorry for this."

"Seems to me you brought some of it on yourself."

Most of the tension he'd lost by going for a run was back. He rubbed the stubble on his chin. "What's that supposed to mean?"

Pandora shrugged. "You kicked her out. And you didn't answer her phone call."

"I did neither of those things." Something wet and rough touched his ankle. He jerked back as he glanced down. "Your cat just licked me."

"You'll live." Pandora spoke to Kaley without turning around. "Did he kick you out?"

"He doesn't even believe in witches." Kaley put on her best the-world-is-out-to-get-me face. "And I *might* have dialed the wrong number."

Cole did his best to ignore the cat as he exhaled a hard sigh. Now his neighbors, however temporary, were going to think his kid was crazy. "Kaley, we talked about this. I don't care what your mother says, there's no such thing as witches and you are not one. Now it's time to go home."

Pandora twisted to face Kaley, giving Cole a chance to sneak a peek at her very nice backside. Her voice came out in a much more serious tone that, this time, wasn't aimed at him. "I thought your mother was dead."

Kaley wrapped a strand of hair around her finger. "Well, she's *kind of* dead. I mean, like, I never see her, so…"

Pandora let out a long sigh and came back around to face Cole. She looked up at him through her lashes, her mouth set in a perturbed line. "Seems I was fed a little story. You're probably completely pro-witch, too, right?"

Cole laughed. "Oh, no, she's right about that part. The whole witch thing is complete BS."

Her arms went back to being crossed. "Don't you think it's important to support your daughter in whatever lifestyle she chooses to live?"

"I…what? Ow!" The cat had bitten him. Kaley was smirking. Cole had had enough. He wanted to take a shower, not discuss his parenting with a stranger and her carnivorous cat. A smoking-hot stranger, but still. Why were all the hot women he met also loony?

Pandora scooped up the cat. "Pumpkin, you can't eat the neighbors." She looked at Cole. "Sorry."

He nodded tersely, ready to be home. "Kaley. Backpack. Now."

Kaley rolled her eyes. How they weren't strained, he had no idea. "So mean," she muttered. "I swear, I will run away again if—"

"Run away again, and you're grounded."

"Dad, you're being so unfair."

"Really? What exactly would be fair in this situation?"

Kaley scrunched up her nose. "Let me stay here tonight."

Cole and Pandora said "No" in unison. Huh. At least they had that much in common.

Pandora went to stand beside Kaley. "I know what you're going through, I really do, but you need to go home with your dad and apologize for running away. That's not cool. Bad things could happen to you, even in a town like this. Although, it's highly unlikely. In this town, I mean. Anyway, maybe, if you do what your dad says, you can come over some day after school and we can talk some more."

Kaley looked up at Cole, eyes bright and eager. "Can I, Dad?"

Pandora seemed saner than Lila, but that was based on five minutes of interaction. The jury was still out on her cat. "I don't know. That's quite an imposition, and we don't know Mrs...." He looked at Pandora.

"Miss," she corrected him.

Single. That was interesting.

"And the last name is Williams." She walked back toward him and dug something out of the purse sitting on the small front table. A business card. She handed it to him. "I'm a regular upstanding citizen."

Pandora Williams
The House Witch
Making Real Estate Magic in Nocturne Falls

He chuckled. The House Witch. No wonder she was all about Kaley believing she was a witch. This whole town was so into the Halloween thing. Crazy, but great marketing. He flicked the card against his hand. "Thanks."

"Dad, we could have Miss Williams over for breakfast." Kaley nodded eagerly, suddenly the sweet and obedient child. "That would help you get to know her."

"I don't think—"

"Please, Dad?" She batted her lashes at him.

Crap. He was a sucker for that face. "I'm sure Miss Williams has to work tomorrow."

Pandora nodded. "I do. At ten. What time does school start?"

"Eight thirty," Kaley offered. "Breakfast is at seven thirty, sharp. We live on Shadows Drive. That big old ratty thing."

Pandora turned to him, odd sparks dancing in her eyes. "I know most of the folks that live over there. Which house?"

"Six-oh-nine."

Pandora did a double take. "You mean the Pilcher Manor?"

"I guess. Is that what people call it?" A *manor*? Maybe he was underestimating how much the house would sell for.

She nodded, her gaze somewhere far away. He recognized the look from when his female students would talk about a boy they liked. Or lip gloss. *Women*.

"Does this mean you're coming for breakfast?" he asked.

A slow smile turned up the corners of her mouth and gave her the most endearing dimples. "I wouldn't miss it for the world."

Shadows Drive wasn't just any street in Nocturne Falls. It was *the* street in Nocturne Falls proper.

Outside of some of the gated communities that skirted the town, Shadows Drive and its companion streets of Boo Boulevard, Eerie Avenue and Phantom Lane had been designed to replicate the kind of small-town, all-American streets featured in trick-or-treating scenes in many Hollywood movies. Big, elaborate houses on spacious lots with mature landscaping and architecture that was just the right mix of creepy and welcoming.

But Shadows Drive was the jewel in that gem-encrusted fantasy. It had the Gothic Victorians, and of those, Pilcher Manor was the shining diamond.

But as Pandora stood outside the wrought-iron fencing complete with spider web design, she thought Pilcher Manor had become less of a shining diamond and more of cracked cubic zirconia.

In the bright light of early morning, all its flaws and defects were plainly visible. The old manor reminded Pandora of a once-great beauty queen who'd gotten really drunk, slept it off at a friend's house (in her makeup) and then walked home barefoot in the rain.

Pilcher Manor looked both sad and embarrassing.

Of course, the house had sat empty since Ulysses Pilcher had passed more than two years ago. He'd become a recluse after his wife, Gertrude Pilcher, had died some ten years before him. Gerty had been a witch, not one Pandora had ever known well, but there were still stories told about the vivacious woman.

Apparently, she'd left Ulysses so distraught, the poor man had closed himself off from the rest of the world to grieve her loss.

Pandora couldn't imagine what the inside of the

house looked like now. Gerty had often held lavish parties—Pandora's mother, Corette, had been to several of them. But after sitting vacant for two years and the time that Ulysses had been cooped up in there…who knew?

Cole couldn't have bought the house. It had never been up for sale. Last Pandora had heard, the lawyers were still trying to find a relative. Which must mean handsome-but-stubborn Cole was that person.

How could a man who was related to a legendary witch like Gerty not believe in witches? This was going to be an interesting breakfast.

She locked her car, marched past the dumpster in the driveway and onto the porch. A board creaked beneath her kitten heel. She stepped over to one that seemed sturdier and lifted her hand to knock.

The door opened, and Kaley beamed at her. "You made it!"

"I'm a woman of my word."

"Come in." Kaley pulled the door wide.

Pandora stepped inside. And tried not to gape. On either side of the foyer were two rooms—a living room and a library maybe? Both were indistinguishable thanks to the stacks and stacks and *stacks* of papers, boxes and…stuff.

Apparently, Ulysses had become a hoarder.

"Yeah, it's totally gross, right?" Kaley's lip curled. "My dad is working on it. Oh, and I'm supposed to apologize for lying to you yesterday. Sorry about that."

Pandora nodded. "Thank you." Please don't let the kitchen look like this too. "Do I smell coffee?"

"Totally. Come on, this way." Kaley practically skipped through the foyer toward the back of the house.

Pandora followed, trying not to give in to the sudden phobias kicking in. Claustrophobia and germaphobia. Neither of which she'd suffered from before entering this house. She focused on her breathing, which is what her sister Charisma, life coach extraordinaire, would probably recommend.

Fortunately, the rest of the downstairs, including the kitchen, was in much better shape. Cole was at the big antique gas stove, looking very nice in blue jeans and an old T-shirt as he juggled pans of bacon and scrambled eggs. He was also wearing black-rimmed glasses that made his eyes even more piercing. What was it about hot guys in glasses? The combination of hot and vulnerable got her every time. Toast sailed out of a four-slice machine with a loud pop.

"Morning," he offered.

"Morning."

He turned and gave her a nod. "It's a mess. I already know that's what you're thinking."

She nodded back. "I wasn't going to say anything."

"But you *were* thinking it." He pointed to the coffee maker. "Cups and sugar are in the cabinet above, creamer's in the fridge."

"Thanks." She took the cue and helped herself.

He looked at Kaley, who was practically balancing on her tiptoes with excitement. "Are you ready to go? Just because we have a guest doesn't mean you can be late."

"*Da-ad*." Somehow she turned the three letters into two syllables. She went flat on her feet. "My backpack is still upstairs, but I want to talk to Miss Williams."

"Go get it. Then you can talk to her."

Pandora watched Kaley leave with a bounce. Teenage energy. That was its own kind of magic. What sort of witchy wisdom Kaley thought Pandora could impart over breakfast, Pandora wasn't sure, but they'd figure it out. Pandora went back to watching Cole. "How long have you guys been here?"

"About three weeks." He used a fork to turn the slices of bacon. "But I estimate it'll take me six to eight months to get this place in shape to sell."

Pandora's realtor side sat up. "You're going to sell it?"

He nodded while stirring the eggs. "It's too much house for two people. Six bedrooms? Way too big."

She couldn't argue with that. The place must be

forty-five hundred square feet. "It's going to be a lot of work."

He shrugged and started plating food. "I can handle most of it. What I can't, I'll hire out."

"You're a contractor?"

"I'm a math professor, but like most of us in the teaching industry, I've had to work through the summer to pay the bills. Construction has been my job of choice since I was a teenager. So, yeah, I know what I'm doing. Not all of it, but most. Like I said, the rest I'll contract out."

A math professor who also worked construction? That explained the lean, tight body she'd seen yesterday. She had a sudden vision of him standing in front of a classroom. If her math professor had looked like Cole, she'd never have passed. Or she'd have done a lot of extra credit. "I'd be happy to help you with that. Recommending contractors, I mean. I know most of them. And which ones you should avoid."

"Thanks, I'd appreciate that." He handed her a plate. "I'm impressed you didn't put the hard sell on me to list the house with you."

She sat at the large round table in the seating nook. A hammer and tape measure lay beside a jar of strawberry jam and a stick of butter in a cut-glass covered dish. "I don't believe in the hard sell."

He laughed. "Are you sure you're a realtor?"

"You say that like you think we're in the same

category as personal injury lawyers and used car salesmen."

Kaley moaned as she bopped back into the room and took a seat at the table beside Pandora. "*Dad.*" Her eyes went skyward. "Enough with the boring house talk."

He gave his daughter a look. "Did you apologize?"

"She did," Pandora offered. "Thank you."

Kaley sighed. "Now can we talk about witch stuff?"

Cole balanced his plate, Kaley's plate and a third plate of toast on one arm, then dug a handful of silverware out of a drawer and came to the table. He dropped the silverware with a clatter. "Kaley, how many times do I have to tell you? Witches aren't real."

Pandora passed out the silverware. "I hate to eat your food and tell you you're wrong, but you're wrong. And Kaley really needs a mentor."

"See, Dad?" Kaley said.

He handed Kaley her plate and sat before addressing Pandora. "I get that the town is invested in this whole Halloween shtick, but you can't tell me you think witches are real."

"I don't *think* they're real. I know they are." Pandora helped herself to the jam. A big dollop fell off the knife and onto the table. "Bother."

He looked at her. "Did you just say *bother*?

What are you, a Disney princess?"

"I don't curse."

"Why not?"

Because her magic was broken, and a curse from a witch's mouth, however casual, could still mean something. "I'm a witch and witches' words have power. We have to be careful."

"Witches." He shook his head in plain disbelief.

Pandora considered the facts. If his daughter was a witch, and considering her lineage and ability to see auras, there wasn't much question about that, then he needed to face the truth. If Kaley didn't get a mentor to teach her, she'd never learn. Or she'd learn the hard way, and that was a dangerous path. "Well, I am one. My mother's one. So are my two sisters. And so was the woman this house once belonged to."

"Get out!" Kaley's eyes rounded. "That is so cool."

Cole stared at Pandora with obvious unhappiness in his eyes.

She shrugged and spread jam on her toast.

He took a long slug of coffee before finally putting his cup back down. "How can you make that claim?"

"Because it's true."

Kaley nodded, smiling. "See, Dad, I *am* a witch. Also, like, is that all the bacon there is?"

"Kaley, give us a minute, honey."

"Yes," Pandora said. "Let me educate your father, then you can worry about bacon." Pandora made a face at him. "You inherited this house, right?"

"Yes."

"So how can you not know your own family? Gertrude Pilcher was a witch. And a fairly well-known one, too."

"I'm not related to her. I'm related to Ulysses. He was my great-uncle on my mother's side."

"Why didn't your mom inherit the house?"

"She passed away five years ago. Cancer. I might have met Ulysses and Gertrude once, at a family reunion when I was a kid. That was it. And I don't remember it."

"I'm so sorry about your mom." She couldn't imagine losing her mother. Pandora's heart ached for Cole. And for Kaley, who'd lost her grandmother. "That must have been hard."

"It was. Still is."

She was quiet for a minute. Then she spoke softly. "Related or not, your distant great-aunt was a witch."

Cole got a look on his face like he suddenly knew how to put an end to the conversation. Pandora recognized the look because it was one witches got from normies a lot. Normie was what witches often called the non-magical. The younger generation had kind of glommed on to *muggle*, though.

"You honestly believe you're a witch."

"I know I'm one."

"Then prove it."

And there it was. The challenge that always came from the disbelieving. *Turn my ex into a frog. Make a million dollars magically appear. Show me your broom.* "No."

"Because you can't."

"I could if I wanted to, but I don't want to." Because her magic never worked right. Sometimes, it went horribly wrong. And neither was a humiliation she enjoyed. She put her fork down. "Time for me to go."

"Dad!" Kaley grabbed Pandora's arm. "See? Now you know what I'm dealing with. Please don't go."

The legs of Pandora's chair squeaked across the tile as she got up. "Sorry, kid, I have to get to work. Have a good day at school."

Then she looked at Cole. Pretty, pretty, naïve Cole. "You have a good day, too. You and your small little mind."

She turned and stormed out before he could say another word. He was damned lucky too, because at that moment, if she'd been capable of it, she totally would have turned him into a frog.

3

A sullen, angry Kaley sat across from Cole as their front door slammed shut. He'd known that would be the outcome of his challenge, and while he wasn't happy Kaley was upset with him, it was better she understood now what was real and what wasn't. He sipped his coffee. "Eat your breakfast. School's in twenty minutes."

She glared at him. Probably wishing she *could* do witchcraft. "I'm not hungry."

"You will be later."

More glaring. Now with sighing. "Did you do the same thing to Mom?"

He looked up from his plate. "What do you mean?"

"Make her leave too, because you didn't believe she was a witch."

His turn to sigh. "Your mother left because she wasn't—"

"Ready to be a mother and she had to work on herself. I know all that. But why did she really leave? You made her, didn't you?"

"No, Kaley, I didn't, but the truth is, your mother wasn't a witch any more than you are or Miss Williams is."

"You didn't give her a chance."

"Who? Your mother or Miss Williams? Actually, I did. Both of them."

"It wasn't nice what you did to Miss Williams. She was going to teach me things. She was going to help me find a mentor."

"Kaley, she's a real estate agent. Not a witch. It's all just a gimmick because of this town. People like to pretend they're something more than they are. That's what they do here."

"It's not just a gimmick."

"Yes, it is. This town makes its money on the idea that every day is Halloween. Honey, I know you're disappointed. But being a teenager is hard enough without trying to be something you're not. Now, please eat your breakfast."

"What's so wrong with pretending? You can't even do that."

Math wasn't about fantasy and pretending. Math was about practicality and absolute truths. Just like construction. You couldn't pretend to put a header in or your wall would only pretend to stand up. "Because that's not how life works, Kaley-did."

"I hate that nickname."

"You didn't used to."

Kaley went quiet, and her plate remained untouched. She stared at him with strange intent. Then her dark brown eyes narrowed down to slits. "Your aura is really ugly."

He'd had enough. "So is your attitude. If you're not going to eat, then you can clean up. I have work to do before I drive you to school." Because the sooner he could get this house in shape, the sooner he could sell it and they could get out of this weird town and back to North Carolina. Back to where life was normal and the only one pretending to be something they weren't was Agnes Houston, the drama professor, who had *never* played opposite Brando, no matter how much she claimed she had.

Kaley jumped up from the table and grabbed her backpack. "You don't need to drive me, I'm walking." She stormed out of the room.

For the second time that morning, his front door slammed shut.

He sat right where he was, watching the ripples on the surface of his coffee until it went smooth again.

Kaley had been so excited about Pandora coming over. Now he had two women mad at him. And he deduced that the only way to make Kaley stop being mad at him would require Pandora no longer being mad at him also.

The Professor Woos the Witch

He drank the last of his now cold coffee and jogged upstairs to his bedroom. There on his dresser was the thing he needed.

Pandora's business card.

Clearing out the front rooms would have to wait a little bit longer. Cole had some groveling to do.

"I'm telling you, Mom, she's a witch." Pandora cradled the phone between her head and shoulder while she brought up the MLS (aka Multi List System) to update a few of her listings. "She can read auras pretty spot-on."

"How old did you say she is?" Corette asked.

"Thirteen."

"That's the right age. Poor dear. Does she have a mentor?"

"No. And she's going to need one."

Corette sighed. "That's for sure. And the father doesn't believe?"

"Nope. Total normie."

Corette tsked. "And him living in Gertrude's house. She's not going to like that."

Pandora squinted. "You know she's dead, right?"

"I know, dear, but there's always a possibility that a witch with that much life in her might not be *entirely* gone."

Pandora laughed. "Oh, that would serve him right."

"Now, Pandy, we shouldn't wish ill will on anyone. That's not our way."

"I know. But he was such a…butthead."

"Very mature response, darling."

"Hey, you want to have lunch today? I could call Marigold, have her meet us too." Pandora's youngest sister ran the flower shop in town.

"I can't. I already have a lunch date."

"Stanhill?"

"Yes." The honeyed tone of Corette's answer spoke volumes. For the last four years, Pandora's mother had dated Hugh Ellingham's rook, a position that was basically like Batman's Alfred. Stanhill was universally adored by Pandora and her sisters. Didn't hurt that he and Corette were well suited and deeply in love.

"All right. Well, keep your hands on the table." Pandora giggled. "We don't want people to talk."

"*Pandora.*" Corette mock-scolded. In the background, Pandora could hear the chimes that sounded when her mother's shop door opened. "One of my brides just came in for a fitting. I have to go."

Corette's shop, Ever After, was the go-to destination for all things bridal and formal in town. "Love you."

"Love you, too." Corette hung up.

Pandora set the phone down. The irony that her mother ran a bridal boutique and yet all three of her daughters were still single was not lost on Pandora. Someday, she might make good use of her mother's shop.

And someday Pumpkin might lose weight.

Maybe she'd call Willa, see if she wanted to do lunch. Pandora could even pick it up and take it over to the jewelry store. They did that at least once a month. Willa's back room had heard more Nocturne Falls gossip than Birdie Caruthers, the sheriff's nosy aunt and receptionist. Okay, maybe not more than Birdie. But close.

The bells above Pandora's office's front door jangled, and she looked up. Right into the face of Mr. Doubter McDoubty Pants. She leaned back in her chair. "Thought of an insult you forgot to hurl at me?"

Cole frowned. Which sadly, did nothing to make him ugly. "I didn't hurl insults at you."

Pandora tipped her hand back and forth. "Let's call that a draw."

He stopped in front of her desk. "I came to apologize, actually. I'm sorry about breakfast. That's not how I planned for it to go."

"That's good to hear. How *did* you plan for it to go?"

His mouth crumpled into an uneven line before he answered. "I don't know. But not like that."

"Do you plan everything?"

"Yes. Don't you?"

"No. That's not a very fun way to live your life."

He shifted uncomfortably and pushed his glasses back. Goddess, he was pretty.

"Something else you wanted to say?" she asked.

He took a deep breath. "I could use some help with Kaley."

Her brows popped up. "And you think I'm your best shot?"

"She likes you a lot. She got really mad at me this morning."

"That makes two of us." She nodded at the chairs across from her desk. "Sit down."

"Thanks." He took a seat and crossed his long legs, one ankle on one knee. "I really am sorry about this morning."

"Only because Kaley got mad at you. Doesn't change the way you feel, does it?"

His mouth did the crumpling thing again. "No."

Pandora rolled her eyes. *Normies*. "What is it that you think I can do for Kaley?"

"She thinks she's a witch."

"Because she is."

Cole opened his mouth, then closed it again. Maybe he was figuring out something new to say. "I was thinking maybe you could…play along with that."

Pandora narrowed her eyes. "What do you mean, play along?"

"She thinks she's a witch, you claim to be one, so help her figure out how to be one, too. At least until this phase passes, because it will. When she was six, she wanted to own a zoo until she realized she'd have to have more animals than just cats and dogs. When she was seven, she wanted to compete in the Olympics until she found out jump rope isn't an Olympic sport. Something will happen to make her realize this witch thing isn't for her."

"I like Kaley."

He smiled, which was some kind of dark magic, because for a moment she forgot she didn't like him. "She's a great kid."

"But I don't like you." There. She'd said it.

He shrugged. "Fair enough. I'm prepared to sweeten the deal."

She hadn't been expecting that. She'd been ready to say she'd help for Kaley's sake, but now she was curious. "How so?"

He paused like his next words were going to be painful. "If you help Kaley, I'll give you the house listing."

An electric charge zipped through her, but she maintained her composure even as her brain went crazy. *The Pilcher Manor.* Not only would it be a killer commission, but she could make sure it ended up with the right family. She picked up a pen and twirled it through her fingers. "So you're basically paying me off."

He sighed. "Yes."

Something bold entered her bloodstream. "No."

"What?" He stared at her. "You don't want it?"

"I do, but I have no idea what sort of...*work* you're going to do to it. Or what kind of shape it's going to be in when you expect me to get top dollar for it." If he didn't believe in her, she damn well wasn't going to let him think she believed in him.

"I do excellent work."

She lifted one shoulder. "I'm sure you *believe* that."

His eyes tapered like he'd just figured out what she was up to. "What do you want?"

"I want the listing, but since I know what buyers look for in this town, I also want equal say in how you renovate the house."

"Are you going to put up equal funds?"

"Are you going to cut me in for a share of the sale?"

He uncrossed his legs and recrossed them in the opposite direction. "You can help with decisions. I promise to run everything by you. But it's my money, so I get final say."

That was fair. "Deal."

He smiled again. "Deal. Thank you."

She wove the pen between her fingers. "So, Cole. What exactly do you believe in?"

"The infinite value of pi. Prime numbers. The strength of an engineered beam. Measuring twice but cutting once."

She blinked. "Hoo boy, I can see why Kaley needs my help. Were you ever a kid? Did you ever believe in Santa and the Tooth Fairy and that stepping on cracks could break your mother's back?"

"Sure, but I was a kid. I'm an adult now. And a realist."

"But Kaley's not. She's still a kid. And there are things out there beyond human comprehension, so before you go telling her not to believe in things, why don't you let her enjoy being a kid?"

He held his hands up. "Point taken. I'll try to be more open-minded."

"Don't worry, I'm not going to drag you to a coven meeting or anything like that."

He laughed. "You won't let it go, will you?"

"What?" But she knew.

"The witch thing."

So help her, she wanted to zap him. Anger bubbled through her. "It's not a *witch thing*. It's who I am. It's who Kaley is, and it's who her mentor will be."

He shook his head. "I said it before, and I'll say it again. Show me."

Her fingers twitched to do exactly that. Because

even when her magic went wrong, he'd still have to admit she'd done something.

She snapped her fingers, and the boysenberry candle sitting next to her pen holder blazed to life. She hoped it didn't explode and cover them both with hot wax, but the flame died down to a dull flicker and danced happily atop the wick like every other lit candle she'd ever seen. It was rare that even a small use of magic went right for her, but thank the goddess it had.

He nodded. "Good one." He picked up the candle and looked underneath it. "Is there a magic shop that sells these in town? Because Kaley would love one."

"No, you...*muggle*. I did that."

He winked at her. "Right."

She pointed at the door. "I think we're done here."

"We haven't talked about how this is going to work."

"I'm not sure it's going to."

"You said deal."

Fiddlesticks. So she had. She tried to remember this was for Kaley, not Cole. And the commission on the Pilcher Manor. "Fine. I'll see if I can get Kaley a mentor. Shouldn't be a big deal. I just have to find someone with the time and inclination, but most witches are happy to do it."

"Why not you?"

Because of her broken magic, but that wasn't a discussion she wanted to have with him. "I'm too busy. But I know a lot of witches."

"I bet you do."

She scowled at him.

"Sorry, sorry, I'll work on that." He stood. "Come to dinner tonight. You have my word it will go better than breakfast. In fact, we can go out. Neutral ground that way. Your choice so long as it doesn't involve me wearing a tie."

She took a breath and let that thought marinate. He might be less likely to get into an argument in public. Which would give her a chance to talk to Kaley. "Howler's. Six forty-five." That would be enough time to go home, change and feed Pumpkin.

"Howler's. That's down at the end of Main, right?"

"Right." Because a werewolf bar was the perfect place to take a guy who didn't believe in things that went bump in the night.

"Great. See you then. I have to get back to work." He started for the door.

"What are you doing on the house today?"

He stopped and turned back to face her. "I'm ordering the new kitchen. Cabinets, counter tops, faucets."

She canted her head to the side. "Shouldn't I be helping you with that? Per our new deal?"

He closed his eyes and opened them back up very slowly, like he was trying to keep himself from reacting. "I guess so."

She grabbed her purse, thankful she didn't have any showings until this afternoon, and blew out the candle.

He held his hand toward the door. "On to the cabinet shop we go."

4

Cole drove a pickup, which wasn't unexpected, but Pandora had figured it would be dirty inside from whatever construction jobs he'd been working and okay, because he was a guy, littered with food wrappers and random pieces of two-by-fours and those odd flat pencils carpenters used. Instead, it was neat as a pin and smelled like the beach.

She tapped the palm tree air freshener dangling from the rearview mirror. "Kaley?"

"Yes."

Pandora put her purse on the floor and strapped her seat belt on.

Cole gave her a funny look, then put on his own.

"What was that look for?"

His brows lifted as he shifted into drive and pulled the vehicle onto the road. "You're pretty trusting to get in a truck with a stranger."

She gave him a funny look right back. "Are you

saying I shouldn't be? What are you trying to tell me?"

His eyes lit with amusement. "Nothing. Just making an observation."

"You're not exactly a stranger. I know where you live. I know your first and last name and your daughter's." And she'd zap him with magic if he tried anything. Not that it would necessarily work, but hope sprang eternal.

"I guess."

She smiled. "Plus, it would be a pretty high coincidence that we're *both* serial killers."

He laughed, his black eyes flashing. "For a potentially crazy woman, you're pretty funny."

"Thanks, I think." She sat back, wondering if he had any idea how handsome he was when he smiled. It was a bit disarming, because he didn't seem like he had a clue.

He didn't smell bad, either.

Oh boy. Was she getting a little infatuated? She'd always had a thing for stubborn boys who didn't believe. A sadness welled up inside her. It was like high school all over again.

She shoved that thought out of her head. Now was neither the time nor the place to rehash that horrible memory. "So, Melworth's Kitchens and More?"

"What? No. I was going to the DIY Depot."

She scrunched up her nose. "A big-box store?"

"Yeah, why not?"

"Because they're not local, they don't do custom cabinets and—"

"Custom? Whoa, what kind of money do you think I'm putting into this place?"

She raised her brows and gave him her best disdainful glare. "The kind it deserves. Pilcher Manor isn't a starter home. You can't just throw any old fixtures in it and call it done."

He kept his eyes on the road as he drove. "Custom cabinets are expensive."

"And how much did the house cost you?"

"That's not the point."

"Do you understand what it could potentially sell for?"

He sighed. "Not really, no. But I'm guessing you can tell me."

"If you do it right—"

"You mean your way."

"Sure, let's go with that. If you do it right, it could be worth one-point-two, maybe one-point-three. I mean, I haven't pulled comps, but—"

Cole pulled off onto the shoulder, and the vehicle screeched to a stop. He threw the truck into park and twisted to face her. "Are you saying one-point-two as in million?"

"Did you think I meant doughnuts? Yes, million. Are you that clueless about the house you inherited?"

He sat back and stared out the windshield, his long fingers gently rapping the top of the steering wheel. A few moments passed before he spoke again. "I guess I am."

He finally looked at her. "Where's this place you mentioned? Melvins?"

"Melworth's. Past the DIY Depot and on the left."

"You're sure you can get that kind of money?"

"Positive. No one sells more real estate in Nocturne Falls than I do."

He put the truck back in drive and pulled onto the highway.

She settled into her seat a little more. "Does this mean custom cabinets?"

"Damn straight." He glanced over, a slight smile bending his lips. Lips that probably didn't suck at kissing. Or did suck, but in the good way. "It also means I want you to come back to the house tonight after dinner and tell me what else I need to do to get the place in the kind of shape you think it should be in."

Huh. Maybe he wasn't so stubborn after all. "That kind of sounds like you're actually going to honor us being partners on this."

He nodded, eyes back on the road. "Hey, I'm a man of my word. You okay being partnered up with a muggle?"

She laughed. "I'll make a believer out of you yet."

"I doubt that. But I'm happy to have your expertise."

"Thanks." Then it struck her that in less than twenty-four hours, she'd gone from not knowing Cole Van Zant existed, to almost having breakfast with him, to agreeing to dinner with him and partnering with him on the rehab of one of the most potentially beautiful old homes in town. Which meant she'd be seeing a lot of Mr. Van Zant.

It was the closest thing to a relationship she'd had since high school.

And there it was again, the memory of her past. This was why she didn't have relationships. Too many reminders of how fast things could go tragically wrong. Too much potential for life-altering, soul-shattering heartbreak.

She turned to look out the passenger-side window. There was no stopping the memory now. The image of Ren's face flashed through her mind, and she sucked in a breath. A barrage of images came after. The crash. The ambulance.

The funeral.

"Hey, you still with me?"

She turned. "What?"

"You seemed lost in thought."

She forced a smile. "Just thinking about the possibilities." The DIY Depot was up ahead. She pointed to it. "After you pass the Depot, you'll see Melworth's in another quarter mile. It looks like a warehouse, but trust me, it's the place you want to be."

"I do trust you." He tipped his head. "Mostly."

"No one would expect more than that right away." She pointed again. "There, that's Melworth's."

"You're right. It does look like a dumpy old warehouse."

"I never said dumpy."

"It was implied." He parked the truck on the gravel lot, throwing up a small cloud of dust. "Shall we?"

If Melworth's was dumpy on the outside, it was a curious mix of showroom fancy and busy warehouse on the inside. She'd brought many clients here to show them what was possible for their home.

Cole nodded approvingly as they walked through the displays. "You're right. Much nicer stuff than at the Depot."

"Told you."

Gary Melworth came up to Pandora with a big smile on his face. "Pandora! Nice to see you." He glanced at Cole. "New client?"

"Sort of. This is Cole Van Zant. He just inherited the Pilcher Manor. I'm going to help him with some selections to bring it up-to-date. Cole, this is Gary Melworth, the owner."

The two shook hands. Gary was a good enough

businessman not to let the dollar signs show in his eyes, but Pandora knew he understood the magnitude of the job she'd just brought him. He nodded. "Whatever you need, you know I'm happy to help."

"That's why we're here."

He gave her a nod. "You know your way around. You need anything, holler."

"Will do."

Cole nudged her as Gary walked away. "You getting a kickback from that guy?"

She frowned at him. "No."

Cole shrugged. "You should be."

"I don't work that way." She walked toward a display that caught her eye. "But he does send me a three-pound box of handmade chocolates every year at Christmas." He'd also redone her kitchen at half-price, but she didn't mention it because it suddenly seemed like that might qualify as a kickback.

She put her hand on the vanilla glazed maple cabinet in front of her. "What do you think of these?"

He made a face. "That's not how I was picturing it."

"Let me guess. Dark wood, dark granite."

"No?"

"That kitchen is dark enough already. Which reminds me, that wall between the kitchen and the dining room should come down. If it's not load bearing, of course."

"Oddly enough, I was already thinking about that." He stared at the cabinets. Then looked at her. "I see what you're saying about the lighter cabinets, I really do. But maybe we should walk through the house together before we go any further?"

She took her hand off the cabinet. "Okay, we can wait until after dinner, then."

"No," Cole said. "I mean right now."

When they walked into the old house, Cole was instantly struck by how alone he was with a very beautiful woman. He still considered her a little batty for thinking she was a witch, but he'd underestimated her when it came to the house stuff. She clearly knew what she was doing, and if she could get the kind of money she'd talked about for this place, he could live with the batty part until the job was done. That kind of money would set him and Kaley up for a long time. Even her college would be paid for.

He could also stop worrying about getting another job during the summers. In fact, maybe he and Pandora could go into the remodeling business on the side. Okay, he wasn't sure why he was thinking about going into business with a woman he'd just met. He needed to slow down and focus on the task at hand. One thing at a time and all that.

He shut the door behind them. "Give me a sec to grab my notepad from the kitchen."

"Sure."

When he came back, legal pad and pen in hand, she was doing a slow circle, taking a close look at the foyer from top to bottom.

He leaned against the stairs. "What do you think?"

"The bones are really good, but the balusters need work."

He nodded. "I was going to strip them and refinish. Okay?"

She scrunched up her nose, an expression he was coming to recognize as her way of softening bad news. "I don't think so."

"What, then?"

"The hand railing and newel posts can stay, because that's a nice touch and a nod to the history of the house, but for the balusters, I'd go wrought iron. Not only would it modernize this entrance, but it would tie into the wrought-iron fence outside."

He shook his head as he took notes. The woman was brilliant.

"You don't like it."

"No, I do," he said. "I never would have thought of that, and it's perfect. It's going to cost, but—"

"You'll make it back."

"I know." He smiled. "What else?"

They walked through the house together, her giving her thoughts for each room and him jotting down her design plans. By the time they'd finished the second story, he had fifteen pages of notes and a solid idea of her vision, which frankly, was so superior to what he'd been planning that he just kept nodding and writing.

He flipped the pages of the legal pad back and tucked it under his arm. "I guess that's it. I have a lot of work to do, namely clearing the rest of the junk out of here, but after that, it's full steam ahead on the remodel."

She glanced up. "What about the attic?"

He looked at the stairs that led to what was technically the third story of the house. "I figured I'd just leave it as storage for whoever buys the house. If they want to do something with it, that's on them."

She cocked one eyebrow.

"You want to see it?"

"I do."

"It's a little…weird up there."

"Weird?"

"You'll see. Follow me." He led her up the steps,

pushed open the door and moved aside to let her in.

Natural light filled the space from the dormers and, at the rear of the house, three large Gothic arched windows that looked over the backyard. It didn't look nearly as creepy as it had the first night he and Kaley had come up here.

"This doesn't seem weird." She walked over to the middle window. "Great view of the yard. And wow, is it overgrown. You could hide an elephant in there."

He stood by one of the sidewalls that held rows of shelves filled with odd bottles, random trinkets and as-yet-unopened boxes. "Really? You don't think all this is weird?"

She turned to look at him, her gaze going past him to the shelves. "Hmm." She walked over, picked up one of the bottles and studied it before putting it back on the shelf and facing him again. "I can take these things off your hands."

"Why? What is it?"

She gave him a piercing look. "You don't want to know."

"Humor me."

Her lips twitched like she was suppressing a smile. "Witch stuff."

He frowned. "Now you're just screwing with me."

"No, I'm not." She picked up one of the boxes,

lifted the hinged lid, took a look, then held it out for him to see. "Who else would have a collection of cat whiskers? This proves Gertrude was a witch."

He glanced briefly into the box. "It proves she was a crazy cat lady, but that's about it."

With a deep sigh, Pandora closed the lid and put the box back. "Okay, how about this?" She took a small brass mirror off another shelf and offered it to him. "Look into that and tell me what you see."

As he took the mirror from her, their fingers touched. A fraction of a second of contact. A centimeter of skin on skin.

That was all it took. A shock jolted through him, and a barrage of sounds and images filled his being. The iridescent gleam of sunlight on black feathers. The brush of wings through the air. The distant cawing of birds. The view of a town—this town—from a thousand feet up.

Then the sounds and images were gone as quickly as they'd come.

He shook himself and blinked as the attic filled his vision again.

"You okay? You look funny." Pandora leaned forward to peer at him.

"I'm good. Fine. I just...never mind." He held the mirror up. "What am I supposed to do with this thing again?"

Her staring took on a new intensity. "You felt something, didn't you?"

"No." Yes. Crap. "It's just warm up here."

She made a small noise and straightened. "We can finish this downstairs."

"Good." He put the mirror back on the shelf and, letting her go ahead of him, headed for the steps. His mind fixated on what he'd just experienced. What the hell had that been? Then he realized she'd said something. "What was that?"

She stopped on the landing to face him. "I said I could go for some coffee."

"So could I." They both turned toward the kitchen. "I'll make a fresh pot." Which gave him exactly enough time to process whatever had happened and then pack it away as something that no longer needed any further mental energy.

"What's your plan for the attic?" He brought the pot and two cups to the table, handing one to her as he set the pot on a folded towel. She got up and grabbed the sugar and creamer, and he kicked himself for not remembering that's how she took her coffee. "Sorry. I should have got those for you."

"No biggie." She sat back down and fixed her cup. "My plan for the attic is to keep it pretty much the same. Clean it up, definitely, but otherwise, you're right that it's a space the new owners can do whatever they like with." She took a sip of her coffee, then set the cup down. "What we really need to talk about is Kaley."

That surprised him. "I thought we already talked about her."

Pandora shook her head, her green eyes sparkling even in the dim kitchen. "Yes, but not enough. I don't know how I'm supposed to help her when you refuse to bend on your stance about the supernatural. Her mentor, if I can find her one, will feel the same way, I can promise you that."

He turned his coffee cup so the handle sat at a right angle to the wood grain of the table. This was the last thing he wanted to talk about right now, but how did he tell her that without coming off as a big grump? "I don't know."

"You could give me free rein."

"And then what?" The spark of indignation in Pandora's eyes put an end to his words. He threw his hands up. "I don't know how to respond without making you angry, and I don't want to do that."

"Really," she snarked. "What's changed?"

"I like you. You're smart and business-minded, and besides the witch thing, you seem totally sane."

"Wow, thanks." Her mouth bunched to one side.

He sighed. "I know Kaley needs some female influence in her life. I just don't want her getting…disillusioned again."

"You want to explain that? I'm sensing it has

something to do with her not-really-dead mother. What's the story there anyway?"

He drummed his fingers on the table. Pandora was bound to find out sooner or later. Better he give her the story so she'd truly understand what Kaley was going through. "Lila is...not a great mother, and wasn't even in the early days. I think she tried. Or maybe she didn't. Who knows with that woman?"

He took a breath, thinking his words through before he spoke them. "She was beautiful in that sort of earth-child, free-love, everything is always cool kind of way."

Pandora nodded. "And you dug that because that's your opposite. Makes sense."

"What do you mean my opposite?"

She smirked. "Cole, face it, you're a little uptight."

He made a face but continued. "We were young and dumb and got married before I even realized what had happened. She treated me like I was a king. I was always right. I was the smartest man she'd ever known. She laughed at all my jokes. Waited on me hand and foot. It was nice, at first. Then it got really old."

He paused, thinking back. "But by then I was already in love with Kaley."

Pandora squinted. "I don't get it."

"Kaley was two when I met Lila." He smiled. "She was this chubby little doll with an infectious laugh and these big brown eyes that looked up at me like I was her very own superhero. Her first word to me was *Daddy*. How do you not fall in love with that?"

Pandora's lips parted, but she said nothing.

"I adopted her when Lila and I got married."

She canted her head. "I never would have guessed Kaley's not your flesh and blood."

That pleased him. "She might as well be. When Kaley was five, Lila's cheating started. Or at least that's when I figured it out. I confronted her, and she cried and pleaded and swore it was over. It wasn't. Long story short, she moved out six months later, leaving Kaley behind. When Kaley turned seven, I filed for divorce and custody. Maybe I was too hasty, but it was a rough year. My mother was dying. And at that point, Lila hadn't seen Kaley in thirteen months. That didn't change in the two years it took for the divorce and the custody to be granted."

"Wow. Rough is an understatement. I guess the judge didn't struggle with that decision."

"It helped that Lila didn't show up for the hearing." Or his mother's funeral.

Pandora grimaced. "What kind of woman does that to her own child? That poor kid."

"Hey, Kaley's done great with me."

"I can see that."

He exhaled, pushing some of the bad memories out. "Since then, Lila's contact consists of occasional phone calls and a package on Kaley's birthday. Oh, she shows up every once in a while, but that's gotten rarer as the years have gone on."

"And this last package is the one that set everything off."

He stared at his coffee. "Yes. Except it wasn't a package. Just a letter and a packet of stickers." He snorted and looked at Pandora. "Stickers? For a thirteen-year-old girl? Lila has no clue what that kid likes."

"And this letter was about Kaley becoming a witch?"

He nodded.

"And Lila would know about that because she's a witch too, right?"

He scowled. "She thinks she is, yes."

"I'm starting to get the picture."

"Good. Then you understand why I'm reluctant to let you—or anyone—teach her to be a witch only to have her grow out of this phase and blame me for subjecting her to some kind of crazy brainwashing with another nutty wom—" He stopped himself from finishing the sentence, but the damage was done.

Pandora pushed back her chair, rolled her eyes and muttered something under her breath.

"What was that?"

She glared at him. "I said I really ought to turn you into a frog."

"You're welcome to try."

"You and your smart mouth. You should shut it until you can learn not to insult the people who are trying to help you." She lifted her hand and flicked her fingers at him.

He tried to respond, but couldn't make a sound. He put his hand to his mouth. His lips were sealed shut.

Her eyes rounded. "I didn't think that would work."

She flicked her fingers at him again, and his voice returned as his mouth opened. "What the hell did you just do to me? What was that?"

"Reason number one why you should never make a witch angry."

"That wasn't witchcraft. That was—" He faltered, unable to come up with an explanation.

"Because it's *warm* in here? Because your lips got tired? A vitamin deficiency? When are you going to understand that there are things beyond your comprehension? I'm sorry you had such a bad experience with your ex-wife, but I'm not her."

"Pandora, I didn't mean—"

"Yes, you did." Pandora grabbed her purse and stood. "Don't get up. I'll see myself out."

And she did, resulting in his door being slammed for a third time that day.

5

After a long day of work, Pandora took refuge in her sister's flower shop. She perched on a stool and inhaled the gorgeously sweet, green fragrance that permeated the space. It was like nature on steroids in here. Of course, it would be. It was a flower shop. But Marigold had a knack for flowers that went beyond the ordinary thanks to her superior witchy gifts with plants. She supplied most of the witches in town with their herbal needs and was generally considered the most adept green witch in the area.

As Marigold lifted a bucket of flowers onto the work table, Pandora resumed her conversation about Cole. "So he's very hot. But kind of a butthead. I mean, I get why he's a butthead, but still."

Marigold stuck a spray of something bright orange into the arrangement she was working on.

"You should cut him some slack. He's clearly not had an easy go of things." She looked over at Pandora. "And as a single parent myself, I know of which I speak."

"How is Saffie?"

"Madly in love with Charlie Merrow, which worries me a little."

"Why? Because he's a werewolf or because his mother's a werewolf or because his dad's the sheriff *and* a werewolf?"

Marigold made a face. "None of those. Because she's eight and already in love with a boy."

"Tell her to sit down and have a conversation with him. That ought to cure it."

Marigold smiled as she added a few yellow roses to the vase. "I think you like this guy."

"Don't go there."

"He *is* your type."

"Seriously, Mari, don't go there."

Marigold went to the cold storage and brought back a bucket of orange lilies. "I'm sure he'll come around. He has no choice if his daughter's a witch. Sooner or later, he's going to experience something that can't be explained away."

Pandora shifted, leaning against the counter behind her. "You know, something weird happened while we were up in his attic. I handed him this old scrying mirror, and when he took it, he got this kind of blank look on his face but his eyes went sort of wild. Like he was getting some strong vibes off it. Or seeing something. But when I asked him about it, he clammed up. Refused to acknowledge anything had happened."

Marigold stopped what she was doing and stared directly at Pandora. "Are you saying there's a bunch of Gertrude Pilcher's things still in that house?"

Pandora laughed. "I'm pretty sure all her things are still in that house. Based on what I saw, Ulysses threw nothing away."

"Those are powerful goods, Pandy. They shouldn't just go to anyone." Marigold picked up a lily and snipped the end. "At the very least, the coven should put them into safe keeping."

"I told Cole I'd take care of cleaning out the attic, but technically shouldn't that stuff go to Kaley? I mean, it's sort of her inheritance."

"When she's ready, yes. Thirteen is no kind of age to take possession of tools that powerful. Who's her mentor?"

"She doesn't have one yet. I'm trying to help her with that. You know anyone who might be interested?"

"Not offhand, but bring it up at the next meeting."

"I will. Hey." Pandora slipped off the stool to stand. "Do you think touching that mirror could have…fixed my magic?"

"What do you mean?"

"I got a little mad at Cole and cast a sealing spell on his mouth. And it worked."

Marigold's brows shot up. "Has he been silenced for life?"

"Very funny. No. I took it back and he was fine."

Marigold shrugged. "I've never heard of touching another witch's artifacts having that kind of effect, but Gertrude was a…unique creature. You should talk to Mom about that. Congrats on the working magic, by the way."

"Thanks. I'll talk to Mom about it tomorrow. Right now I just want to go home, have a glass of wine and tell Pumpkin all about my day."

"You live such a full life."

Pandora flicked a petal at her sister. "Tell my favorite niece I love her. Gotta run. I need to hit the Shop and Save before I go home. I'm almost out of that diet cat food."

Marigold made a skeptical face. "Didn't you just put Pumpkin on that diet like three days ago? How are you already out of food?"

"She clawed the bag open in the middle of the night and ate most of it." Pandora shook her head. "Don't judge. She gets *hangry*."

Marigold laughed. "See you at dinner Saturday?"

"Wouldn't miss it for the world," Pandora said as she headed for the door.

The Professor Woos The Witch

Saturday nights were family dinner night at their mother's house, which meant Stanhill would be there. He was basically family at this point anyway. Charisma, their other sister, always came too when she was in town. Her job as a life coach meant she traveled a lot, although Nocturne Falls would always be her home. Pandora stopped with her hand on the knob. "Charisma here?"

"Yep."

"All right, see you then." Both sisters, her mother *and* Stanhill? Oh boy. Pandora would get some serious grilling this Saturday. No way her new friendship with Cole wasn't already a main topic of conversation. The Williamses liked to talk. Especially about each other. It was born out of love and caring, but there was no escaping the family scrutiny.

By the time Pandora got home, she was more than ready for her evening glass of wine and a little snuggle with Pumpkin.

Her cat, however, didn't meet her at the front door. Instead, Pandora found Pumpkin sitting in front of the sliders, staring at the backyard.

"Nice to see you not sleeping for a change." Pandora decided to pour her wine first and take it with her into the bedroom. She could drink it while she put her comfies on.

Pumpkin meowed pitifully.

Pandora stared at her cat. "Have you lost that much weight that you suddenly want to go out and run around?"

More meowing, this time with longing.

"All right, keep your panties on, I'm coming." Pandora opened the slider and Pumpkin shot out. Well, maybe not *shot* out. Lumbered with haste was a more apt description.

Pandora took her wine into the bedroom and came back five minutes later, hair up, tank top and shorts replacing her work clothes, and joined Pumpkin in the backyard, wine in hand. There was no chance Pumpkin could escape. There was a gate in the wooden fence around Pandora's property, but that led out to the front of the house and definitely required opposable thumbs.

She took up her spot on the glider and looked around for Pumpkin. Her Royal Fatness was sitting in front of the shed door, pawing at it with no real effort. Still, just the fact that Pumpkin had put in the work to get to the shed was saying something. "What's in there, Plumpkin?"

The cat ignored her and kept pawing.

Pandora's witchy senses kicked in. Even if they hadn't, she still could have guessed what Pumpkin wanted. She sighed, set her wine down and headed toward the rear of the yard. She opened the shed door. "Out, Kaley. Before Pumpkin has a beef-jerky seizure."

Kaley heaved out a sigh and looked at Pumpkin. "Traitor."

"You're the one with the delicious meat products."

Kaley trudged out. "Please don't send me home."

"I have to. But you can come hang out on the porch for a bit if you want."

The teenager exhaled another sigh that made it seem like the weight of the world was on her shoulders. "Okay."

They walked back to the porch, Pumpkin at Kaley's heels in a last-ditch effort to cute some jerky out of her.

Pandora rolled her eyes. "Give it up, Pumpkin. You're not getting any people food." She picked up her wine and sat back in the glider. "What's up?"

Kaley flopped down on the wicker chair and ottoman, her backpack slumped on the floor. "I love my dad, but he can also be a jerk."

"Kaley, don't say that. He works hard to take care of you, and I know you don't agree with him, but he means well. He's just trying to protect you."

She slanted her eyes at Pandora. "Great. You like him now, so you're siding with him."

"I don't *like* him. I mean, I don't dislike him. Too much. But I'm definitely not romantically interested in him. We're going to work on the house together. It's the deal I made with him so you and I can spend more time together. And while I do that, I'm going to work on him too."

Kaley sat up a little. "What do you mean?"

"I mean, I'm going to get him to believe."

"Really? Does that mean I'm getting a mentor?"

"It means I'm working on it. But I need you to help me out with your dad."

"Is this the part where you tell me to behave and do what my dad says?"

"Basically, yes."

Kaley treated Pandora to yet another bodily sigh. "Yeah, all right. But you're still going to give me witch lessons?"

"Someone will."

"Why not you?"

"Because I'm…I have a lot on my plate already."

Kaley squinted. "This has something to do with your aura being all cracked, doesn't it?"

Rotten child. "I'm going to talk to my mother about where to start, and then at the next coven meeting, I'll ask about a mentor."

Kaley's mouth fell open. "There's a coven meeting?"

"Yep. Once a month."

"You guys are so lucky. Can I get in on that?"

"We'll see." Pandora wasn't sure how Cole would react to that. Actually, she had a pretty good idea.

"Hey, you said your mom's a witch too, right?"

"She is. And my sisters."

"Can I meet them? Please? It would be so awesome."

"Sure. I'll figure something out. But you have to promise me you're going to be on your best behavior with your dad."

"I will." Kaley grinned. "You do like him, though, don't you?"

"He has his moments. When he's not hating on witches."

"I hear that, sister."

Pandora gave Kaley a raised brow in response.

Kaley just laughed. Then Pumpkin jumped up into Kaley's lap, and Kaley let out an "oof" as the breath was pressed out of her. "Your cat really needs to lose weight."

"Why do you think I don't want her having beef jerky?"

"Yeah, I get it." She ruffled Pumpkin's fur. "You too fat, kitty, but you're very cute and super soft." Kaley looked at Pandora. "I wish my dad liked cats. I'd love to get one."

"Not into cats or witches, huh? He gets better by the second." Pandora went to take another sip of her wine, but thought better of it and put it on the coffee table instead. "I should drive you home. I'm sure your dad is worried about you."

"Weren't you supposed to meet us for dinner at that place?"

"How did you know about that?"

"Dad texted me at school to say he'd apologized to you and that we were going to dinner at Hooters."

"Howler's. If you knew he apologized, why did you come over here?"

"Because when I got home, he was grumpy and snapped at me when I told him he should put on a nicer shirt."

"Yeah, well, I think dinner's off anyway. I'm sorry he was grumpy, that's probably my fault too."

"Why? What happened?"

"I…" Pandora wasn't sure how to explain, but Kaley was a sister witch. Young, maybe, but Pandora decided to use what had happened as a teaching moment. Isn't that what they called it? "I sort of zapped your dad with some magic this afternoon. I got mad and I wasn't thinking. It was wrong, but—"

"Cool!"

"No, not cool. You should never use magic to harm another person. We take an oath about that and everything."

Kaley's eyes got big. "Harm? What did you do to him?"

"I didn't hurt him. I just…sealed his mouth shut so he couldn't speak."

Kaley went blank for a split-second, then burst into laughter. Pumpkin ran for it.

"It's not funny," Pandora said.

"No wonder he was so mad," Kaley choked out. "That's epic."

"No, it is not." Pandora stood up and grabbed her wine to take it inside. "Let's go. I'm driving you home."

"Aw, c'mon, it is a little funny." But Kaley got up, hauling her backpack over her shoulder.

"Okay, maybe a little. It wasn't at the time, though." Pandora led Kaley and Pumpkin inside, locked the slider behind them and headed for her purse by the door.

"Are you mad at me for coming over?"

Pandora opened the front door and shooed Kaley out, car keys in hand. "No. I'm glad you think of this as a safe place, but you still need to work on cutting your dad some slack."

"I will."

"Good." Pandora probably needed to take some of that advice herself. "Get in the car."

Cole stood in the attic, staring at the shelves of books and bottles and other random junk. Everything he believed was suddenly in question. It wasn't just what Pandora had done to him, but the moment of contact between them that had blown his sense of reality to smithereens.

Worse, he couldn't stop thinking about her. Especially about how he wanted to touch her again.

Which was why he was up here. He was going to pick up the mirror again and pray that's what had caused his weird vision. *Not* touching her.

Because he'd already convinced himself that the temporary muteness had been nothing more than the worst possible case of a frog in the throat. *Not* magic.

The mirror was right where he'd left it. There was nothing unusual about it. Just a small brass hand mirror with a few flowers and ornaments engraved on the handle. Ordinary. He flexed his hand. There was nothing to think about. Just pick it up.

He grabbed the handle. Nothing happened. He let out the breath he'd been holding and put the mirror back. "See? You idiot. All worked up over—"

A dull thump interrupted him. He turned to see a puff of dust curling through the air. A book had fallen off one of the shelves. That wasn't weird at all. "Houses shift. Stuff moves. Totally explainable."

He walked slowly to the book and picked it up. The heat from the attic made the back of his neck prickle. The book was a slim volume, bound in dark blue leather. Here and there on the spine and cover, gold decorations had worn away, leaving only the imprint of the embossing visible. The title on the front read *Concerning Familiars*.

It meant nothing to him. He reshelved it and headed for the stairs.

A dull thump sounded the moment his back was turned.

He twisted around. The book was on the floor again. He hesitated. Then got angry. He picked up the book and jammed it onto the shelf. "Stay," he muttered.

He went for the stairs again, and this time there was no more noise behind him. He shut the attic door firmly and started down the steps. He swung by Kaley's room to apologize to her for snapping earlier.

This whole thing with Pandora was setting him on edge, but that was not Kaley's fault. Plus, she'd been right. He really should put on a nicer shirt. He tapped his knuckles on the door. "Sweetheart, can I talk to you?"

Nothing. That kid and her earbuds. She was going to ruin her hearing. He knocked louder. "Kaley, turn your music off a sec."

Still nothing. He opened the door. She wasn't in her room.

He jogged downstairs. "Kaley? You down here?"

A car pulled into the driveway. He recognized the well-maintained late-model Mercedes. Pandora. With Kaley in the passenger seat.

He opened the front door and leaned against the

frame while his daughter got out. This running away business was getting old.

She climbed the porch steps and glanced at him sheepishly. "I went to Pandora's."

"Miss Williams'."

"I went to Miss Williams'."

There were worse places she could go. "Because I snapped?"

"Yes. You mad?"

"Not really." He was. At himself for having another argument with her. "But I would like you to go to your room and do your homework."

"Okay." She trudged past him.

"I love you, Kaley."

"Love you, too, Dad."

He stepped onto the porch and peered into Pandora's car. Didn't seem like she was getting out. He walked down to the driver's side.

She unrolled the window as he approached but didn't say anything.

"She cause any trouble?"

"No." Pandora eyed him warily.

"You don't look like you're dressed for dinner." Not that he disapproved. Her love for tank tops was fast becoming one of his favorite things about her.

"I didn't think we were still going after…what happened."

He took a breath. Being this close to her

exponentially ramped up the desire to touch her again. "You, uh, could come in and we could get pizza. Or something."

"I think I should just go home."

"I'd really like to talk."

Uncertainty lifted her brows. "We've tried that. Doesn't seem to work out so well between us."

"Maybe we could start over."

She studied him. "I'm sorry about what I did to you. That was not the correct use of magic."

It wasn't *any* use of magic. But that conviction didn't ring as true as it would have the day before. "The thing is...I'm starting to have doubts. Not doubts. Questions."

"About?"

He braced himself and forced out the words. "What's true and what's not."

She grinned and turned off the engine. "Pizza sounds great."

He opened her car door for her, and she slid out, her shapely legs tanned and a little freckled and utterly sexy. He leaned past her to close the door.

"I see you didn't take Kaley's advice." She poked at the hole in the sleeve of his T-shirt. Her finger went through and connected with his bicep.

A flash of moonlight and the caw of birds filled his senses. Wind rushed over his skin as the earth fell away beneath him. The sensation gave him a moment of vertigo, and he stumbled, coming in contact with the side of her car. Losing contact with her.

He blinked hard. The images were gone. His heart was pounding, and his breath was coming fast.

Alarm distorted Pandora's face. She reached for him. "Are you okay?"

He put his hands up. "Don't touch me. Please. Something's not right."

She retreated. "Are you sick?"

"No." He straightened as he caught his breath. "But we really need to talk."

6

As soon as they got into the house, Cole called upstairs. "Kaley?"

"In my room," she yelled back.

"Okay," he answered, then said to Pandora, "Let's go into the kitchen."

"Sure." She headed there with him, dying with curiosity over what was going on. It almost seemed like he'd had the same kind of episode as he'd had in the attic, but he hadn't touched anything witchy.

Except her. And, technically, she'd touched him.

She took a seat at the table and waited for him to do the same.

"You want a beer?" He pulled the fridge open. "Because I do. Definitely." He held up two cold bottles.

"Since I'm missing my wine, sure. Plus, it goes good with pizza."

He twisted the tops off both bottles and handed

one to her as he sat down, his fingers well away from hers. They each took a drink, his slightly longer. When he set his bottle down, he shook his head. "Something is happening to me."

"So you said. What kind of something?"

"I...don't know." He swallowed. "I'm having these...visions."

She knew her facial expression probably wasn't helping the situation, but to hear a guy who flat-out refused to believe in witches say he was having visions was pretty jaw-dropping. "What kind of visions?"

More head shaking. "Like I'm flying. And there are always birds in them. Or the sound of birds."

She pursed her lips. "I don't know what that means. Wait. You said always. When did they start?"

He let out a breath. "The visions started when you handed me the mirror..."

"I sense a *but* coming."

He ran a hand through his dark hair, his eyes troubled as he nodded. "I've been having dreams like that since I was a kid."

That was a little concerning. She sat back, scrunching up her nose. "Okay, that's weird."

He flicked his gaze at her. "That's not helpful."

"I'm sure."

"Maybe we should go back to the attic and take a look at that mirror again."

"I already did that."

"And?"

"Nothing. But when you touched me in the driveway, it happened again."

"That doesn't mean these visions aren't connected to the mirror."

His brows bent. "It doesn't?"

"No. If that's where the visions started, it could definitely be involved." She put her hands on the table. "You mind if I run up there and have a look at the mirror?"

"Be my guest." He stood. "I guess I should go with you."

"Actually, no."

"No?"

"Just trust me on this." Despite opening up about the visions, she wasn't convinced Cole was ready for the full-on witch experience, and she wanted to try a little summoning spell while she was in the attic. Without him going all Judgy McJudgerson.

"Okay." He looked relieved and sat back down.

She got up. "I won't be too long."

He nodded and sipped his beer. "I'll order the pizza. Any toppings you hate that I should know about?"

"Pineapple. Don't go there."

"Got it."

She headed upstairs. She added residential elevator to the list of things the house could use. At least the two flights would count as some kind of cardio.

The attic was exactly as she remembered it. Big, dusty and crammed with all kinds of witchy things. She poked around. Some really great witchy things. Maybe Cole would let her mom and sisters come over to help catalog this stuff.

She went to the shelf with the mirror and picked up the scrying glass. She turned it over, tested its weight. There was nothing unusual about it. She put it back.

Her magic had been rather cooperative lately. She hoped that would hold out for her summoning spell. It was very possible Gertrude had left some unfinished or lingering magic behind.

She stood in the middle of the room and spread her arms out. "Any spells that remain undone, show yourself in a beam of sun."

She turned slowly, but not a single thing was illuminated.

"I didn't leave any loose ends."

Pandora spun toward the unfamiliar female voice.

Behind her stood a ghost. *Stood* maybe wasn't the right word. *Hovered* was more correct. The ghost was about five feet tall, eighty years old and had a helmet of cotton-candy-pink hair that matched the pantsuit she was wearing.

Pandora took a wild guess. "Gertrude?"

"One and the same. You the new lady of the house?"

"No, I'm just visiting." Pandora had seen her share of supernatural weirdness in her time, but this was the topper.

Gertrude nodded. "You sleeping with the disbelieving man candy?"

"I—no."

"You should be. He's got it going on for a normie." Gertrude tapped a finger against her chin. "Technically, he's not a complete normie, though."

"He's not?"

Gertrude's eyes narrowed. "Is he some relation to my Ulysses?"

Pandora nodded. "Distant nephew."

Gertrude slapped her thigh. "I knew it. Same eyes. Plus, I can tell a familiar when I see one."

"A familiar?"

"I tried to give him a hint." Gertrude wiggled her fingers at the bookshelf on the other side of the room, and a narrow book slid out and floated over. "But he's got a classic case of denial going on."

The book bobbed in the air in front of Pandora. She plucked it free and read the cover. "*Concerning Familiars*?"

Gertrude waved her hand at Pandora as if assessing her. "Your magic's a little wobbly on a good day, isn't it?"

Pandora lifted her chin. "I do my best."

"Oh, it's not your fault, dearie." Gertrude levitated so she could look down her nose at Pandora in a very conspiratorial way. "But around the stud muffin, it works just fine, am I right?"

"No one says stud muffin anymore." Pandora bit her lip as she thought back. All the magic she'd done that had actually worked had been performed in Cole's proximity. The candle and the sealing spell. And maybe the summoning spell. He was just a few floors down, after all.

And while the spell hadn't found any unfinished magic, it had brought Gertrude out of the ether. Whether or not that was actually a positive remained to be seen. "What does it mean that my magic works around him?"

"He's a familiar. And not just any familiar, he's yours." She gave Pandora a naughty wink. "Touching him will awaken feelings in both of you, but to seal the bond and keep him from bonding with any other witch, you need to get a little more intimate. You know what I mean? You need to get—"

"I know what intimate means, so settle down. Let's go back to what you first said, because I don't understand all of this. Familiars are like cats and birds and rats. There's a member of our coven who has a bearded dragon."

"You could at least kiss him, that's all I'm saying." Gertrude hovered close enough that Pandora realized she was wearing false eyelashes. "And yes, familiars are usually animals. Sometimes, they're people who can shift into animals."

"Cole's not a shifter."

"Ah, but he *is*. You can see it in his aura."

"I can't see auras."

"Didn't get that gift, eh? It's all right. Not many do. But trust me, being a familiar is an essential part of who Cole is. After all, my Ulysses was one."

Pandora did a quick mental check on all the stories she'd heard about Gertrude and her husband. "I've never heard that about you two."

Gertrude's drawn-on eyebrows rose abruptly. "So you've heard things about me, then?"

"My mother knows—knew you."

"Who's she?"

"Corette Williams."

Gertrude nodded. "I remember her. You ask her about human familiars. You'll see. They're rare, and those of us who are fortunate enough to get one, don't talk about it, because there are less-scrupulous witches out there who'd like to steal them away. Some witches spend their whole lives trying to find one, but human familiars don't work that way. They find the witch who needs them, not the other way around. And if one finds you, then you are a very lucky witch indeed."

Pandora's head was spinning. "But why doesn't he know he's one, if that's what he is?"

Gertrude shot up into the air and hovered several feet above the floor, her gaze shifting over Pandora's shoulder. "Gotta go!"

"Wait!" Pandora put her hand out, but Gertrude was gone.

Behind her, the attic door opened.

"You okay up here?"

She turned. Cole stood at the landing. Gertrude was right. He really was a stud muffin. "Yeah, I'm fine. I was just coming back down."

"Were you talking to someone?"

"No. Yes. I don't know." She rubbed her forehead. "I don't know where to start."

He walked over, his gaze on the book in her hand. "Please tell me that book wasn't on the floor when you came up here."

"No. Why?"

"It kept falling off the shelf earlier."

Pandora nodded. More like it kept getting pushed off the shelf by a crazy old woman with drawn-on eyebrows and a penchant for glitter. "I think I know what's going on with you, but you're not going to like it."

"I don't like it now. Tell me your thoughts. I'll be as open-minded as I can be."

Gertrude's words rang in Pandora's brain. "This is going to sound crazy, but you might be something called a familiar."

"Familiar with what?"

"No, *a* familiar. A witch's companion."

His expression didn't change for a moment, then he started laughing. "Okay, you got me. Good one."

"No, I'm serious." She held out the book to him. "You should read this."

He held his hands up. "Pandora, c'mon. That's so bananas I don't even know where to start. Certainly not with that dusty old book."

Reluctantly, she put the book back on the shelf. "You said you'd be open-minded."

"Yes, but a witch's companion? As in your companion? Is this your way of trying to get me to believe? It's cute, I'll give you that."

Kiss him, a voice whispered in her ear.

So she did.

Cole registered Pandora getting closer, her eyes closing, her lips puckering. He knew on some level what all those things meant. And yet he was still surprised when her mouth made contact with his.

Not so surprised he couldn't react. His growing desire to be near her, to touch her and hold her, spiked into incalculable territory. His arms slipped around her of their own volition. She was as warm and soft and curvy as she looked. Maybe more.

Her lips fit his perfectly, and as her tongue

brushed the seam of his mouth, he groaned in pleasure, unable to hold back the sheer joy of tasting her. Kissing Pandora was torture in the most amazing way.

She kissed with the kind of tentative pressure that made him realize she had no idea how he felt about her. And why would she? He'd been a jerk.

Then, maybe because she'd figured out he wasn't resisting, she leaned in and *really* kissed him.

Heat rose up through his body like he was standing on a steam vent. Every muscle and nerve came alive. He wasn't even sure he was still touching the floor.

The rush of air stripped the heat from his skin and everything *changed*. No matter which way he turned his head, his field of vision was filled with the sprawl of forest and rising hills. He flapped his wings and—*he flapped his wings?* Cole opened his mouth to cry out.

The screech of a bird filled his ears.

Pandora was gone. He couldn't feel her or sense her presence. All he saw was sky and the earth below. Things started to contort, and his vision went blurry. His heart pounded, thundering with the unknown and the known. More bird cries filled his ears. Everything about this moment was strange and, somehow, déjà vu.

There was a brief pinch of discomfort, then all went black.

He opened his eyes and saw the wood ceiling of the attic. And Pandora, looking down at him with big eyes and a slightly awed expression.

"Are you okay?"

He blinked up at her. "I don't know. What just happened?"

She glanced down the length of his body before making eye contact again. "For about thirty seconds, you were...a raven."

"It sounded like you said I was a raven."

"I did."

He really didn't want to unpack that, but somehow it made perfect sense. And no sense. "An actual bird."

"An actual bird."

He stared at the ceiling for a long, quiet moment, hoping he would suddenly awaken and realize this was all a dream. No such glorious thing occurred. "I might need professional help."

She nodded. "I can arrange that."

"You mean professional witch help, don't you?"

"In this situation, that seems like the best choice." She helped him sit up.

He leaned on his bent knees. "What the hell is going on with me, Pandora? This isn't normal. You can't tell me this is normal."

"If you're a familiar, which it seems you are, then yes, becoming a bird is normal. But you shouldn't be shifting spontaneously or blacking out when it happens. It seems pretty obvious you weren't in control of the shift and that's not how it should be, but then how could you control it when you didn't even know what was happening to you? Or...I don't know. But we'll figure this out."

As his common sense returned, he managed to process his thoughts a little better. "Pandora, I'm not a familiar. I'm not anything but human, so there's no way I just changed into a raven. I'm sure it was just the rush of blood and endorphins brought on by our kiss."

"Cole, I know what I saw."

He closed his eyes for a moment. "I can't believe this is possible. I just can't."

"I thought you might need convincing. So I pulled this off you." She held up an iridescent black feather.

7

Pandora chewed without really tasting. She sat between Kaley and Cole with the pizza in the middle of the table. She knew Cole and Kaley were talking about school, but Pandora's mind was on the feather in her pocket, what she'd just seen and what it meant.

And how much she'd liked kissing Cole.

She studied him. He was in an animated conversation with his daughter, as if nothing had happened. How he could manage that, she had no idea. Maybe it was a skill set that came with parenthood. Whatever, it was impressive.

Kaley tapped her arm. "Hey, are you in outer space?"

"Kaley, that's not nice," Cole reprimanded.

"Sorry." Kaley shot her father a look before talking to Pandora again. "You seem really far away."

"Yeah, I guess I was." Pandora glanced at Cole, but he was getting another slice. She turned her attention to Kaley. "What did I miss?"

"Nothing. Boring school junk. I'm so glad tomorrow is Saturday. Do you have to work?"

"Yes. I have to show a house in the morning. Hey, can you see everyone's aura?"

Kaley perked up, apparently happy to talk about witchy stuff. "Yep. Yours doesn't look nearly as broken as it used to."

Good to know—and telling—but not what Pandora was after. She pointed the tip of her pizza slice at Cole. "What's your dad's aura look like?"

Kaley made a face. "His is weird. I've never seen anybody else's like it. Except for Grandpa's."

Which made perfect sense. If Cole was a familiar, one of his parents had to be too. "Weird how?"

"It's all dark and floaty. Like black snow."

"Or maybe...feathers?" Pandora watched Cole's face.

"Sure, could be." Kaley stuffed another bite of pizza in her mouth.

Cole's everything-is-fine expression blanked out. He stared at Pandora, the look in his eyes like that of a drowning man searching for a life preserver.

Pandora's heart went out to him. She could only imagine how it felt to have your life—and your beliefs—turned upside down like that. Not to mention finding out your parents had clearly kept some big secrets. "Why don't you guys come to my mom's house for dinner tomorrow night?"

Cole nodded, but it seemed more like an acknowledgment that she'd said something rather than an acceptance of her invitation.

Kaley answered around a mouthful of pizza. "Cool! I can't wait to meet more witches. Will your sisters be there?"

Pandora smiled at Kaley. "Sure will."

Kaley tipped her head toward Cole. "Dad, can we?"

Pandora turned her gaze back to him as well. "I think my family could be...helpful."

He appeared lost in thought a moment longer. "I guess so." Then he addressed Pandora in a softer voice. "I don't like this."

"I know." Pandora made herself smile. He also really wouldn't like it if he knew the ghost of the witch who'd owned this house was still in it.

Kaley dropped her half-eaten slice of pizza on her plate. "I'm done. Can I be excused?"

"Yes." As Kaley took off, Cole seemed relieved that he could stop pretending. He laced his hands behind his head and stared at the ceiling. "What am I going to do?"

"You're going to take it one day at a time. I'll help you."

He dropped his hands to lean on the table, closer to her. "What does this mean for my life? Why didn't my parents tell me?"

"You'll have to take that up with your dad."

"I plan to." He shook his head. "Let's say I am a familiar, which still makes no sense to me, then what does that have to do with me being a raven?"

"Familiars are traditionally animals. I guess for human familiars, it means you can shift into that form. Yours just happens to be a raven. Birds are definitely one of the more popular types of familiars with witches, although cats are high on the list too. Hmm. You being a raven shifter might explain your dislike of cats."

"And why yours tried to eat me."

"Pumpkin did not try to eat you."

"I felt teeth. Look, if I'm a familiar, why haven't I been chased by witches all my life?"

Pandora thought about what he'd told her about his ex-wife. "I think you have been. At least once."

"What do you mean?"

"You said Lila claimed to be a witch. Based on what I've observed in Kaley, I'd say that's true. Kaley had to get it from someone and it sure wasn't you. Did Lila also claim to see auras like Kaley does?"

"Yes."

"That explains it then."

"Explains what?"

"You said that in the early days, she treated you like a king."

He nodded. "So?"

"She saw your aura and understood exactly what you were. I think she was trying to get you to bond with her. Or at least reveal yourself as a familiar. When that didn't happen, she split."

Cole swore softly. "She was using me. I guess I always kind of thought that, especially when she left Kaley behind, but hell, I never knew to what extent."

He sighed and pushed his glasses back. "Is Kaley really a witch?"

Pandora nodded. "Yes. And seeing auras like she can? That's pretty special stuff. A lot of witches claim they can, but most just see vague colors. Kaley seems to be able to read them with the sort of clarity that's rare." She hesitated. "Gertrude could read them too, I think."

"You mean the old woman who used to live here?"

Pandora rolled her lips together, wondering if she should say more.

"What?" Cole asked. "You're not telling me something."

"I don't know how much more you can take."

He laughed. "You're a witch. From a family of witches. My ex-wife is a witch. Apparently literally and figuratively. Plus my kid's a witch. And I am probably some kind of animal shifter. All that, and I'm still upright and functioning. I don't think there's anything you could tell me that would break me at this point."

She kept her mouth shut.

He reached out and put his hand as close to hers as possible without touching. "C'mon, Pandora. What is it?"

Goddess help her, she wanted to touch him, but she didn't want to throw him into that weird shifting fugue state again. She sighed. "Gertrude is still here. Sort of. I ran into her ghost in your attic."

He swallowed. "You're sure?"

Pandora nodded. "She's the one who told me what you are. Your great-uncle Ulysses was a familiar too. It's in your bloodline. And based on what Kaley said about your dad's aura, he's also a familiar."

Cole pulled his hand back and took a deep breath, exhaling before he spoke again. "You think your family can help? Not just me, but with Kaley?"

"Yes, absolutely, to both."

"Good." He smiled with weak resignation. "We'll come to dinner tomorrow night. I don't know how I'm going to live with this. And Kaley's going to need guidance I'd never be able to give her."

He stared at Pandora's hand, then slid his back across the table toward her. "I like you, Pandora. I feel…drawn to you in a way I've never felt with another woman. If that's whatever's inside me responding to who you are, so be it, but I don't like being afraid of touching you."

He raised his head to meet her eyes. "I don't think I can stop feeling this way either."

She lifted her fingers, her instinct to lay them on top of his, but she stopped herself and dropped them back to the table. "I'm okay with that. I feel drawn to you too, despite the fact that I don't really like you much. *Didn't* really like you much."

"I'm sorry about that. I'll work on being more likable. I swear."

"I'll believe that when I see it." She smiled. "We'll figure this out. I promise."

He stood, putting some distance between them. "I need to call my dad. He owes me a big explanation for why he and my mom kept this from me all these years. I'd really like to know what the hell they were thinking."

She got up. "I should go anyway. Work tomorrow and all that. I'll text you with the time for dinner."

"Sounds good. Thanks for not giving up on me. I'm sorry I was such a bonehead about the whole witch thing."

"You were just being human." She smiled, her heart thudding a little at how handsome and vulnerable he looked.

A thin half smile lifted his mouth. "I'd like to kiss you good-bye, but I'm not sure that would be a good idea what with the shifting and all."

"Right. We totally shouldn't do that then." But she couldn't bring herself to move toward the door. "Or I could try to…help with that."

"How?" He took a step in her direction.

"A little suppression spell. That's the best thing I can think of. You willing to give it a shot?"

His answer came without hesitation. He threaded his fingers through her hair and tipped her mouth up to meet his.

She sank into his kiss with none of the hesitation she'd felt the first time. If he wanted to kiss her, she was going to give it her complete effort. She was also going to do her witchy best to keep him from shifting again and freaking out. He could learn to manage that in his own time. With that in mind, she pushed a little spell over him.

His mouth was hungry and searching and fit hers as perfectly as if they'd been made for each other, which she guessed was kind of the case.

She could practically feel his pulse thrumming through his skin. Or maybe that was hers. For a moment, it seemed like they were one person, one being, one perfect entity. A whirlwind spun around them, lifting them, making them lighter than air…

And then he broke the kiss and backed up. His eyes were a little wild, wide and feral with the kind of animalistic need she'd seen in him right before he'd transformed in the attic. She whispered a calming spell on top of the one to suppress his shifting.

He relaxed and took a breath. "Did you just use more magic on me?"

She nodded. "A calming spell. You looked a little freaked out. Like you were going to shift."

"But I didn't, right?"

"No."

"Thanks for the help, but it makes me think we need to practice more."

"Practice more what?"

"Kissing." He reached for her again.

Half an hour later, Cole had said good-bye to Pandora three times. This time they'd somehow made it stick, and he gave her a wave as she pulled out of his driveway.

He was crazy. He knew that. But at a certain point, you couldn't fight the inevitable. So if he was going to be crazy, he was at least going to enjoy himself.

And Pandora was very enjoyable.

But it wasn't just a physical attraction. He felt complete around her. And that wasn't a feeling any part of him wanted to fight.

He watched her car until it was out of sight, then went to the kitchen to grab his cellphone and call his father. He walked out onto the back porch to sit as the line connected.

"Hello, Cole."

"Hi, Dad. How are you?"

"Good, son. How's that granddaughter of mine?"

Where to start? This wasn't exactly a conversation about the weather. "She's good. We're settling in."

"Glad to hear it."

There was no way to ease into the tough questions, so Cole stumbled through them as bests he could. "I know about the...that is, I *think* I know. What I mean to say, without sounding like I'm losing my mind, is that I know about the whole familiar thing. Including the shifting. And we really need to talk about it."

His father didn't respond right away.

Cole cringed, wondering if he was losing his mind. If his dad said there was nothing to discuss—

Jack Van Zant let out a pensive breath. "I could pretend not to know what you're talking about, but we're both too old for that. I owe you an apology and an explanation, but I'd rather talk to you in person about this. You okay with that?"

Cole would have rather heard everything

immediately, but he was just thankful his father was willing to talk. And that he wasn't crazy. "Sure, but this house isn't exactly in visiting shape."

"I don't care about that. Any chance to spoil that granddaughter of mine is a good one. I'll leave first thing in the morning. Be there by noon."

Wilmington, North Carolina, was six hours away. "Dad, you don't have to leave at six A.M."

"And miss lunch with my granddaughter?"

"Uh, Kaley and I have a dinner thing to go to tomorrow night. I'd invite you, but it's not my place to add someone. I'm not telling you you can't stay, just that you'll be by yourself tomorrow night."

"I'm happy to sit someplace and read. That house have a back porch?"

"I'm on it right now." Not that you could see much past the railing thanks to the riotous overgrowth.

"Good. See you tomorrow."

Cole hung up. The feelings inside him almost defied labeling. He was as unsettled as he was excited, which was plain odd, because to think he'd be excited about being something more than...human went against everything he believed in.

But if being a familiar meant more time with Pandora, he was all about that. Just the thought of being near her again pumped endorphins into his system. That had to be this other side of him at work. He hadn't been interested in a woman in ages. Not after the scar Lila had left.

He closed his eyes and tipped his head back, the buzz of insects and the melody of birdsong creating a natural white noise that let him drift into his thoughts. Pandora was beautiful and had curves that wouldn't quit, but there was more to her than just a stellar exterior. She was kind and sweet and funny and smart. Also not afraid to speak her mind or stand up to him, which he loved.

But above all that, she was good with Kaley. If there was one way to his heart, it was through his daughter.

After the divorce had been finalized, he'd dated a few times. Mostly set-ups put together by some of his colleagues at school. But after watching the change of expression on his dates' faces when he mentioned Kaley, he'd quickly decided his need for companionship could take a backseat until his daughter was off to college. Apparently, it took a special kind of woman to accept another woman's child.

He hadn't really needed another woman in his life that badly anyway. And Kaley sure as hell hadn't needed another mother figure walking out on her.

But Pandora had started out liking Kaley better

than she liked him. He grinned. For a witch, she was all right. Hell, for a human being, she was spectacular.

Which brought him right back around to thinking about kissing her again. He sighed deeply, remembering the sweetness of her mouth on his and the lush curves of her hips under his hands. And after seeing her in those skimpy shorts and too-tight tank tops, he could imagine very well what she'd look like—

"You're thinking about her, aren't you?"

He opened his eyes and sat up abruptly. "Hey, Kaley. I didn't even hear you come out the door."

She sat in the chair next to him. "That's because you were dreaming about Pandora, weren't you?"

"Miss Williams."

"Hah! So you admit it." She got a big goofy grin on her face. "You're in luh-ove," she sing-songed.

"Kaley. I just met Miss Williams. No one falls in love that quickly." Although it wasn't out of the question to say he was headed toward deep *like*.

Kaley shrugged. "Whatever. You like her."

He gave her his best fatherly look. "Did you come out here to harass me or did you have another reason?"

Her smile turned sly. "I thought I heard you call me for ice cream."

He laughed. "Oh, you did, did you?" For a moment, he was overwhelmed with how beautiful his daughter was. How perfect and smart. This child had been a gift to him. If he loved her any harder, he'd explode. "Come on, let's get in the truck."

She sat up straighter. "Why?"

He stood. "You said you wanted ice cream, didn't you? Well, let's go into town and get some."

She jumped up. "You mean it?"

"Get your shoes on, young'un. They don't serve the barefoot."

She ran back into the house. "Okay!"

He walked in behind her and shut the door. If Kaley was a witch, he was okay with that. And if Pandora could help Kaley, then he needed Pandora. No matter what he was or what he had to sacrifice, he'd make sure this worked out.

8

Pandora had over an hour to meet her buyers at the house she was showing them, which gave her the perfect opportunity to swing by her mother's place. Corette didn't open Ever After until ten anyway, allowing them plenty of time for coffee and an interesting chat about Mr. Cole Van Zant.

She knocked on the front door, then walked in. As always, her mother's house was pin-straight and picture perfect. "Mom? It's me, Pandora."

"In the kitchen, honey."

Pandora set her purse and briefcase on the granite counter, then leaned in and kissed her mother's cheek. "Morning."

"Morning." Corette stood at the island, scrambling eggs in a Pyrex bowl. She smelled like Chanel No. 5, her signature perfume. "Hungry?"

"No, I ate at the house, but I'd love another cup of coffee."

"Help yourself. What brings you by this morning?"

Pandora filled a cup, then added cream and sugar. "I need some advice. And help. And I might not be the only one."

Corette's precisely sculpted brows went gently skyward. "Are you in trouble, honey?"

"Oh no, it's not for me..." Pandora frowned. "Well, it might be a little for me."

Corette stopped whipping the eggs. "What's going on?"

Pandora stared at her coffee for a second, choosing her words. "What do you know about familiars?"

Corette poured the eggs into a buttered pan and put the bowl in the sink. "The same as any witch, I suppose. A familiar is an animal that can help a witch focus, and often strengthen, her craft." She smiled, but it was bittersweet, and Pandora knew why. "I wish we'd been able to find one for you. I still think it would have made all the difference."

If only her mother knew. "What about the human kind of familiar?"

Corette blinked a few times. "They're very rare. I haven't heard about one in ages. Some people think they've died out." She shrugged. "I don't think that's true. I think the familiars that aren't bonded yet keep a low profile, and any witch who has one guards that knowledge dearly."

"I'd say that's right." She took another sip of coffee. "Ulysses Pilcher was one."

Corette laughed. "I don't think so. Gertrude wasn't known for keeping secrets. I'm sure she wouldn't have held on to that one. If it were true."

"He was."

Corette looked over at her. "How do you know? You seem so sure."

"Because...I talked to Gertrude."

Corette turned the heat down on the eggs. "Start from the beginning."

"You know that guy I told you about? The one who inherited the Pilcher Manor? The one with the daughter who's a witch—"

"Just turned thirteen, right? And she can see auras?"

"That's the one. Kaley. I agreed to help him with her as she comes into her powers, and in exchange, he offered to give me the listing on the house when he sells it. I negotiated and got him to let me help with the renovation decisions too so I could get top dollar, because you know I know how to sell houses in this town."

"You do."

Pandora took a breath. "So, I was in the attic of the Pilcher Manor, and Gertrude showed up. Did she have pink hair?"

"Pick a color, she had them all at one time. She was a true eccentric." Corette added a little sea salt and fresh ground black pepper to her breakfast and stirred.

"It was her, then. She told me about Ulysses and human familiars and said that Cole is one too."

"How does she know?"

"She can see auras. I don't know how clearly, but enough that she figured Cole out. And me."

"That much I knew about her." Corette made a soft, throaty noise. "Wait, I thought you said this Cole was Ulysses's great-nephew. How did his daughter inherit Gertrude's abilities?"

"She didn't. Kaley is his adopted daughter. And her mother was a witch."

"So Cole was bonded?"

"No. It's a long story, but his first wife basically did whatever she could to get herself bonded to him, but it never took. Which is why she left him."

"Maybe he's not a familiar."

"No, he is. Definitely. A raven shifter."

"Definitely?"

Pandora slipped the feather from the side pocket of her purse and laid it on the counter.

Her mother stared at it for several long moments. Then she took a breath as she slid her eggs onto a china plate. "Pandy, I know this must be very exciting for you, but from what I understand, human familiars are not only rare, they don't just bond with any witch who comes along. His ex is proof of that. I'm sure he sounds like an answer to your craft troubles, but I'd hate for you to get your hopes up only to find out he makes no difference."

Pandora put the feather away. "What happens when a witch and a familiar bond? Besides her powers strengthening?"

"When the familiar is in his animal form, the witch can communicate with him telepathically. She can also see through his eyes in that form." Corette pursed her mouth. "This is only what I've heard and read. I imagine Gertrude could tell you more."

"I'll have to talk to her again the next time I'm at Cole's."

Corette sighed. "I can tell you like this guy, and with you two working on the house together, that's probably not going to change. I worry you're going to end up hurt. You need some distance, honey. Get to know him, sure, but take your time."

Pandora swallowed. "It might be too late for that. I already know my magic works perfectly around him. And when we...touch, he gets these visions of himself in his raven form."

"And more than visions, apparently." Corette's brows lifted as she shifted her gaze toward the pocket of Pandora's purse that held the feather.

Pandora nodded slowly. "Until we made contact, he had no idea what he really was."

Corette sat at the counter across from her daughter, her eyes filled with concern. "So his parents never told him about his true identity? I can almost understand that. There was a time when familiars were practically hunted. Not in the shoot-to-kill sort of way, but witches with mediocre powers—even those with decent gifts—starting aggressively seeking out human familiars. A human familiar became a kind of status symbol. And a chance to increase one's power. Many human familiars were coerced into relationships against their will."

"That's horrible."

Corette took a delicate bite of her breakfast before she answered. "I agree. Most covens frowned on it, and eventually the ACW declared that any attempt to coerce a human familiar into a relationship against their will would be dealt with by a minimum of a five-year power nullification."

Pandora made a little eek sound. The American Council of Witches had the final say in all things witchy. If they decided you were going to lose your powers for five years, that's exactly what would happen, and they had the witches on staff to back that punishment up. "I wonder if that's why Cole's ex-wife finally gave up on him."

"You're sure they didn't bond?"

"Doesn't seem that way. I don't think he'd ever shifted before he met me."

Corette lifted her fork, then put it back down. "You say your magic works around him?"

Pandora nodded. "I haven't tried any big spells." She hadn't done any of those in years. "But the two simple things I did went off without a hitch. And Kaley said my aura didn't look so broken now."

Corette smoothed the cloth napkin on her lap. "It could very well be his influence, but it may also be your craft is finally straightening itself out."

"I think we both know that's not the case."

"No, maybe not." Corette sighed. "I just don't know if you should get involved with him, Pandora. I understand what a temptation it must be to think that another person could fix everything you think is wrong. But a human familiar is nothing like an animal familiar. You're talking about having a relationship with a man you know nothing about. And he's got a child."

"Who I like."

Corette held up a hand. "I have nothing against the girl. Or the idea of taking on the role of parent to a child who's not your blood. Look at Sheriff Merrow and Ivy's boy, Charlie. They get on like a house on fire."

"I hear Saffie's rather fond of Charlie too."

"She's got herself a crush, that's for sure." Corette smiled, but her expression quickly turned serious again. "But it's not fair to the little girl if you waltz into her life on a whim only to waltz back out again. Children need stability. If this child falls in love with you, and things don't work out between you and Cole, she'll end up hurt too. That's not right, Pandora. You have to understand what a relationship with this man entails. However enticing it may be to be around him."

"I get what you're saying, Mom, but I just met the guy. There is no relationship yet." Kissing, but no relationship. A detail her mother didn't need to know.

"You said you agreed to help him with the house."

"Okay, there's a business relationship. If anything else comes of it, we're going to take it very slow. I swear."

"Good. You have no idea if you're compatible. Just because you're a witch and he's a familiar means nothing. That's not a basis for a marriage. And working well together might be a basis for a business, but trust me, a marriage is a very different thing."

"Hold the phone. Marriage isn't even a word that should be uttered yet."

"And what if you bond? What then?"

"I, uh, I don't think that's going to happen." Pandora looked down at her coffee, acutely aware of how that bonding happened. She wondered if the warmth in her cheeks was turning her cheeks red.

"I take it Gertrude told you how the bonding works?"

Apparently it was. Pandora's eyes stayed on her cup. "Yep."

"You're a grown woman. He's a grown man. But if you sleep together and bond and end up not liking each other, I can promise that you will both be miserable. And not just because things don't work out."

"I get it."

"Pandora, look at me."

For a moment, Pandora felt like a child again. She lifted her head. "What?"

"Bonding with a familiar and then losing that familiar would be worse than a bad breakup. Worse than living with faulty gifts. It would destroy your magic for the rest of your life. And you'd both end up with holes inside you that would eat away at any happiness you find."

"Like Ren."

Corette nodded. "Like Ren."

Pandora stared at her mother as the words sank in. She certainly didn't want that for Cole or herself. One tragedy on her conscience was enough. "I never intended to get involved with this guy. Now I'm not sure I want to."

Corette took her plate to the sink. "Familiars have a way of finding the witches who need them the most and, in the case of human familiars, the witches they belong with. There's a good chance you could be meant for each other as a fated pair.

But like I said, that doesn't mean you'll get along as man and woman. Just witch and familiar. It's a lot to consider."

"That's for sure." But clearly it had worked for Ulysses and Gertrude.

"I know this must be overwhelming for you to take in. Did I answer the question you came over to ask?"

"Not really." Pandora sighed. "I wanted to see if I could bring Cole and Kaley to dinner tonight. Kaley still needs a mentor, and she's dying to be around other witches. Plus, I thought maybe being around my family would help Cole see there's nothing weird about us."

Corette laughed. "Pandora, there will be four witches and a rook at dinner. You want to add a fledgling witch and a familiar and you think it's not going to be weird? Bring them, but don't expect miracles."

Pandora grabbed her stuff. "Thanks. All I want is for him not to be afraid of who he is."

Because no matter what the risks were, Pandora couldn't help but be attracted to Cole. He was handsome and sexy and smart and, yes, her magic worked perfectly around him, but beyond all that, she felt drawn to him. Ever since that kiss.

She gave her mom a little wave. "See you tonight."

Her mother nodded back as Pandora left the

house. She walked to her car with a sinking feeling. What if the lure of being a witch with unencumbered powers was why she really liked Cole?

Getting to know him better seemed like the only way to know for sure. But then she could be setting herself up for a disaster, and she'd already had one of those in her life. She couldn't be responsible for ruining another man's life.

She got in her car, closed the door and started the engine, but didn't pull out of the drive. Liking Cole for Cole was one thing. Liking him because he was a familiar was another. There was only one way she could think of that would keep both of them safe.

Under no circumstances, no matter how sexy Cole was, no matter how much she was tempted, not even if he did some kind of familiar magic spell on her (if that was even possible), there was absolutely, positively no way she could end up in bed with him.

Jack Van Zant arrived at Cole's house earlier than expected. He greeted Cole with a hearty handshake. "Good to see you, son."

"You too, Dad." He raised his brows as he looked at his watch. Quarter to noon. "You made good time."

His father shrugged. "What else have I got to do these days?"

"Grandpa!" Kaley came down the stairs. Despite being a thirteen-year-old, she hadn't yet lost the ability to be affectionate, at least with her grandfather. Maybe it was because he was the only grandparent she had any regular contact with.

Jack scooped her up in a hug. "Hello there, baby girl."

She returned his hug until he deposited her back on solid ground.

Then he started with the questions as he came into the foyer. "How's the move treating you? You like your new school? Keeping your grades up? Have you made any friends? I hope none of them are boys."

"Grandpa, no. No boys. And my grades are fine." She rolled her eyes. Not even Grandpa Jack was spared that.

"Good. Just checking." He dug into his pocket and pulled out an iTunes gift card. "You have any use for this thing? I won it playing poker. It says it's worth twenty-five bucks, but it looks like a fake credit card if you ask me. If you don't want it, I guess I'll just throw it away..."

Kaley squealed. "Don't throw it away!"

Jack put on a confused face. "You mean you want this old piece of plastic?"

"Yes, totally. Can I?" She held out her hand,

playing up the cute factor with big eyes and a winsome smile. It was a look Cole had a hard time saying no to as well. And it was one of the few things Kaley had inherited from her mother.

"Sure, but I want a kiss first." Jack offered her his cheek.

She gave him a long peck as she grabbed the card out of his hand. "Thank you!"

"You're welcome, baby girl."

Kaley popped her hip to one side, the card firmly in her hand. "Can I go upstairs?" she asked Cole.

"Sure, but we're having lunch in a few minutes." Normally, he'd make her stay and talk to her grandfather, but Cole needed some time alone with him.

"Okay, I won't be long." With that, she scampered back to her room to fill her iPhone with new music.

"Thanks, Dad. That was nice of you." Cole shut the front door.

"I don't see that kid enough since you've moved."

"You know it's just temporary. We'll be back as soon as I get this place fixed up and sold."

Jack looked around. "I might be dead before then."

"Dad, please."

His father took a hard look at the stacks of paper

still filling the dining room. "You've got your work cut out for you, that much I know."

"It's well underway, I promise." But Cole hadn't contacted his father to talk about the house. There would be plenty of time for that topic at lunch when their conversation would have to be tempered for Kaley's ears. "Let's go out on the porch so we can talk."

"Sure." Jack nodded, his face serious. "After you."

Cole led his father out to the back, and when they were both settled in, he went silent for a moment trying to find the right words. But what those were, he wasn't sure. All he knew was that he needed answers. "Why didn't you tell me what I am? What we are? I know you're the same thing I am. Kaley can see it in our auras."

"Right to it, then." Jack took a deep breath. "Yes, we're both familiars. Your mother and I kept the truth from you for many reasons. But your safety and personal happiness were paramount."

Cole's brow furrowed. "Was I in some kind of danger?"

"It was a distinct possibility."

"Why don't you just start from the beginning?"

Jack glanced at his son, then out beyond the porch to the overgrown backyard. "What you need to know is that your mother, may she rest in peace, was a witch. And I was her familiar."

Cole stared at his father. "Mom was a witch?"

Jack nodded.

"But you raised me not to believe in any of that."

"Which was part of keeping you safe."

None of it made any sense, but Cole hoped that would change. A thousand questions flew into his head, but he tucked them away for later and let his father talk. "Go on."

"We made the decision to shield you from the truth around the time you were three. A very aggressive witch in your mother's coven made it plain that she wanted me for her familiar. Now, granted, it doesn't work that way. A witch and a familiar must be a bonded pair for the connection to reach its full power and remain that way, but a lot of witches think they can circumvent the natural bonding with magic. Anyway, this woman took it upon herself to interfere with our lives and our marriage."

Jack sighed. "It was mildly annoying at first. We didn't pay much attention to it, really. In fact, it became something of an inside joke between us." A faint smile played on his lips. "Whenever anything bad happened, we blamed it on Zarina. Paper cut? Must be Zarina. Rained-out picnic? Zarina had cast a weather spell. Milk spoiled before we could use it all? More of Zarina's dirty tricks."

The smile disappeared. "Then your mother became very sick, very fast. Couldn't eat, couldn't sleep, and the doctors couldn't diagnose her. So she called a few trusted members of the coven. It took a complicated discovery spell but they found the reason for her illness. She'd been placed under a hex. And Zarina had cast it."

"The coven must have done something. Punished her."

"They did. The ACW stripped Zarina of her magic for five years, but the damage was done. Your once fierce mother was afraid. Not so much for herself as for you and me. We left Portland and moved to North Carolina. Your mother refused to join another coven for fear there would be a new Zarina and that you would be the target this time. After a while, she stopped practicing altogether. We both agreed that you should be raised as normally as possible."

"Because of that one incident?"

Jack shook his head. "It wasn't one incident. Covens all over the country were reporting similar events. Human familiars had become something of a status symbol after it was revealed that the head of the ACW had one."

"What is that?"

"The American Council of Witches." Jack let out a breath. "I knew if you moved into this house, something like this would happen. Did you find some of your uncle's things? Is that how you figured it out?"

"No. I...met someone."

Jack gave him a hard look. "Explain."

Cole told him what had happened when he and Pandora had touched, about the visions he'd had, and how she'd seen him shift.

Jack frowned and swore softly. "This is Lila all over again."

"No, it's not. Don't compare Pandora to her." Anger stormed through Cole at that accusation, instantly needing to protect Pandora. Then he hesitated at what his father had just revealed. "You and Mom knew Lila was a witch?"

"Yes, we did. In the beginning, your mother wanted to confront her and run her off, but then it became clear you weren't going to bond. We made the decision to let things run their course so long as Lila didn't seem like she was resorting to any kind of black magic. We figured she'd give up at some point, which she did."

"Lila had to know the truth about you two, though. She said she could read auras."

"She knew exactly what we were. But your mother made it very plain that if she said a word, or used any kind of magic to influence you, Lila would find herself hauled before the ACW. That seemed to do the trick."

"I'm surprised Mom didn't make her leave." Cole couldn't remember his mother ever being afraid to stand up to anyone.

"She would have. Except that we fell in love with Kaley the same way you did. For her sake, we held our tongues many, many times. And then it didn't matter anymore."

The memory of Maxine Van Zant's death put them both in a somber mood.

After a long pause, Jack's smile returned. "Kaley was the only good thing to come out of that marriage."

"That's for damn sure," Cole agreed. They sat quietly for several minutes. Then Cole looked at his father. "So you know that Kaley's a witch obviously."

Jack nodded. "I do. And I wish your mother was still alive to help her out now that she's thirteen and will be coming into her power soon. Poor kid. She's going to need someone to guide her through this."

Which brought them back to Pandora. "A mentor. I know. Dad, my…friend has already agreed to help her find one. She comes from a family of witches. That's where Kaley and I are going tonight. To their house for dinner."

Anger filled Jack's eyes. "You're making a mistake. You don't know this woman. You don't know what witches can be like. They look at a familiar and they see an opportunity."

"Pandora is nothing like that. I doubt her family is that way either."

"How do you know?"

"I'm a good judge of character."

"Lila says otherwise."

Cole sighed in frustration. "Pandora had no idea what I was when we met. In fact, she didn't even like me. She liked Kaley. I was just"—he shrugged—"the bothersome muggle who didn't believe his daughter was a witch."

"But she warmed right up to you after she figured out what you were, am I right?"

Sort of. He scowled. "That's not how it happened."

"Then tell me."

"I told her if she helped me with Kaley, I'd give her the listing when I put the house up for sale." At his father's curious expression, Cole added, "She's a real estate agent."

Jack's grimace hardened. "Even better."

"You have no reason to have an issue with her. You haven't met her."

"I know witches."

"Are you saying Mom wasn't trustworthy?"

Jack's face softened. "She was the best woman I've ever known. She changed my life for the better. She was…my other half. Emotionally. Spiritually. Physically." He closed his eyes. "I have never stopped missing her."

Cole gentled his voice. "And how do you know Pandora isn't that person for me?"

Jack took a few breaths before answering. "Are you in love with her?"

"It's too early to say anything like that. I've only begun to get to know her. But I do feel drawn to her in a way that's unlike anything I've ever felt before. Do you think that means we're connected?"

"Just because she's a witch and you're a familiar? Maybe. Maybe not."

"Are you saying she's not the one I'm supposed to be with?"

"I'm not saying anything about it one way or the other. Listen…" Jack twisted in his chair to face Cole a little more. "It's our fault you're not prepared for this, so for that, I apologize, but I'll tell you now the only thing you need to know. The relationship between a witch and a familiar benefits both sides, but it can hurt both sides too."

Cole doubted that was the only thing he needed to know about being a familiar. He had more questions than he could count. "How so?"

"If you bond with a woman you aren't emotionally compatible with, you will be miserable the rest of your days. It can be soul sucking."

"Doesn't seem to me like I have much choice in whether or not we bond."

"Sure you do. Keep things slow, get to know her as a person first." Jack glanced toward the door. "But most of all, you can keep it in your pants."

"Dad."

"I'm serious. Sleeping with her is what seals the bond. But the closer you get to her, the more difficult it will become to resist the temptation. Your inner spirits will start to crave each other. I don't know what it's like from the witch side, but for a familiar, the witch becomes your sole focus. You'll think about her constantly. Dream about her. Find ways to be near her."

Cole tried not to react. That was sort of already happening. "Good to know. But what about everything else involved in being a familiar? What can you tell me about that? Do all human familiars shift into an animal form? Do you? Are you a raven?"

"Yes, I'm a raven. All the men in our family have been. Familiars are almost always men. And all familiars have an animal form."

Well, that was some information. Cole tried for a little more. "What changes when you're bonded? How do even know if you are bonded? Is it automatic if you sleep together?"

Jack shook his head. "I'm not going to tell you anything else. Not yet. All you need to know is these next few weeks will be critical. You've got to keep your distance."

The fact that his father wasn't willing to help him fully understand what it meant to be a familiar came as no surprise to Cole. Not after years of being told nothing. "Keeping my distance is going to be pretty hard to do considering she's promised to help Kaley and assist me with the renovation of this house. Not to mention the dinner with her family tonight."

Jack cut his hand through the air. "Cancel."

"No. It would be rude, and who else am I going to get to help Kaley? I can control myself."

"You think that now, but—"

The porch door opened, and Kaley popped out. "I'm, like, starving."

Cole stood. "Then you can help me with the sandwiches."

Jack got up as well. "I'm serious. You should get out of it."

"Get out of what?" Kaley asked.

"Dad, for the last time, I'm not doing that." Cole put his hand on Kaley's shoulder and aimed her back inside. "It's nothing, sweetheart."

Jack followed them. "What your father meant to say is I'm going to dinner with you tonight."

"You are?" Kaley turned, her eyes lit up. "That's awesome. I didn't know Miss Williams invited you too."

"She didn't," Cole muttered.

"Not yet, but she will. And she'll be happy about it too." Jack took a seat at the table and winked at Kaley. "Especially if you and I go into town after lunch and get a fancy dessert to bring from the bakery I passed on the way in."

Cole shook his head as he pulled sandwich fixings from the fridge. He loved his father and generally understood where the man was coming from, but this was too much.

He shut the fridge door, arms full, and headed for the counter. His father and Kaley were laughing about something. If Jack didn't want to teach Cole how to be a familiar, he could deal with that. If Jack tried to ruin things between him and Pandora, Cole could deal with that too. But if Kaley ended up hurt because of Jack's meddling, that was something else entirely.

Cole's mind was made up. He set out slices of bread and started building the sandwiches. "Forget it, Dad. I'm putting my foot down. I'm not going to impose on Pandora and her family that way. I'd be happy to introduce you to her, but dinner tonight is about Kaley and getting her a support system."

He could feel his father's gaze on him. "Cole, you need to rethink this."

"No, I don't." Cole scraped mayonnaise out of the jar. "The decision's made." He glanced over his shoulder. Kaley looked upset.

He immediately felt like a heel. "What's wrong, sweetheart?"

Her mouth pulled down at the corners. "Why are you and Grandpa fighting? Why can't he come to dinner?"

"Honey, Miss Williams invited *us*. It's not polite

to assume we can bring someone else without asking."

"So let's ask her."

Jack nodded. "The kid's got a point."

Cole sighed. Being in the middle was a hard place, but he needed to take a stand. His parents had made decisions about his upbringing that were affecting him in some tough ways. Now he was the parent and the decisions were up to him. He would not let his father jeopardize Kaley's future. She would grow up knowing everything she needed to know about who she was. "Next time Grandpa's in town, we'll have a cookout and invite everyone over, okay, Kaley?"

She crossed her arms and slumped in her chair. "Yeah, okay, but I still don't see why we can't ask Pan—Miss Williams if Grandpa can come."

"Because it's short notice and impolite. End of discussion." Let Kaley be mad at him. It was easier than explaining that her grandfather might interfere with her chances at getting the witch tutoring she needed.

She let out an enormous sigh.

Cole went back to making sandwiches. Maybe he wasn't going to win any Father of the Year awards, but he'd bet good money she'd forget all about Jack not being there once they got to dinner.

9

Pandora arrived at Cole's promptly at six thirty, dressed a little nicer than usual for Saturday-night family dinner. She'd started to put on her usual jeans and cute tee, then realized Cole had seen her mostly in ratty tank tops and gym shorts. That had been impetus enough to slip into white ankle pants and a turquoise wrap top that showed off her assets and made her skin glow.

Pumpkin had given her the side eye for white pants after Labor Day, but what did cats know about fashion? Plus, states below the Mason-Dixon Line weren't under the same rules when it came to wearing white. Heat and humidity had a way of negating those things.

She parked her sedan and walked to the front door, the click of her strappy high-heeled sandals accompanying her. She knocked and stood back to wait, but Cole answered quickly.

He looked...dreamy. He wore dark jeans with a pale blue and white checked shirt rolled up to show off his hard forearms. His hair was neatly combed, and his face was freshly shaved, revealing the chiseled line of his jaw.

She was definitely hot for teacher.

He stepped outside and shut the door behind him, but not before she heard laughter from inside. "I'm really sorry."

"About?"

"Kaley's in a mood. I thought she would have shaken it by now, but she's holding a grudge. Hard."

"Really? Because I could have sworn I heard her laughing just now. What happened? You didn't try to convince her witches aren't real again, did you?"

"No, I'm past that, I promise." He glanced back at the house as he adjusted his glasses. "It's just...my father is here, and he tried to invite himself to dinner tonight, but I told him no. Now Kaley thinks I'm being mean."

"You kind of are."

"What?"

She shrugged. "Bring him. It's no big deal. These dinners are very fluid. We're constantly bringing friends at the last minute."

"But you don't even know him. In fact, your family doesn't know us."

"But I know you and Kaley, and after tonight that'll all be moot anyway."

He sighed.

"Okay, seriously, what's up? Do you not like your dad or something?" Her eyes widened a bit. "Did you have a big fight over your parents not telling you about your true nature?"

"No. Not exactly." Cole closed his eyes for a moment, then opened them again. "I'm worried he's going to cause problems with your family. And you. He's convinced you're after me only for what I can do for you."

"You mean because you're a familiar."

Cole nodded. "He's also convinced you're going to lure me to bed to bond with me as fast as you can."

"Yes, I'm a regular seductress." Pandora rolled her lips in, but snorted in laughter anyway. "As if."

One of Cole's inky brows lifted over the rim of his glasses. "Have you seen yourself in this outfit?" His gaze traveled down to her cleavage and lingered. "It's pretty seductive from where I'm standing."

She crossed her arms, realized that only hefted her chest higher, and then uncrossed them. "I was trying to look nice."

"Nice?" He raked a hand through his hair. "You look"—he swallowed—"edible."

Heat swept through her, leaving her dizzy and

on the verge of bad decisions. "You shouldn't say things like that unless you mean them."

He stared her down, his dark gaze taking on the feral look she'd seen before. "You tempt me, Pandora."

Without thinking, she licked her bottom lip.

He made a growly sound, and the next thing she knew, his mouth was on hers. For several long seconds, all she could do was feel. The pressure of his mouth, the grip of his hands on her shoulders, the intoxicating scent of a man fresh from the shower. He *became* the heat coursing through her, then a soft breeze seemed to lift her off the ground. She was floating. Or they were floating.

Or they were *flying*.

In a moment of panic, she pushed a stabilizing spell at him.

Then a throat cleared.

They broke apart. A man stood in the open door behind Cole. He was an older version of Cole, hair more salt and pepper than pitch black, stockier, maybe an inch shorter and wearing different glasses.

Pandora felt a new kind of heat rise up in her. The kind that came from sheer embarrassment. Cole's dad had just caught them kissing, except kissing didn't really encompass what they'd just been doing. Making out like horny teenagers was probably more on point.

He cleared his throat again and looked at Cole expectantly. "Are you going to introduce us?"

Cole showed no signs of mortification. Pandora wished the same was true for her, but she knew her face had to be the same color as her hair. Cole rested his hand lightly on her back. "Dad, this is Pandora Williams. Pandora, this is my father, Jack Van Zant."

She stuck her hand out, pleased that it wasn't shaking. "Nice to meet you, Mr. Van Zant. Cole's spoken highly of you."

Jack shook her hand, his grip a tiny bit tighter than comfortable. "I'm not sure that's true."

She didn't know what to say to that.

Jack released her hand. "You're the witch who's going to teach my granddaughter the craft, are you?"

Cole spoke before she could answer. "She's the witch who's going to help her, and speaking of Kaley, would you let her know it's time for us to go?"

Jack gave his son an unreadable look. "Ah yes, the dinner that I'm not invited to." He turned his gaze back to Pandora. It held a clear challenge.

For a moment, she felt completely intimidated. Then she decided she wasn't going to let him make her feel that way. If he thought she was up to something despicable, how better to show him that she wasn't? She straightened her spine and put on her best realtor smile. "Actually, we'd love to have you."

It was enough to erase the judgmental look right off his face. "You would?" He glanced at Cole. "Did my son put you up to this?"

Honesty was always the best policy. "Nope. He actually told me not to invite you, but it's my family and I can invite whomever I please."

Jack smiled broadly at Cole as if to say, *So there*. He gave Pandora a little nod. "That's very kind of you."

"You know how we witches love familiars." She widened her smile, knowing that was a bit of a jab but unable to help herself. "You are a familiar too, aren't you?"

"Yes." He gave her a strange look. "I'll go get Kaley."

"We'll be right here."

He disappeared back into the house.

"Why did you invite him?" Cole hissed. "And don't think I missed that crack about witches loving familiars."

"Maybe I shouldn't have said that, but I couldn't help it. And I invited him so he can see I'm not after you for *naughty* reasons." Although after that kiss, she had a lot of naughty reasons to think about. "If you and I are going to work together on this house and your daughter, the last thing you need is for your dad to be on your back."

He shook his head. "You're something else, you know that? That was very kind and completely unnecessary. I just hope this doesn't come back to bite you. My father can be a real handful."

She laughed. "You haven't met my mother or my sisters yet. Which reminds me, I should send my mom a heads up to put out an extra place setting." She pointed at her car. "My phone is in my purse."

"Go ahead. Hey—I got a bottle of wine. I hope red is good."

She started for the car. "It's perfect."

"Good. I'll grab it, collect the stragglers and lock up the house."

Ten minutes later, they were pulling into Corette's driveway. Stanhill's Bentley was already there.

"Nice car," Jack called out from the backseat. "Your mother must do pretty well."

"That's her beau's car." Although her mother did own a gorgeous white Mercedes, which never left the garage unless she was driving it.

"Is he a familiar too?"

Pandora shot Cole a look as she parked. "No, he's a rook."

Kaley leaned up between the two front seats. "What's a rook and a familiar?"

Cole opened his mouth, but the look on his face said he didn't know how to answer.

Pandora twisted to face her. "A familiar is

usually an animal but is sometimes a person who forms a deep bond with a witch in a way that strengthens the witch's magic. A rook is a like a vampire's assistant."

Kaley's eyes rounded. "Whoa. There are vampires? Like, for real? Is there going to be one here tonight?"

Pandora looked at Cole. "I feel like we should have talked about this sooner."

He nodded. "I see that now."

Pandora smiled at Kaley. "Yes, there are vampires for real, but there won't be any here this evening. There are several who live here in town, so at some point, you'll meet them. All kinds of fun supernaturals reside in Nocturne Falls. Stanhill, the rook, is my mother's boyfriend. You're in absolutely no danger from him, though, okay?"

"Okay." Kaley sat back and scooted closer to her grandfather.

Cole put his hand on Pandora's thigh. "This is sort of news to me too. What kind of fun supernaturals are you talking about?"

She tried to hold onto her train of thought while the heat from Cole's touch warmed the skin several inches above her knee. Holy goddess. What was the question? Something about supernaturals, right? She swallowed and checked her answers off on her fingers, mostly to give herself something to do. "Uh, vampires, werewolves—and other kinds of shifters. Witches, obviously. Fae and fae-adjacent creatures, gargoyles, valkyrie, ghosts, mer-people. You name it, we probably have it."

Cole nodded. "I see." But he looked a little overwhelmed.

And clearly unaware that he'd just set parts of her on fire. She cleared her throat as he finally moved his hand. "Hey, listen up, all three of you. They're all friendly. They live here because that's the benefit of this town. The whole thing of celebrating Halloween every day means we can live in peace and pretty much out in the open about who we really are, and no one suspects anything."

Jack made a noise. "You're telling me you've never had a tourist figure out the truth?"

"No." Pandora made eye contact with him in the rearview mirror. "The spring that feeds the falls and supplies the town's water was enchanted years ago by the witch who helped establish the town. It prevents humans from grasping the truth about this place."

"Pretty clever." He snorted. "Remind me not to drink the water."

"That's not something you have to worry about."

He frowned. "Why not?"

"Because it only affects *humans*, Mr. Van Zant." She gave him a wink and got out of the car. Let him explain that to Kaley.

Cole got out at the same time, shutting his door

in sync with hers. "Hey, Kaley doesn't know about me yet."

"Well, you'd better explain that to her. It's going to come up in conversation. She's a witch, Cole. She's going to learn this stuff sooner or later. Don't you want her to hear it from you?"

"Yes. You're right. Give us a few minutes? I'm probably not going to tell her about the animal-shifting part. Not yet."

"Whatever you think she's ready for. Let me just grab the wine I brought out of the trunk, then I'll go in and see what I can help my mom with. Come in when you're ready."

"Thanks."

Jack and Kaley got out. Cole turned toward his daughter. "You, me and Grandpa are going to have a little talk before we go in."

She rolled her eyes. "I'll be on my best behavior, I swear."

"It's not about that."

Pandora grabbed the wine and gave the trio a wave. "See you inside." Then she left them to talk.

The house smelled of garlic and herbs and roasting meat. "What are you cooking? It smells crazy good in here." She walked into the kitchen to see her mother and Stanhill smooching on the other side of the island. A big pot of red sauce bubbled away on the center stove. "Okay, that's enough of that."

They stopped kissing, but not embracing. Stanhill tipped his head at her, his wry smile challenging her to disagree. "I'll kiss your mother whenever I bloody well please, thank you."

"I see that. Just maybe not over the food." Pandora put the wine on the counter and took a seat at the island. "You're getting love germs in the sauce." She stuck her finger in the pot and licked it clean. "Oh, that's good. Germs and all."

"It's very good. It's pork roast with spaghetti marinara." Corette eased out of Stanhill's arms. "Where are your guests?"

"Having a little conversation outside. Kaley and Cole just found out that witches aren't the only supernaturals in Nocturne Falls, and Kaley's also getting the explanation about what her father and grandfather really are. And, yes, Cole's dad is also a familiar." She took a deep breath. "And I should probably tell you that Cole's dad thinks I'm out to use his son for all the benefits of his familiar status. Including the hot sex."

Corette narrowed her eyes. "Get him in here. I'll talk to him. The nerve of that man assuming my daughter is—"

"No, Mom, don't. We need to kill him with kindness. Not get up in his face. He already doesn't trust witches. Cole had a bad first marriage, so…" She shrugged. "Just be nice to him, okay?"

"Whatever you think is best, darling. But I'm not

going to let him disparage you in my house." Corette tapped her finger on the counter. "I draw the line there. A sharp one."

"I understand."

The front door opened. "Hello?" Cole's voice rang out.

Pandora hopped off the seat and headed for the foyer. "In here."

She met him halfway. Kaley looked like she'd taken the news about her father's and grandfather's true identities pretty well. Pandora nodded toward the kitchen. "Come on, I'll introduce you."

Cole pushed his glasses up. "Lead the way."

She took them back into the kitchen, and after Cole had handed his bottle of wine to her mother, Pandora made the introductions. Everyone shook hands, including Kaley, who then retreated a few steps and stared at Corette and Stanhill like she expected them to do something magical at any moment.

Thankfully, before the silence got awkward, Pandora's sisters arrived. Marigold came in with an enormous salad bowl, a large bouquet for the table and her eight-year-old daughter, Saffron, in tow. Charisma was right behind them with her own contribution of freshly baked Italian bread in crisp paper sleeves.

More introductions were made, and as everyone headed to the table, Pandora found a moment to fill her sisters in on the situation with Cole's dad. They nodded as she spoke.

"We've got your back." Marigold glanced toward the dining room. "I get the protective-parent thing, but Cole's a grown man. He can make up his mind about you on his own."

Charisma nodded. "The father's projecting his own fears onto his son. Classic emotional transfer."

Pandora cut her eyes at her life coach sibling. "Can you not psychoanalyze him at the table?"

"I'm just stating the obvious. And if he thinks he's getting away with dumping all that on you, he's got another think coming."

Pandora rubbed her forehead. She appreciated her sisters' protectiveness, but she was already getting visions of just how badly the night could go. "I didn't bring enough wine for this."

10

Cole wasn't surprised by how pretty Pandora's mother or sisters were. After all, Pandora was a knockout. He'd expected the gene pool to be strong. What he wasn't prepared for was the amount of noise the clan made. There were nine of them seated around a dining room table meant for eight. For someone who'd been raised an only child, it was somewhat overwhelming. It also filled him with a curious longing to be a bigger part of something this loud and raucous. There was an abundance of love and joy in this room, and despite the craziness of it, the feeling was infectious.

Kaley and Saffron, Pandora's youngest sister's girl, were seated next to each other and, despite the five-year age difference, seemed to be becoming fast friends. At least, they were talking up a storm and laughing, so it looked like they were having a good time.

In that moment, an ache filled him at the thought that Kaley was growing up an only child too.

Pandora, seated on his left, bent closer to him. "You okay? Or just overwhelmed by all this?"

He smiled, thankful for the easy out. "A little overwhelmed. But good. I like it. Just not used to it."

"I totally understand." She lifted her gaze toward his father. "Your dad and Stanhill seem to be getting on."

Cole nodded. Stanhill was at the head of the table with Jack directly across from Cole. The two men had been engaged in conversation since dinner started. "It helps that they have cars in common. Especially British cars. My father's been in love with British machines since as far back as I can remember. He has an old Jag in the garage that he's been working on for the last couple of years, but he loves Aston Martins and Bentleys, too."

"My mother excels at hostessing. She knows how to pair people up at the table."

"I'd say." He tipped his head toward his daughter. "Look at Kaley and Saffron. I'm not even sure they know the rest of us exist."

Pandora smiled. "I'm happy about that. I think they could be good for each other."

"I agree." Just like he thought Pandora could be good for him.

She blinked at him. "You're staring."

He held her gaze. "It's hard not to." He wanted to kiss her with the kind of intensity that almost made him lean in, but this was her mother's house and her mother's table. He was not about to cross that line.

As if sensing his thoughts, Pandora retreated a few inches.

Corette, who was at the opposite end of the table, must have picked up on something, because he heard his name a second later. "Cole, what is it you do for a living?"

"And so it begins," Pandora muttered.

He smiled. He'd been waiting for the inquisition. "I teach math. Most recently at East State University."

"But not anymore?"

"I took a sabbatical. Getting this house remodeled is my job now. I've worked construction almost every summer since I was sixteen. I don't mind getting my hands dirty." He nodded at his dad. "A job worth doing is a job worth doing well."

Jack smiled. "That's right."

"I agree," Corette said. "Pandora told us you inherited the Pilcher Manor. Your skills will come in very handy. I'm glad someone who cares about it will be in charge of fixing it up. It's going to be a big job, though."

He smiled. "It is. Huge. But the money that

came with the inheritance will help. That's what made it possible for us to move here while I fix the house up. Once it's sold, Kaley and I will be set."

"I'm sure Pandora will get you a fabulous deal." She picked up her wine. "I know you haven't been in town long, but do you know what neighborhood you want to be in then?"

He hesitated. "I'm not sure what you mean."

Corette finished her sip and set the glass down. "Well, most of the neighborhoods here have their own sort of flavor. Pandora can tell you better than I can, but her section tends to have large ranch-style homes, while the houses on the streets in this part are almost all two-story cottages."

Marigold chimed in. "I live one street over. It's a small house, but this is a great neighborhood. They all are, really. This is a well-planned town."

"You could always get a condo," Charisma said. "I live in the Excelsior. It's a fabulous building. We have an indoor pool and a gym, not that I get to use them that much. I travel a lot, so having a house to take care of isn't really feasible."

Pandora, her mother and her sisters all looked at him, waiting on his answer.

He put his fork down. "That sounds great, but we're not staying."

Beside him, Pandora frowned. "What do you mean you're not staying?"

He blinked in confusion. "We have a house in

North Carolina, where I work. We're only here as long as it takes to fix up my uncle's house and sell it."

The table went silent. Even Kaley and Saffron. Kaley looked at him. "But we could stay, right?"

"No, Kaley, we can't. I have a job to go back to."

Kaley frowned and crossed her arms. "But my mentor will be here." She looked around the table. "Right?"

Pandora shook her head. "You and your mentor need to live in the same town. Or at least the same state."

"*Dad.*" Kaley glared at him.

He gave her the look that said they'd talk about it later. Then he glanced at Pandora.

Her mouth was open, and it seemed like she'd started to say something. Instead, she snapped her jaw shut, pushed her chair back, put her napkin alongside her plate and stood. "If you'll excuse me for a moment." Then she walked into the kitchen.

Corette's brows lifted gently. "I guess this is news to all of us."

He sat there, feeling about as awkward as could be. "I thought she knew…"

Marigold snorted softly. "Nope."

He looked at his father.

Jack shrugged as if to indicate this was one more reason not to get involved with Pandora.

"Excuse me." Cole got up and went after her.

She stood in front of the sink, staring out the window.

"Hey, I thought you knew this whole thing was temporary."

She frowned and kept her gaze straight ahead. "Clearly not, but you don't owe me an explanation."

"I feel like I do."

She finally turned toward him and smiled, but it was too bright and didn't reach her eyes. "You don't. And, really, this just makes things easier, doesn't it?"

"Pandora, it doesn't mean—"

She put her hand on his chest. "Yes, it does. I'll help you with the house, and I'll help you with Kaley as much as I can, but it would be silly to pursue anything between us. You're a math professor. You understand being practical. And you and me? We're not practical." Her smile wavered. "And I don't do casual."

He took a step back, his gut coiling like he'd been punched. "You're right." His voice sounded flat. It matched how he felt. But then, what had he thought? Well, he'd thought she'd grasped he wasn't here for good. And he'd thought she was okay with that.

The fact that she wasn't...sucked.

She turned back toward the window. "I'd like a moment alone now, thanks."

He knew when he'd been dismissed. "Okay."

He went back to the table. The joyous energy that had been in the room earlier was gone, replaced by whispers and long looks and tension. All of it caused by him. He made himself smile as he took his seat. "It's all good."

Corette and her daughters smiled back like they knew that was a lie but they understood.

Jack reached for the bread. "Excellent meal, Mrs. Williams. Haven't had home cooking like this since my wife passed."

Another lie, Cole thought, but one that smoothed things out and restarted the conversation. He stared at his plate, not quite able to join in. He'd hurt Pandora. He hadn't meant to, but he still felt terrible about it. Maybe she was right, though. Getting involved was risky for both of them.

He'd spent this long not being anyone's familiar. He could certainly live the rest of his life the very same way.

Out of the corner of his eye, he saw Marigold pick up the wine carafe and mention something about refilling it. She got up and headed for the kitchen. He hoped she was going to talk to Pandora. Comfort her. Commiserate with her. All that stuff that sisters did.

That gave him some peace. If he couldn't be the one to fix things, at least she had her family to lean on.

The truth was, he didn't feel that great about leaving now. It *was* the plan he'd made and it was the path that made the most sense. Leaving his job wouldn't be a practical or smart decision. He was working on tenure after all. And his dad was in North Carolina too. The only other family Kaley had.

But he also saw how much Kaley liked it here. He didn't exactly hate the place. Sure, it was hands down the oddest town he'd ever been to with the strangest inhabitants, but he was one of those strange inhabitants now.

The other thing that bothered him was leaving meant disappointing both Pandora and Kaley. That made him sad. Neither one deserved to be hurt like this. And he didn't like being the cause of that hurt. But what were his choices? Practical things were practical for a reason. They made the most sense.

At least on paper.

He took a drink of his wine and tried to feel better about the whole thing.

He failed.

A wave of nausea hit Pandora with enough strength to make her close her eyes and hold on to the counter. She'd made a huge assumption about Cole. This was her mistake to get over, not his. Of course he had a house somewhere else. He was a professor on sabbatical. Had she thought he just moved himself and his daughter around the country willy-nilly?

No. But she had thought he would stay. Especially with Kaley being a witch and needing a mentor.

How wrong she'd been.

And how could she hurt this much when she'd known him only a few days?

Because she was being ridiculous, that's how.

She took a deep breath and tried to exhale the shock as she stood up a little straighter and gave herself a strong mental talking-to.

Snap out of it. You're acting like a silly teenager. You just met this guy. You're not in love with him or anything. You just feel drawn to him because he's a familiar and you're a witch with wonky magic. That's all.

Soft footsteps filled the kitchen, followed by Marigold's voice. "Hey, are you okay?"

Pandora did her best to keep her voice steady. "No. And it's absolutely stupid of me to feel like this."

Marigold put a wine carafe on the counter, then slipped her arm around Pandora's waist. "It's not stupid. You like him, and you just found out he's basically a tourist. A long-term tourist, but still. Whatever you're feeling is perfectly okay."

Pandora smiled without too much effort. "Thanks. But I'm fine. Really." And then she meant it a tiny bit. Like saying it had made it so.

"Are you sure?" Marigold wiggled her fingers. "I could cast a little happiness spell over you."

"No, I'm good. I swear." She leaned her hip against the counter. "Mom told me I shouldn't get involved with him anyway. All this stuff about what happens if we bond as witch and familiar but end up not working as couple. It's just bad news. And I want no part of it."

Marigold looked skeptical. "If you say so."

"I do." She gave her sister a quick hug. "And now I'd better get back out there before it gets any weirder."

Marigold handed her the carafe. "Fill this and take it out. It's good cover."

It wasn't actually, but Pandora appreciated the gesture. She topped off the carafe and went back to the table. Marigold rejoined them a minute later and instantly went to work keeping the conversation going.

Pandora poked at her food, now lukewarm. She took a bite. Nothing had any taste.

She sensed Cole sneaking a look at her, but didn't react.

"You okay?" he whispered.

"Great," she muttered back. Enough already. Time to shift his attention to other things. Like his daughter. "So, Mom, Kaley needs some tutoring in the craft, seeing as how she didn't grow up with witches around her. You have any suggestions? Other than a mentor, obviously. Which might be tricky with them leaving."

"I don't know if a mentor is completely out of the picture," Corette said. "True, most witches expect it to be a long-term relationship, but there might be someone who'd be willing to do it for a couple months."

Corette turned to Kaley, who had stopped chatting with Saffie at the mention of her name. "Why don't you come with Pandora to the coven meeting tomorrow night? You can meet some of the other witches in town and get a feel for what a meeting is like. We can talk about mentoring some more then. How does that sound?"

"Epic," Kaley said. She looked at her father, her questioning gaze mixed with accusation and expectation. She wasn't happy with him so he'd better allow her this much. "Can I, Dad?"

"I guess." He looked at Corette. "What time is it?"

"Six thirty. And it won't go past eight. I know there's school the next day."

He glanced at Kaley. "I guess we can go."

Corette laughed softly. "Oh my dear. A familiar at a coven meeting? I don't think so. Only witches allowed."

Cole's father harrumphed, like a witches-only

meeting was underhanded business of some sort.

Cole ignored the noise and looked at Pandora. "Are you willing to take her?"

"Absolutely." Kaley was the innocent party in all this.

"Okay." He nodded at Kaley. "You can go."

"Yay!" She finished with a reluctant and slightly snide, "Thanks, Dad."

Stanhill pushed his chair back. "Are we about ready for dessert?"

He got loud yeses from Kaley and Saffie.

He laughed. "You two are getting chocolate cupcakes with vanilla cream filling. As for the rest of you, I hope you don't mind being guinea pigs. Delaney sent me over with a test cake. It's a triple-layer chocolate bourbon cake with maple frosting. She assures me we won't need after-dinner drinks with it."

Marigold, Charisma and Pandora all answered him with oohs and aahs. Corette stood up. "I'll put some decaf on, then."

She and Stanhill went into the kitchen.

Charisma stood and picked up her plate, but directed her attention to Saffie. "You and I are on table-clearing duty, love bug."

Kaley jumped up. "I'll help too."

She and Saffie went to work picking up plates. Pandora smiled, and it wasn't lost on her that Cole did too.

Kaley fit in well here. Too bad her father was going to take her away.

Pandora tried to ignore that thought. That path wasn't going to take her anywhere good.

Marigold shifted in her seat to face Jack now that there weren't two children between them. "What line of work are you in, Mr. Van Zant?"

"Please, call me Jack. I'm a warehouse foreman for Greenway, the big grocery store chain. I run the number fifteen facility in Wilmington."

Cole nodded. "He's been there for twenty years."

"Twenty-one," Jack corrected. "What business are you in?"

"Twenty-one years is impressive. I run the little florist shop in town," Marigold said.

"It's not that little," Pandora corrected. She looked at Jack. "She does practically all the weddings in town."

"Funerals too?" Jack asked.

Pandora smirked. "Considering who lives here, we don't have many of those."

Jack lifted his chin. "No, I suppose you don't."

"We have some." Marigold smiled. "Thankfully, not that many."

Stanhill and Corette walked back in. Stanhill carried a tray laden with small plates and big slices of cake. Corette had a silver coffee urn. Charisma and the two girls followed with cups, saucers, creamer and sugar.

Cake and coffee were distributed, and everyone dove in.

Pandora glanced over at Kaley and Saffie and laughed. "Stanhill, those are *not* cupcakes. They're big enough to be the top tier of a wedding cake."

Cole looked up and raised his brows. "I'd say. Those are huge. Kaley, maybe just half of that."

Stanhill put his coffee down. "Delaney has a hard time with moderation. Being a vampire means calories don't count."

Charisma pointed her fork at him. "They do for the rest of us mortals."

Kaley's eyes rounded. "This was made by a vampire?"

Stanhill nodded. "Yes. Does it taste any different?" he teased.

She took another bite. "Just extra awesome."

"Yeah," Saffie said. "Extra awesome." She laughed and made a face, and the two of them went back to stuffing their faces.

Pandora tucked her head to hide her smile as she leaned toward Cole. "I think Kaley has a not-so-secret admirer in Saffie."

"I see that." He paused, his head bent to match hers, his voice so low and husky it sent a shiver over her skin. "She's not the only one with a not-so-secret admirer."

She stilled. That was *not* fair. He couldn't flirt

with her and pretend nothing had changed when he was leaving.

She sat up and dug into her cake, putting a big forkful into her mouth so there would be no polite way to answer him. The cake was all that was right in the world. It would mean extra time on the treadmill tomorrow, but right now chocolate and bourbon seemed like the answer to everything.

Stanhill noticed. "What do you think of the cake, Pandora? Delaney will want to know."

She finally swallowed. "It's perfect. I mean, chocolate and booze?" She paused to gesture dramatically with her fork as the need to jab back at Cole rose up within her. "With cake this amazing, who needs a man?"

11

Cole gave Pandora her space for the rest of the evening, which thankfully wasn't much longer. After dessert, she seemed very ready to go. And very ready to be away from him.

On the way home, he let Kaley ride up front while he sat in the back with his father. Kaley did exactly as he'd hoped and kept up a steady salvo of questions about the coven meeting.

Jack was staring at him. Cole could feel it. Finally, he turned toward his father and lifted his brows in question.

Jack took the opening. "Good meal."

Cole nodded. "Very."

"Nice family, too." In other words, Jack no longer thought Pandora or her family was out to get him.

"Yes."

"You probably should have brought more than

wine." Translation: The wine hadn't been enough to make up for upsetting Pandora.

"I didn't know what else to bring."

Jack hmphed and turned to watch the scenery out the window.

Cole caught Pandora looking at him in the rearview mirror, but as soon as he made eye contact, she snapped her gaze back to the road.

They pulled into the driveway five minutes later, although it felt like the trip had taken an hour. Cole jumped out and opened Kaley's door. As soon as she vacated, he leaned down. He had to say something to Pandora. "I'm sorry about tonight. I really am."

"I told you, it's no big deal." She was flip and casual and completely on the defensive. "I'll be by around six fifteen tomorrow to pick Kaley up."

She shifted the car into reverse, ready to go.

He exhaled. She obviously didn't want to talk. Or listen. "Okay. See you then."

"Yep." She stared straight ahead.

He shut the door, but stood in the driveway as she reversed and pulled away through the gate. She'd be back tomorrow. He knew that. But he couldn't get past the fact that her leaving right now felt like it was forever.

Kaley was in the house already, but Jack stood on the porch. "Let her go."

"What's it look like I'm doing?" Cole knew the

tone in his voice was less than respectful, but he was angry and didn't care. He strode up the drive to join his father on the porch.

Jack shook his head. "This is for the best. Trust me."

"Maybe Pandora and I wouldn't both be so upset right now if I'd known what I was before she and I met." Cole faced him. "Still think my not knowing is what's best?"

Jack's eyes narrowed. "I'll tell you what you need to know when you need to know it, and yes, it's what's best for both of you. Plus, you have a house, a job and a life back in North Carolina. You going to give all that up to move here on the chance things *might* work out between you? What kind of teaching job are you going to get living in a town where pretending every day is Halloween is the main industry? Pull yourself together, son."

"Hard to do when so much in my life has been upended."

"And you think Pandora's going to fix all that?"

"No, but that's not her job. What if things did work out between us?"

Jack grunted. "All I know is you have a daughter to provide for."

"I'm well aware of that." A daughter who wasn't all that happy with him right now. What else was new? He tried to focus on that and not the burgeoning ache in his chest. He had no right to feel this way about Pandora anyway. They'd kissed a few times. That was all. "I should go talk to Kaley."

"They seem like good people, but—"

"Dad, I really don't want to discuss it anymore. It's late. I need to talk to Kaley, and then I'm going to bed. This house isn't going to remodel itself."

Jack held his hands up. "You got it. I'll be on the couch tonight and out of your hair in the morning."

"Dad..." Cole took a breath. He didn't want to leave things like this with his father. "I appreciate you coming down. I'm still not happy about you and Mom not telling me the truth, and I don't agree at all with your decision not to tell me much now, but I guess I get that you were doing what you thought was right to protect me."

"You'd do the same for Kaley."

"Yes, I would." He took his glasses off and rubbed the bridge of his nose. "I'll get you a blanket and a pillow." He headed into the house, his father behind him, and went for the stairs. "Tomorrow morning we can go out for breakfast. There's a diner in town that looks good. Kaley's been wanting to go there."

Jack smiled. "Sounds like a plan. You want me to talk to Kaley?"

"No, but I appreciate the offer. I need her to understand that impulsive decisions can have negative consequences later on. Moving here permanently on a whim...it'd just be...impractical."

Jack nodded. "She's a good kid. She'll understand. Maybe not tonight, but she will."

"I hope you're right." Cole ran upstairs, got his dad a blanket and pillow and tucked them under his arm. He knocked on Kaley's door.

"Yeah?"

"Can I come in?"

"Yeah."

He opened the door. She was already in bed. One earbud dangled free while the other was still in her ear. "We're going to try that diner in town for breakfast tomorrow. Sound good?"

She shrugged and stared at the screen of her iPhone. "I guess."

He sighed. "I know you're mad at me."

No response.

He came in and sat on the edge of her bed. "Kaley, we can't stay here. I know you like this place, but I have a lot of years invested in my job at home. I can't just walk away because this place seems like fun."

She cut her eyes at him. "You could get a teaching job here."

"There aren't any colleges in the area. And a high school isn't going to pay what I'm making now."

"It's not all about money, you know."

He laughed. "You think I found that iPhone in a

cereal box? You're right that money isn't everything, but it is important. We need a certain amount to pay our bills and eat."

"What about all the money from selling this house?"

"That will definitely help, but we're not just going to spend it. A lot of it will go into your college fund."

She frowned. "Maybe I'm not going to college."

"We're not having that discussion."

She rolled her eyes. "I want to stay here."

"What about all your friends back home?"

"I'm already making new ones."

"I'm glad to hear that. But our plan isn't changing. We're fixing up the house, selling it and moving back. That's it. End of discussion."

She huffed out a breath, her eyes narrowing. "What about Miss Williams?"

The question caught him off guard for a moment. "She's...she's going to help me with the house and you with your witch stuff. Nothing's changed there either."

Kaley tipped her head, mouth bent in obvious skepticism. "Really? *Nothing's* changed? She's totally mad at you."

"No, she's not. Everything is fine between us."

Kaley laughed. "Dad, you have a lot to learn about women."

He kissed her on the cheek and stood. "On that

note, it's time for you to go to bed. Earbuds out, iPhone off."

"Fine." She yanked the other earbud free, then flung the covers over herself.

He hit the light switch on the way out, still shaking his head as he headed downstairs. Kaley was right. Pandora *was* mad at him.

He thought for a moment about going to see her, but it was after ten. She was probably in bed. And probably wouldn't want to see him. He rolled his shoulders, but the prickly energy from the night's events was stuck in his bones. He needed to do *something*.

He put the blanket and pillow on the couch. Jack was sitting on the porch. Cole stuck his head out. "You okay?"

"Yep. You?"

"I'm going out for a run. Don't wait up."

Jack smiled like he knew what his son was up to. "All right."

Cole went back upstairs to change into his gear. If Jack thought Cole was going to see Pandora, he was wrong.

Running by her house was *not* the same as going to see her.

Pandora pulled away from Pilcher Manor with

one clear thought. She wasn't ready to go home. She was too wound up from Cole's revelation, too buzzed on hurt feelings and the disbelief that he thought everything was still hunky dory between them. How the hell was she going to help him with that house and spend time with Kaley and pretend that they were nothing more than friends?

Practical. Not freaking likely.

She needed a drink. And she didn't want to imbibe alone. That would only put her in a worse state of mind. She needed company. She pulled over and hit Willa's speed dial.

The fae jeweler answered a couple rings later. "Hey, woman, what's up?"

"Are you busy? You want to come over for a glass of wine?"

Willa made a disappointed sound. "I'd love to, but Nick and I are watching a movie. How about tomorrow?"

"No, it's cool, don't worry about it. I was just in the mood to hang out. Have fun. Tell Nick I said hi."

"Will do. Talk to you soon."

Love ruined everything. Pandora hung up and pulled back onto the road. As much as she wanted Willa's company, the lack of it wasn't going to stop her from having one drink. And since she still didn't want to be alone, she made a few turns and five minutes later she was walking into Howler's.

The bar and grill was busy—it was Saturday night, after all—but with kids back in school, there were slightly fewer tourists in town, so the place wasn't unbearably crowded.

Bridget Merrow, owner of Howler's and a werewolf, waved at Pandora before she'd reached the bar. "Hey, Pandora! What brings you in?"

"I need a drink." Pandora wriggled in between two occupied bar stools to lean on the bar.

Bridget's brows shot up. "That bad?"

"Sort of."

"Sorry to hear that. What can I get you?"

Pandora glanced to her side. "A seat would be nice. But I'll settle for a glass of cabernet."

Bridget grinned. "I can handle both of those." She leaned forward and jerked her thumb toward the other end of the bar. "Did you see who's here?"

Pandora turned to look. Sitting at the opposite end of the bar was a stone-faced man with a shaved head, a multitude of tattoos and a bent nose that made a lot of sense in conjunction with his heavily muscled body. He had the kind of tensed look that said he could strike at any moment and when he did, you weren't going to see it coming.

She grinned. "I didn't know Van was in town."

Bridget nodded. "Just got here. Go ahead, I'll bring your wine."

"Thanks." Pandora headed toward the hulk of

a man and got two steps away before he saw her.

His face broke out in a huge smile as he slid off his seat and threw his arms wide. "*Kotyonok*! Is good to see you."

She hugged him and laughed. To have a man who looked like him call you *kitten* was a very unique thing. "You too, Van. How are you?"

"Good, good." He kissed her on both cheeks, then pulled back and looked her up and down. "I would ask how you are, but I see you are also very good. You look like you are on the prowl. Have you come to pick up men?"

His Russian heritage still accented his words. She shook her head. "Definitely not. In fact, I'm here to drink one out of my head."

He frowned. "You have man troubles?"

"Sort of, but nothing a few drinks and a good mope won't cure."

He looked past her. "You have seat already?"

"No, I just got here. Bridget's getting my wine."

He glared at the man on the bar stool next to his. "You. Get up."

The guy turned to see who was talking to him and paled. He grabbed his beer and vacated.

Van pointed to the empty chair. "You sit by me. Tell me everything."

Laughing, but knowing there was no point in trying to get the poor man his seat back, she took the chair. Ivan "Van" Tsvetkov wasn't a man who took no for an answer. He was a dragon shifter, and while he was a resident of Nocturne Falls, he was here only between fights. He made his living on the MMA fight circuit where he was known as The Hammer.

Pandora had first met him when he'd come to town looking for a house. A retreat, really. He'd wanted a place in the mountains where he could recoup between fights and get away from the press and publicity. Nothing on the market had fit his needs, so she'd ended up finding him the perfect piece of land and then being his right hand during the building process.

He'd trusted her implicitly, and she'd gained a friend for life. He'd become almost like an older brother to her, which was fine, because he certainly wasn't her type romantically.

Sadly, Cole was. The giant poophead.

Bridget showed up with Pandora's wine. "Ivan, you ready for another beer?"

He nodded. "We need two shots of vodka."

Pandora held her hand up. There were some things she could say no to. "I can't do a shot."

"Why not?" He looked at her. "Do you work tomorrow?"

"No, but..." Really, why not? If there was ever a night to drown her sorrows, it was tonight. "Okay. But only one."

If Van thought Pandora didn't see him wink at Bridget, he was wrong. He held up two fingers and nodded. "Vodka."

Then he sat down and turned to face her. "What man has caused you trouble?"

She sipped her wine. "It's a long story. With a quick end." She smiled. "Why don't you tell me what's going on with you? How long are you in town for?"

"Not long. A week." He finished his beer. "I should talk to this man."

She almost choked on her wine. "No, Van, you should not. I appreciate that, but it's so over it's not even funny."

"You are sure?"

"Positive."

Bridget returned with their shots. "Here you go, kids. Enjoy."

They did. Two more rounds later and Pandora had told Van everything about everything. She put her hand on her head. "Ooof. I need to go home. I'm kinda smashed."

He looked concerned. "Are you all right, *kotyonoko*?"

"Yes. But I probably won't be tomorrow." She laughed, even though there was nothing funny about being hungover.

"You cannot drive." He held out his enormous hand. "Keys."

"I'm not going to drive. I can walk from here. My car will be okay."

"But you might not be. I will go with you." He held up a credit card to Bridget.

She gave him a nod and came to get it.

"Everything," he said, pointing to his and Pandora's empty glasses.

"Got it." She glanced at Pandora. "You okay? You want me to call somebody to take you home?"

"No." The last thing Pandora wanted was one of her sisters coming to get her and figuring out she'd gotten so plastered because of Cole that she'd needed someone to walk her home. She sat up as straight as she could. "I'm good. A little wasted, but good."

Van put his hand on the back of her chair and said to Bridget, "I will get her home, don't worry."

"Thanks, Ivan." Bridget took his card. "Be right back."

He leaned toward Pandora. "You must drink a lot of water."

"I will." She crossed her heart. Or her entire body. It was hard to tell. "Promise."

He signed the check, took his card back and helped her to her feet, then made sure she had her purse. They were about halfway to her house when the last shot kicked in. A sudden wave of wooziness came over her, and her strappy gold sandals turned on her. She tilted toward him, grabbing his arm.

He caught her before she fell. "This is no good."

"I think my shoes are—whoa!" Next thing she knew, she was completely off the ground and in Van's very strong arms. "You're carrying me."

"Da. Your walking now is not so good."

She poked at his chest. "You're very muscurly. Muscularly. Muscle-y." She laughed and poked his chest again.

He snorted. "*Kotyonoko,* you are drunk and it is my fault. I am sorry."

"No." She waved her hand through the air. Being carried was really a nice way to travel. "I had a good time and you're a good listener. Thank you."

"You are welcome."

She smacked his chest. "And you paid. You shouldn't have done that. I have money. How much do I owe you?"

"Drink your water and we are good. It's what friends do." He stopped at a crossroads. "Remind me. Which way to your house?"

She pointed toward the street and told him the house number. They started off again. "How's your house?"

"It's very good."

"It's very big." She yawned. Sleep was tugging at her hard. She put her head on his shoulder.

"Pandora. We are here."

"Huh?" She lifted her head. She'd definitely drifted off.

Van was standing on the walk that led to her front steps. "I do not want to put you down. There is someone on your porch."

She blinked and looked toward the door.

Cole was sitting on the bench by the front door. He stood. He was dressed for a run. Basketball shorts. T-shirt. No glasses.

"Put me down, Van. I can walk."

He eased her to her feet as Cole came down the steps. His dark eyes seemed angry. Or maybe hurt. "I thought we could talk, but I see now there's nothing to talk about."

A surge of annoyance sobered her enough to stay upright without wobbling. Too much. "No, there isn't. Unless you've changed your mind about leaving."

He snorted and looked at Van. "Doesn't look like there's still a reason for me to stay."

"What's that supposed to mean?"

"Means you work fast."

Van stiffened. "We are just friends."

"Yeah," Pandora added. "Good friends." Cole was taller, but Van was wider. And Van could breathe fire. Was that a wisp of steam curling out of the side of his mouth? She put her hand on Van's arm to keep Cole from getting scorched. "Thanks for getting me home. Call me for lunch or something."

Van's gaze shifted from her to Cole then back to her. "I should wait until you are inside."

Cole frowned. "She's not in any danger from me."

"I'm a little tipsy, Cole, in case you hadn't noticed." She leaned forward and almost fell over.

His frown softened. "Are you okay?"

"I will be. I need to go to bed."

Van held on to her. "She will be hungover tomorrow."

"No, no." She shook her head, then stopped when that made her surroundings spin. "I'm going to drink lots of water, I promise."

Cole sighed. "She drank because of me."

Van nodded. "Yes."

She pushed at Van's rock-solid arm. "Shh. Don't tell him that."

"Damn it." Cole started to push at his glasses, realizing a second too late he wasn't wearing them, and dropped his hand. "I'm sorry, Pandora. I didn't mean to hurt you. I thought you knew—"

"Stop." Her stomach started doing questionable things. "I just want to go inside and go to bed."

Van helped her forward. "Keys?"

"Purse." She handed the bag over to Van. "Side pocket." Then she looked at Cole. Pretty, pretty, oblivious Cole. "This isn't the time."

He nodded. "I see that. I'm sorry. Tomorrow?"

"Sure. Whenever. Bye." She wanted him gone before she embarrassed herself by blowing chunks all over her yard.

"Tomorrow." He took one more look at Van, then headed for the street, breaking into a run.

She sighed as the sound of his footsteps faded away. Then she sniffed. She felt like crying. She blamed it on the booze.

Before the tears came, Van had the front door open and Pandora back in his arms. He carried her in, then set her up on the couch with a bottle of water, two aspirin and her cell phone at hand. "I should stay."

"No, I'm fine. Really." Embarrassed and way too drunk, but fine.

"You will call if you need me."

"I will. Promise."

He slipped her shoes off and covered her with the throw off the back of the couch. "Call me in the morning, or I will come over."

"Got it."

Pumpkin jumped up and draped herself over Pandora's legs.

With the sound of purring and the front door closing, Pandora gave into sleep.

12

Cole was a well-educated man. He knew the difference between smart decisions and dumb decisions and yet, he thought, as he stood on Pandora's front porch the next morning, he couldn't tell which one this was. But he hadn't been able to stop thinking about her or wondering if she was okay. She'd even shown up in his dreams. He had to do something.

Even if that guy she'd been with last night had been something more than a friend.

The shopping bag he carried was filled with take-out boxes of bacon and eggs, hash browns, biscuits, and blueberry pancakes from the diner where he'd eaten breakfast a half hour ago with Kaley and his dad. A place called Mummy's. It had been very busy, and the food had been very good, so there was no question about the quality of what he'd brought her.

He just had no idea if she'd even open the door for him. Or if her friend from last night would still be there.

Please don't let that be the case.

If she didn't open the door, he'd leave her the food anyway. On the rare occasions he'd been hungover, diner food — once he'd been able to eat — had been just the thing. And since he was the reason she was hungover, he kind of owed her.

With no real hope, he knocked.

A few minutes went by. He'd bent to set the bag on the porch when the door swung slowly open. Pandora's fat orange cat sat in the foyer staring at him.

On the other side of the foyer, Pandora leaned against the kitchen doorway, a cup of coffee in one hand, the other finishing a flourish in the air. Had she used magic to open the door? She was swaddled in a big, fluffy ivory robe, an emerald green P embroidered on the breast. She waved her hand and the door opened wider. She frowned. "I thought you were Charisma or Willa, even though I told them not to come over."

"I was…worried about you. Are you okay?"

"Do I look okay? I'm hungover like a frat boy after a weeklong kegger. I'm never drinking again."

"You don't look anything like a frat boy. You look pretty good, actually." Her makeup was smudged like she'd slept in it, and her hair was a messy knot on top of her head, but it was kind of adorable. And sexy. An image of her sprawled in bed floated through his mind.

He had it bad for her. Bad.

He picked up the bag. "I brought you breakfast."

The cat meowed.

"Pumpkin, you already ate." Pandora stared at him. She'd yet to say he could come in. "From?"

"Mummy's."

She perked up a little. "Any pancakes in there?"

"Blueberry. Also biscuits, bacon and eggs and hash browns."

She swallowed. "You can come in. But I don't feel like talking."

"That's okay." As long as she felt like listening.

He waited until she'd had her first bite of pancake dripping in butter and syrup, both of which Mummy's had provided in ample amounts. She made a happy, that's-delicious noise.

"Good?"

"Always." She glanced at him, then pointed toward the counter with her fork. "You can have some coffee if you want."

"Thanks." He got a cup, then joined her at the kitchen table. "Do you remember much of last night?"

"I remember all of it. I was tipsy and unstable, but I didn't black out."

He nodded. "I owe you an apology. And an explanation."

"I'm listening." She stabbed her fork into another bite of pancakes.

"I'm sorry for not explaining things better. For not telling you upfront that I had no plans to stay in Nocturne Falls. And for assuming you knew. But I didn't expect for anything to happen between us, either. You didn't even like me initially."

She looked up through her lashes at him. "You seem to think I do now."

He nodded. "You certainly seemed to like kissing me."

"I did. I don't anymore."

"You can turn it on and off just like that?"

"When it means protecting my heart? Yes." She got up and refilled her coffee, but stayed at the counter. She held the cup in both hands.

He took a breath, but hesitated, turning his thoughts over in his head before he put voice to them. What if she didn't want the same things he did? What if... *Just say it.* "I came over here because I wanted to see how you were but also to apologize for upsetting you. And I wanted to let you know that I'm willing to give us a shot if you're willing to risk—"

She stared over the cup at him, unblinking. "No."

That wasn't the answer he'd expected. His gut

sank. "No? Really? Pandora, taking risks is part of life."

Her gaze dropped. "Thank you for the food, but I think you should go."

He stood. "Why are you so afraid of getting hurt?"

She closed her eyes for a moment. When she opened them, they held a pain that surprised him. "Because I've been hurt. I don't ever want to feel that way again. And I don't want to be responsible for someone else getting hurt."

"No one does, but—"

She mumbled something else that he swore sounded like, "Not again."

"I'm a grown man. I can take it. Tell me what happened."

She shook her head. "Cole, you have no idea."

He took a step toward her. He wanted to pull her into his arms, but he didn't need an equation to show him how that would turn out. "Then tell me."

She walked past him and went back to the table. She put her coffee down, picked up her fork, then put that down too. "I had a pretty serious high school boyfriend. He was…a lot like you. He didn't believe in magic or witches or anything that didn't have a solid, scientific explanation. My magic was…well, it wasn't stable. It never has been, but in those days it was early still and everyone thought I was just a late bloomer."

She took a deep breath, then let it out. "I couldn't imagine my life without Ren. I thought we'd go to the same college, get married, have kids and live the white-picket-fence life. I also thought I'd make a believer out of him.

"We were coming home from one of the football games one night, and it had just started to rain. I had a stupid impulse to show him just how real my magic was. I don't know why that moment seemed like the right one, but it did. Teenage foolishness, maybe."

She swallowed. "I cast a big spell. Way bigger than I had any right to."

"What was it?" he asked.

"An umbrella spell." She laughed, but the sound was bitter. "How could he not believe if I could make the rain go away, right?"

She continued, her gaze going to a faraway place. "There was a huge flash of light, and he jerked the wheel and the car rolled." The color that had started to come back to her face drained out of it. "He was thrown out of the car and killed instantly. I barely got a scratch."

She'd lived with this since she was a teenager? He tried to imagine Kaley's reaction to such a thing. No wonder Pandora's broken magic was such a big issue for her. "Pandora, it's not your fault a bolt of lightning startled him. I'm so sorry you've been carrying this all these years."

"It wasn't a bolt of lightning. It was my magic gone wrong." She hugged her arms around her torso. "My magic has been crap all my life. My mother tried everything to fix me. We went to see specialists, she tried to find me an animal familiar, we did cleansing rites—nothing worked. I was born broken. And Ren died because of it."

"You couldn't have predicted what would happen."

"I shouldn't have attempted that spell."

"You were a kid."

She didn't say anything for a moment. "I should have been the one who died."

His gut clenched at the thought. "I'm so glad you weren't."

Liquid rimmed her lower lids. "I've never felt pain like that before. I know I was just a teenager, but I loved him. When he died, I felt so responsible."

"I'm sure you did. Anyone would have."

She sniffed and blinked the tears away. "I haven't dated much because of that. I haven't dated at all, really. I couldn't bear the thought of being that unhappy again."

His heart ached for her. He couldn't imagine how devastating that loss must have been for her. And to shoulder the responsibility for the accident must have been crushing. At that moment, all he wanted to do was make her smile. "Your magic works around me, so obviously it's not broken."

She picked her head up and looked at him. "And when you leave? I should go back to being broken after feeling what it's like to be whole? To be who I was meant to be? I can't do that. I'd rather not know. I'd rather stay who I am now. I've figured out how to be that person. I'm...okay with it. But to get a taste of being complete and then having it ripped away..." She stared out the kitchen window. "Let me put it in terms you can understand. I'm zero percent interested in that."

He sat back. He could see her point. "We don't even know if we're compatible. You're not a little interested in figuring that out?"

She glanced at him. "You're really persistent for a guy with one foot out the door."

"What if...what if maybe I was willing to stay?"

She just stared at him.

He took a breath. "I like you, Pandora. I can't stop thinking about you."

"That's just the familiar-witch thing."

"Speaking of, I have a lot to learn since my dad isn't exactly being forthcoming with the information. I thought maybe you'd help me with that. You could tutor me and Kaley."

"I don't know. Familiars aren't my area of expertise."

"We could go through those books in the attic. Maybe figure it out together."

"I guess."

He finally felt like he was getting somewhere. "I like you, and I'm not convinced it's completely related to the witch-familiar thing. What if we've got some real chemistry going on here? Don't you at least want to find out?" Then something occurred to him, and he realized what an idiot he was. "You don't feel the same way, do you?"

"What do you mean?"

"I mean, I'm kind of nuts about you, and you probably want to friend-zone me. That's why you agreed to help with Kaley and the house. You like me, but you don't *like me* like me." He shook his head, laughing softly. "I didn't get that until just now."

"That's not true." She frowned and yanked a wayward strand of hair behind one ear. "I do like you. Unfortunately. You and your stupid pretty face."

He laughed harder. "That's the nicest thing you've ever said to me."

"Oh, shut up. I'm hungover, and you're trying to have a big discussion. I told you I didn't want to talk. I don't know what I'm saying."

"Sorry." But he couldn't stop smiling. "I know you're taking Kaley to the meeting tonight, but what are you doing tomorrow night?"

"Why do you want to know?"

"Because I'd like to take you to dinner. Anywhere. Even places I have to wear a tie."

She scowled at him. "You're trying to take advantage of my weakened condition."

"Maybe I am. So what do you say? Dinner? And we give this thing a real shot. Maybe we'll have a miserable time, and that will be the end of it. And maybe we'll find out we really like each other."

"What about Kaley?"

"She's supposed to go to a friend's house to work on a group project. I'm sure she can hang out there until we're finished." He grinned. So far, so good. "Is that a yes to dinner?"

She let a few moments go by before she answered. "What if we do like each other? What then? Are you still going to move?"

"If things between us work, I'm willing to explore other options. Do you think there's any chance I could get a teaching job around here?"

"I have no idea. Is that more important than your love life?"

"Not if you're willing to date a homeless guy. I'm just being practical. I have a child to take care of. I can't let her suffer for my decisions."

Her eyes narrowed and after a long moment, she responded, "You paint such a positive picture, how can I say no? We can give it a shot."

"All right!" He clapped his hands together, causing Pumpkin to go skittering out of the room and Pandora to cringe.

"My head," she moaned. Her eyes were scrunched shut.

"I'm sorry, I forgot," he whispered. "Can I do anything for you? Get you anything? Run you a hot bath?"

She opened one eye. "We haven't even been out on a date yet, and you're trying to get me naked."

"I *am* a man. And even hungover, you're pretty hot."

"Go away before I change my mind about dinner. Or turn you into a toad. I can do that now, you know."

He stood up. "You're adorable. Never change." He headed for the door. "See you tonight. Call me if you need anything."

She grunted something, maybe a word, maybe not, but it reminded him of someone else.

He stopped and stuck his head back in the kitchen. "Hey, that guy you were with last night. He's not an old boyfriend, or anyone I'm going to have to fight for your hand, is he?"

She snorted. "My hand is mine to give as I see fit, but no, he's not an old boyfriend. Nor does he want to be a new one. And you should be very glad about that."

He stood up taller. Sure, the guy looked intimidating, but that didn't mean he was a threat. "You don't think I could take him?"

"In a battle of wits, maybe. Physically? Uh,

probably not. He's a dragon shifter. And a top-ranked mixed martial arts fighter."

"Dragon shifter. Got it." Cole nodded and made a mental note not to tick the guy off. "I'd say I'd try to stay on his good side, but he already didn't seem to like me very much last night."

"I might have told him you'd been leading me on. He's kind of like a big brother to me. He was the first person I called when I woke up this morning."

Well, that sucked. Cole did his best not to react. "Great. You sure it's nothing I need to worry about?"

"Not unless you break my heart." She smiled with the sort of acid edge that almost seemed like a challenge.

"All right. No pressure." He gave her a little wave as he left again. Monday night he was going to have to wow her. The last thing Cole needed was Puff the Magic MMA Fighter showing up at his door breathing fire.

13

By five o'clock, Pandora had finally begun to feel human again. A hot shower had gone a long way toward making that happen, but, she was reluctant to admit, so had Cole's peace offering of blueberry pancakes.

It was like he'd known that was the perfect thing to bring. Was that because he was an awesome guy or the familiar meant for her?

The whole thing was so complicated she couldn't bear to think about it for more than a few minutes at a time. Any more than that, and her brain tangled in knots.

At least there appeared to be some hope for a future for them if things went well. Cole seemed to be willing to entertain the idea of staying in Nocturne Falls if that was the case. But that was kind of a double-edged sword. If she wanted him around, she was going to have to make him fall for her. Make him want to stay.

She stared at herself in the bathroom mirror. "I'm not sure I need that pressure."

She looked down at her cat. Pumpkin was curled up on top of the hamper lid, a place she could reach only by jumping onto the toilet seat first. "What do you think, Fatness Everdeen? Is Cole worth the effort?"

But Pandora didn't need Pumpkin's opinion to formulate her answer. Deep in her heart of hearts, Pandora *wanted* to love again. She still wanted the white-picket-fence life. A big comfortable house with a tire swing hanging from one of the trees in the backyard. A wonderful husband who was as crazy in love with her as she was with him. Rambunctious, smiling kids who would make too much noise and draw her Mother's Day cards on construction paper and give her gray hair and laugh lines.

But that dream required commitment. And she was scared spitless of going through the same kind of hurt and pain she'd endured with Ren. Right next to the part of her that wanted that dream, however, was a part of her that also wondered if finding a new love might heal a lot of her lingering pain.

But was Cole that guy? Was anyone?

Cole was tempting on so many levels. He was

smart, and she loved smart. He was handy, and wow, that was hot. Physically, there was no question he was her type. That lanky, casually fit guy had always been her go-to dream man. Add to that Cole's piercing eyes and sexy-geeky glasses, and she was a goner.

And that was before she factored in the part about him being a familiar.

A man capable of fixing both her heart and her magic.

She leaned her forehead against the mirror. She had to give it a shot, didn't she? The rewards outweighed the risk.

She hoped.

Pumpkin jumped down and wound around her legs, making a tiny meow that was precursor to the big song and dance that would follow if dinner didn't appear shortly.

Pandora pointed down the hall. "Kitchen."

Pumpkin didn't need to be told twice. She scampered off.

"That's right," Pandora said. "Burn off some of the calories you're about to eat."

She followed Pumpkin into the kitchen and opened a can of diet cat food while Pumpkin went into her frantic "I'm near death with hunger" meowing.

"All right, already." Pandora put the dish on the floor and picked up the old one to put in the sink.

The Professor Woos The Witch

Pumpkin fell on the food with all the grace and etiquette of a prison inmate.

The doorbell rang, and a second later, the door opened and a familiar voice called out, "Pandy?"

"Marigold, hey. I'm in the kitchen." Pandora ran water in Pumpkin's old food dish and let it soak.

"Hey there." Marigold came in with a pretty bouquet in her hands.

"Hey there, yourself." Pandora leaned against the counter. "What brings you by?"

She held up the flowers. "Deliveries."

"I thought you had someone to do those."

"I do, but it's Sunday. I close at five, and this one's for you."

"Really?" Pandora lifted her brows in surprise, then realized who they must be from. "Let me guess. Ivan sent them."

Marigold frowned and set them on the counter. "I didn't know he was in town. And no, these aren't from him."

Pandora reached over and grabbed the card.
Thanks for giving me a second chance.
—Cole
She glanced at her sister. "This is unexpected."

Marigold grinned. "He likes you."

"Yeah, I know."

"You don't seem impressed."

"It's not that, the flowers are really sweet. It's cool that he came in to your shop and got them, but—"

"He didn't come in. The order was called in via Floraline. I was the closest fulfillment center to your address. Still, he had them sent, so same gesture. Just a little less personal. What was the but for?"

"It's just...I don't know. Long story." She stuck the card back in the flowers and opened the fridge. "You want a Coke?"

"No, thanks, I have to swing by Mom's and pick up Saffie before the meeting. I can't stay long. You still bringing Kaley?"

Pandora grabbed a Coke for herself and popped the top. The caffeine was a necessity at the moment. "Yes."

"I'm glad you and Cole worked things out, because I really like him. He's cute and smart and has the tightest little—"

"You already read the card, didn't you?" She watched her sister as she took a long drink of the icy soda.

"Maybe." Marigold toyed with a loose blonde curl. "What second chance are you giving him? Is this about him moving back to North Carolina?"

Pandora swallowed the mouthful of Coke. "You're so nosy."

"I'm your sister. It's my job."

"It's about us going to dinner tomorrow night."

"Ooh. Dinner. Sounds fancy."

Pandora laughed. "You're just saying that

because you're a single mother who hasn't been out on a date since forever."

Marigold cocked an eyebrow. "Says the woman who hasn't been on a date since high school. At least I've had sex."

Pandora almost spit soda all over her sister. Talk about keeping a secret. "When?"

Marigold made a face and mumbled something.

Pandora put her hand to her ear. "What was that? I didn't quite catch it."

Marigold sighed. "I said, nine months before Saffie was born."

Pandora laughed. "So almost nine years ago. Yeah, you've totally got me beat." Unable to stop her subconscious, the idea of sex with Cole danced through her brain.

"What was that look?"

"Huh? Nothing." Pandora's cheeks warmed. "I need to get ready for the meeting. I'm not kicking you out, but I am about to disappear into the bedroom to get dressed."

"Yeah, yeah. I need to scoot too." Marigold headed for the door. "Tell Mr. Second Chances I said hi. If you can stop kissing him long enough."

Pandora rolled her eyes. Then decided kissing him wasn't such a bad idea.

14

Never in his life had the impending visit of a woman given Cole the kind of jittery buzz he was currently experiencing. He'd been to the front door twice to look for Pandora's car. Actually, three times considering this recent trip. But the driveway remained empty.

"Dad, what are you doing?"

Cole jerked back. "Nothing."

Kaley grinned. "You're looking for Miss Williams."

"So?"

"Good comeback."

He made a face at her. "Shouldn't you be getting ready? She'll be here any second."

"I am ready."

He crossed his arms and leaned on the door. "Kaley Van Zant, I don't know anything about coven meetings, but I do know you're not going with BBQ sauce on your shirt."

She looked down as she stretched her T-shirt out. "Oh, man."

"Go change. You have time."

She dashed up the steps to her room.

Cole went back to looking out the sidelight. Pandora was just pulling into the drive.

His entire body tightened with need. He opened the door and walked out onto the porch.

Pandora got out of her car and came toward him. She wore skinny jeans, a T-shirt and a tight cardigan that showed off her incredible figure. "Hey."

"How are you feeling?" he asked.

"Good. Not a hundred percent, but nothing like this morning." She joined him on the porch. "Thanks for the pancakes, by the way. That was really thoughtful."

"Thoughtful enough for a kiss?"

She smiled like she was trying not to. "Kinda pushy, don't you think?"

That wasn't a no. He slipped his fingers into the hair at the nape of her neck and brushed his mouth across hers. A fluttering of wings filled his ears, and the earth around him seemed to disappear beneath his feet. He released her, not wanting to push her goodwill too far.

She sighed, eyes still closed for a moment. When she opened them, she shook her head slowly. "I really hope you don't turn out to be bad for me. The flowers were really sweet, too."

Before he could say anything, Kaley opened the door. "Hey, Miss Williams."

"Hiya. Ready to go?"

"Yep. Do I need to bring anything?"

"Nope." Pandora hooked her thumb toward the car. "Hop in. I need to talk to your dad for a sec."

"Okay."

"Wow," Cole said. "Not a single eye roll. Impressive." He couldn't stop grinning. "What do you want to talk to me about?"

"The whole familiar thing. And us. The two go hand in hand. There's no pretending otherwise. We've got to get you comfortable with this new side of yourself."

"I am comfortable. I guess. Other than the way I feel when you touch me, I haven't really noticed anything different. I haven't even shifted since that first time, although I've felt like it might happen, it hasn't. Are you still helping me with that?"

"I am. Every time I've touched you since, I've pushed a spell toward you to keep it from happening so you don't freak out."

"You have?"

She nodded.

"Then I do need to work on this. Suggestions?"

"Yes. Go into the attic and talk to Gertrude."

He stared at her. "You want me to talk to a ghost?"

"You want this to work or don't you? If anyone can give you the basics on being a familiar, it's her. And you really need to understand this side of yourself."

"How do I...summon her or whatever?"

"Just go on up and say hi. She's not shy. You shouldn't be either."

"Okay, I can do that." He tucked his hands in his pockets. "Looks like I know what I'm doing tonight."

She smiled. "Good. You can tell me all about it when I bring Kaley home."

"Have fun."

She started down the steps, laughing softly. "Yeah, you too. Tell Gerty I said hi."

"You're enjoying this way too much."

Still laughing, she gave him a wave and jumped into the car. He waited until they'd pulled through the gate, then went inside.

He looked toward the attic. Talk to a ghost. What on earth had his life become? With a shrug, he headed up the steps, trying to psych himself up for whatever was about to happen.

The attic was warm but not unbearable. He flipped the light on. How did one start a conversation with a ghost? He walked to the center of the space. "Um...Aunt Gertrude? If you're there, Pandora Williams told me to come upstairs and talk to you."

He stared into the empty space of the attic. This was the most ridiculous thing he'd ever—

"Does that mean you believe?"

He spun around.

A petite woman with fluffy lavender hair and a purple jumpsuit hovered a few feet behind him. He could see right through her. Like a freaking hologram.

She waved. "Hello there, stud muffin."

He swallowed. This was so weird. "My name is Cole."

"I know." She batted her lashes. "You have Ulysses' dark eyes. All you raven familiars do. Oh, I miss that man." She put a hand over her heart. "Best lover I ever had."

Cole tried not to grimace, but talking to a ghost—who was technically his great-aunt—about her sex life was...just weird and not something he'd ever thought he'd do. "So...Pandora told me to talk to you. About the whole familiar thing."

"Ready to face facts, cookie?"

"Yes. Something like that. Can you help me?"

She levitated higher and stared down at him. "Sure. You are family after all. What do need help with?"

He thought for a moment. "Everything. What is a familiar capable of? Can I shift into that bird form anytime I want, or is that not something I can always control? How do I help Pandora with her magic? What happens when we're bonded? What am I not asking that I should be? I really don't have a clue about any of this."

She squinted. "Didn't your parents teach you *anything*?"

"No. They gave up being who they were in an effort to protect me. And my father doesn't think I should get involved with Pandora so he's not keen on giving me too much info right now."

"I see." She floated back and forth, like a person pacing. Then she stopped. "I can almost understand what your parents did. I never told a soul about Ulysses being my familiar. For a while, human familiars were practically hunted down." She clucked her tongue. "Shame, really. They're rare creatures, but they were never meant to be treated like a commodity."

"So I heard. It's why my parents did what they did. My mother had another witch try to hex her out of the picture to get access to my father."

Gertrude shook her head. "Some witches don't abide by the code of ethics. Makes us all look bad. Was she dealt with, this witch who went after your mother?"

"From what I understand the ACW took away her magic for five years."

"Good. That's what should have happened." She smiled at him. "You like Pandora?"

"I do. Very much."

"You do the horizontal mambo yet?"

"Maybe we could keep this on a more professional level?" Was there such a thing as a professional level when talking to a ghost?

She threw her head back and laughed. "I'll take that as a no, then. You know that *being intimate*"—she made finger quotes—"is how you bond, if you're going to."

"Yes, I know. My father told me that much." Gertrude wasn't being much help. "Can you give me answers to any of these other questions or not?"

She waved at him. "Don't get your knickers in a twist. I'll help you. After all, I was bonded and married to a familiar longer than you've been alive."

"Great. What do I need to know?"

"You should be able to shift when you want to, but based on your upbringing, it's going to take some work for you to learn that skill. I'm guessing right now you only shift when you're touching Pandora."

"I probably would be, but she's been using a spell to keep me from shifting."

Gertrude frowned. "She needs to stop that. The more comfortable you get with the change, the easier it will be."

"I'll tell her. How do I practice it on my own?"

"Do you remember what it felt like the first time? Ulysses used to get visions and a sort of full-on sensory experience."

Cole nodded, understanding completely. "Yes. That's exactly what happens to me too. I've been having dreams like that since I was kid. But then I just thought they were dreams."

"You need to focus on those experiences and recreate one on your own. Try a little meditation. That should help."

"And when I do shift? What then?"

She raised her brows. "You've got to get comfortable in that skin too. Fly around. See what it's like. Test your wings, as it were."

"This is so surreal. I really hope I'm not about to wake up in a padded cell and realize I've actually lost my mind."

"You haven't. I can assure you."

"So you say. Okay. What else? What about when and if Pandora and I bond? How does that change things?"

"Pandora will be able to see through your eyes when you're in your raven form. You'll also be able to communicate mentally. You'll hear her in your head and vice versa. Sometimes the sensory communications go beyond that, but not always."

That wasn't weird at all. "Really?"

"Really. But you don't need to worry about that now. What you need to do is practice shifting, then we can work on more when you've got that handled."

That was probably a good idea. Small steps.

"My daughter and Pandora are out at the coven meeting. I guess I'll use the time alone to see if I can get the shifting part down."

She winked at him. "You do that, cookie."

He gave her a nod and started for the stairs. With his hand on the door knob, he stopped and looked back. She was still there, watching. From the angle of her gaze, most likely his backside. He cleared his throat and got her to make eye contact.

"Yes?"

"Can you access all areas of the house?"

She grinned. "Worried I might visit you in the shower?"

"Something like that."

She made a dramatic sigh. "Sadly, no. This attic was my spellroom, and as such it seems to be the limits of my visitation."

He let out a breath. "Thank heaven for small favors." He lifted his hand to his forehead and saluted her. "See you later."

Pandora spent the first few minutes at the coven meeting introducing Kaley to the rest of witches gathered in the fire hall. She'd been firm but clear with Kaley on the ride over that she wasn't to say anything about her father—or grandfather—being a familiar. Pandora explained that, while unlikely, it could put them in danger, which was enough to illicit a solemn, wide-eyed promise from the thirteen-year-old.

Kaley was polite to everyone Pandora introduced her to, but only Pandora's mother and sisters earned a smile. Pandora could understand the shyness. Meeting this many witches had to be intimidating.

Pandora had often felt like a bit of an outsider herself, what with her magic being so flaky. She nudged Kaley. "Want to get a snack? There's all kinds of stuff on the refreshments table. Including brownies. Although, if you hate brownies, I'll happily eat yours."

Kaley gave Pandora one of those adults-are-weird looks. "No one hates brownies."

Pandora nodded sagely. "Correct answer. If you'd said otherwise, we'd have to turn you into a rock."

Kaley squinted. "Can you actually do that?"

Now it was Pandora's turn to roll her eyes. "No, silly. It's just a joke. We don't do that."

"I know it's a joke. But could you?" Then she tipped her head. "You totally could, right? If you wanted to?"

"Not me personally. Animate to inanimate is pretty high-level stuff. Some of us could, yes. But none of us *would*." Pandora put her arm around Kaley's shoulders, and they walked together to the snack table. "We've all taken an oath to do no harm. It's part of the initiation into the coven."

Kaley took a plate and helped herself to a brownie. "Can I join the coven?"

Pandora grabbed a brownie too. "Maybe someday. To begin with, you'd have to be a resident of the town."

Kaley frowned. "That's never going to happen."

"Never say never."

Happiness glinted in Kaley's eyes. "Does that mean you talked my dad into staying?"

"Let's go grab a seat, and I'll tell you." They found two chairs together in the double crescent of thirty or so that were set up, and Pandora explained. "Your dad and I have agreed to get to know each other better and see if there's any kind of possibility for something more than friendship between us. Are you totally grossed-out yet?"

Kaley laughed. "No. I like you. And I know how boys are." She took a bite of her brownie.

"What does that mean?"

Kaley shrugged one shoulder. "You know. They like kissing and *stuff*. Sex," she blurted out. "I'm sure my dad is the same way."

"Hold up, your father and I are not there yet. But for the record, girls like all that stuff too. You will. You'll see. Some day. Not any day soon. Bother. Don't tell your father we talked about this, okay?"

Kaley made a face. "I won't. And yeah, I know I'll like it. Kissing's cool—not that I've done that—and some boys are cute, but some are still jerks. Not my dad. He's not a jerk." Her expression became a little distraught. "Plus, I think he gets lonely sometimes. I don't want him to be lonely. Or sad."

"You think he gets sad?"

She exhaled. "I think he works too much and needs to have more fun."

Pandora winked at her. "That's something I can definitely help with."

"Good." Kaley ate some more of her brownie before speaking again. "Do you think my mom is in a coven like this?"

"I don't know. Not all witches join them. You have to be approved to become a member, and that can be hard to do if you don't know other witches in the area where you live."

"I hope she is." Kaley stared at her half-eaten brownie. "My mom isn't really good at being a mom, but I still love her. She *is* my mom. I want her to be happy too."

Pandora's heart went out to Kaley. Life with an absentee mother couldn't be easy. "That's really nice, Kaley. Do you get to talk to her much?"

"Once in a while she calls me. Sometimes I call her, but most of the time it goes to voice mail."

"I'm sorry. You can talk to me anytime you want to, okay?"

"Okay."

Marigold and Charisma joined them in the next two chairs, but Corette was still chatting with another member.

The buzz of conversation in the room fell away. Pandora looked up to see Alice Bishop, head of the coven, enter. All the witches who hadn't yet taken their seats quickly did so.

"Who's that?" Kaley whispered.

Pandora leaned closer. "Alice Bishop. She's the high priestess of this coven. Mostly because she started it." Although it was generally understood by the coveners that while Alice held the rank of high priestess, it had become more of an honorary title. Alice rarely came to meetings unless there was something major to be discussed. As far as Pandora knew, that wasn't the case this evening, but the woman was here for a reason.

Kaley nodded. "Cool."

Alice came to stand in the center of the half circle. She nodded to those in attendance. "Good evening."

"Good evening," the witches answered back.

"I trust you are all well. I have a brief announcement, and then I'll turn the meeting over to Dominique."

Pandora whispered to Kaley again. "Dominique is a third-degree witch, and she's one of the town's councilwomen." And, for the sake of most coven meetings, the real witch in charge.

Alice shot a displeased look at Pandora, a sign to be quiet.

Marigold slid her hand over and squeezed Pandora's knee. Another sign to shut up.

Pandora took the hint.

Alice cleared her throat. "As you all know, the Black and Orange Ball is fast approaching. Due to unforeseen circumstances, Nella Davis had to step down from the decorating committee. Fortunately, Delaney Ellingham has agreed to take her place. Because Delaney is already providing the cake and other desserts, we're looking for one more person to fill out the committee."

On the other side of the half circle, Martha Trevors raised her hand. "I can do it."

"Very good. Thank you, Martha. Please make sure Delaney has your contact information." Then Alice turned back to the group. "Thank you for your time. Dominique, the floor is yours."

Dominique took over as Alice left. She looked around at those in attendance. "Anyone have any new business?"

Pandora thought about the treasure trove of goodies Gertrude had left behind, but with Cole on board, there was no need for the coven to get involved. That stuff was rightfully Kaley's anyway.

No one had any new business, so Dominique launched the group into a discussion about scrying bowls.

Forty-five minutes later, the meeting was over, and Kaley was beaming. "That was so cool. Can I come to the next one?"

"If you're still in town, sure."

"Excellent."

"Did you meet anyone you'd like to talk to about becoming your mentor?"

Kaley smiled shyly. "I want you."

Pandora smiled back. "That's really sweet, but…"

"But you're still not convinced you and my dad will work out, are you?"

"No, I'm not. No one can know that kind of thing until they give it some time. But it's not that."

Just then Marigold, Charisma and Corette joined them and started asking Kaley how she'd liked the meeting, giving Pandora an out so she didn't have to explain about her broken magic and all the complications that could bring. After a few minutes, Kaley seemed to have forgotten about it.

Eventually, Pandora said it was time to say their good-byes. "School tomorrow," Pandora reminded the reluctant Kaley.

As soon as they were in the car, Kaley started with more questions. "Where can I get a scrying bowl?"

"Probably in the attic. I know there's a scrying mirror up there, but until you learn some basics, I'm not sure what good either would do you. You can certainly try, though."

"You could teach me the basics."

And they were back to the mentoring. "Someone will, I promise."

"Will you at least come upstairs and help me find it?"

"How about tomorrow night after your dad and I go to dinner and your homework is done?"

Kaley rolled her eyes. "Okay."

When Pandora pulled into Cole's driveway, she parked the car and hopped out to follow Kaley in.

Cole was sorting through boxes in the dining room. "Hey, sweetheart. How was it?"

It took Pandora a sec to realize he wasn't talking to her.

Kaley was practically vibrating. "Dad, it was so cool. I learned about scrying bowls, and Pandora—"

"Miss Williams," he corrected.

"Miss Williams is going to help me find one in the attic tomorrow after your *date*."

He smiled. "Excellent." He put down the box he was holding and gave Kaley a hug. "I'm glad you had fun."

"I did, and I'd really like to go again, so we need to stick around. Like live here."

"So noted." And since he apparently wasn't in the mood to discuss that topic again, he changed the subject. "Have you done everything you need to do for school tomorrow?"

"Mostly."

"Kaley."

She sighed. "I have like a chapter to read in Biology, which I'm totally going to do right now."

"Get to it, then. I'll be up to say good night."

"Okay." She gave Pandora a wave. "Thanks for taking me. See you tomorrow."

"See you tomorrow."

Kaley clomped up the steps, leaving Pandora alone with Cole. "How was your night? Did you have a talk with Gertrude?"

"Hey!" Kaley reappeared on the landing at the top of the steps. "Look what I found in the hall."

She held up a black feather.

Cole stiffened. He opened his mouth, but said nothing.

Pandora stepped closer to him and looked up at Kaley. She wrinkled her nose. "I hope you don't find the rest of the bird. Toss that old thing down here and I'll throw it away."

"No way," Kaley said. "It's really pretty. I'm keeping it."

Cole snapped out of it. "Fine, but wash your hands. You never know where it's been."

Kaley shot him a look of disbelief. "Uh, Dad, it's been on a bird."

"My point exactly. Wash your hands."

"Fine." She went off to her room, twirling the feather between her fingers.

"You're going to have to tell her sooner or later," Pandora said.

"I know, but I need to understand the shifting part better before I do."

"Speaking of, did you talk to Gertrude?"

He took a few steps toward Pandora but glanced in the direction of the attic. "I did."

"And?"

He slipped his hands around Pandora's waist. "She said we should practice kissing more."

"She said that."

"Uh-huh."

Pandora resisted his pull. "I know how to kiss just fine, thanks."

"That's not what I meant." He tugged her closer, hooking his thumbs in the belt loops of her jeans.

"You're not very clear. Do your students have trouble understanding you too?"

He narrowed his eyes. "She said we needed to practice touching and me being able to control the urge to shift without you using your magic."

"I'm not using any magic at the moment." She leaned against him. He was too yummy to resist. "And right now it's not your urge to shift I'm worried about."

His smile turned wicked, and he nipped at her jaw, sending a cascade of hot sparks through her. "Is that so?"

"Mm-hmm. What else did Gertrude say?"

His mouth went lower, and his hair tickled her nose. "I can't really remember…"

Parts of her were getting really warm. She broke free, trying to catch her breath and succeeding only in inhaling another delicious lungful of Cole's masculine scent. "You seem to be doing pretty well at not shifting."

He grinned proudly. "I've been practicing."

"I figured that's where the feather came from."

He nodded. "Gertrude gave me some pointers and told me to practice. So I did. I figured with Kaley gone, there was no better time. I'm not saying I'm an expert or anything, but with some concentration, I can shift. I, uh…flew around the house. I might have run into a wall once. Well, clipped it."

Pandora laughed and clapped her hands. The more Cole got in touch with his familiar side, the better chance she had of convincing him to stay. "That's so cool! Show me."

"You've already seen it."

"Yes, but not on purpose."

He glanced up. "What if Kaley comes down and sees me? I don't want her to freak out."

"I think she can handle it. Besides, when I told her that you and your dad being familiars is absolutely to remain a family secret, I also explained that sometimes some really weird stuff might happen, but it's nothing to be afraid of if it involves you or me. Just so she'd be somewhat prepared."

"Good. Thank you."

"Sure. Hey, I'm here to help right?" She wiggled her fingers at him. "So come on, shift."

His mouth flattened to a thin line. "Not here."

"Then where?"

"My bedroom."

She snorted. "Well played, Mr. Van Zant. Is that how you get women up there?"

He grabbed her hand. "Yes, and it works beautifully." He tugged her along while he walked backward through the stacks of boxes.

"Really? How many women have you had up there?"

"Scads. More than I can count."

"That's saying something for a math teacher."

At the bottom of the stairs, he stopped and embraced her. "I went on a few dates after the divorce went through, but only because I was set up. They were awful."

"Setups usually are. Any particular reason you're telling me this?"

"I want tomorrow night to be nice, but I'm sorely out of practice."

She leaned in and brushed her mouth across his. "You're doing fine with the kissing. And you already sent flowers. I'm sure you can't miss the good-date mark by that much."

He kissed her back. Slowly and deliberately. His mouth was soft and firm and the focus of her entire being in that moment. More sparks went through her, accompanied by a warm current of air that spiraled around them and gave her the curious sensation of being weightless.

His hands gripped her hips, possessive and strong. His kiss turned demanding.

She met his hunger with some of her own. She wanted Cole. There was no denying it. As much as she didn't want to be hurt again, she was willing to risk it for him. She was sure she could make him see that this was the right place for him and Kaley. Positive that she could convince him to stay.

And that they were meant to be.

When he broke the kiss, they were both panting. His eyes were as black as the midnight sky. "I don't know if going up to my bedroom is such a good idea after all."

She held his gaze. "Maybe not. But we're both consenting adults." She held a finger up. "And we both know it's not going any further than kissing. Not until you decide to stay in Nocturne Falls."

The heated look on his face eased into one of amusement. "Sexual blackmail, huh? Well played, Miss Williams. Well played."

He took her hand again and started up the stairs.

"What grade would you give that kiss?"

He gave her a quick glance. "B-plus. But you can bring it up with extra credit."

She made a little choked sound. "That's what she said."

He laughed and led her into the bedroom, shutting the door behind them. "You're going to do everything in your power to make it impossible for me to leave, aren't you?"

The room was military-grade neat, which was what she'd expected after seeing his truck. "Yes, but it's a win-win, so relax." She sat on the bed and leaned back. "All right, show me your raven."

He rubbed his hands together.

"Nervous?"

"A little." He closed his eyes. "Here goes."

A few seconds ticked by. Then a shimmer of energy passed over him like a heat mirage.

And an enormous raven sat on the floor before her.

Another shimmer of energy distorted his image again, and Cole stood before her. His eyes were solid black, even where the white should be. He blinked, and they went back to normal.

A surge of desire went through her with such power she flushed with warmth. "Whoa."

"What?"

She stood, reluctant to tell him she felt like she was going into heat. "I should go. Busy day and all that."

"Pandora, what aren't you telling me? Did I do something wrong? Freak you out?"

"No, but..." She hesitated. "You gave off some kind of metaphysical power surge. I think. Whatever it was, I felt it."

He seemed to ponder that. "The shift was much easier that time. Maybe because you were here. You didn't do anything magical to help, did you?"

She shook her head. "Nope. Not doing that anymore. Whatever happens, happens."

She just hoped it happened fast. There was no way she was going to be able to keep her hands off him for very much longer.

15

Cole's Monday zipped by in a blur of getting Kaley off to school, finishing the front living room clean-out, calling the hauling company to come empty the dumpster and finally, getting ready for his date with Pandora.

Around lunchtime, she'd texted to say it would be easier for her to come by after work since she'd had a last-minute meeting with new sellers. He'd planned to pick her up, but he knew how busy she was. Whatever worked for her worked for him.

He took a quick shower, checked in to make sure Kaley was at her friend's house working on their school project, then ran into town to get Pandora more flowers. Maybe it was overkill, but this date was going to be as perfect as he could make it. Which was also why he was doing this in person instead of ordering flowers online again.

Not until he walked inside the Enchanted

Garden florist shop did he remember the business belonged to Pandora's sister Marigold.

She smiled when she saw him. "Hi, Cole. What brings you in?"

"Hi, Marigold. I need flowers."

Her brows did a little wiggly thing. "I'm fresh out."

He looked around at all the flowers and greenery and potted plants. "Uh… Really?"

She laughed. "Obviously, that was supposed to be a joke."

"Oh. Right." He laughed too, feeling weirdly under pressure.

She shrugged. "I'm not really the funny one in my family. Don't sweat it. What kind of flowers do you want? Same as last time?"

"Last time?"

"I'm the shop that fulfilled the order you did online."

"I didn't know that's how that worked." He thought for a moment. "Not the same thing. Roses. I guess."

"These are for Pandora again?"

"Yes."

Marigold's grin reminded him of Pandora's—bright, dazzling and utterly captivating. "Any particular occasion?"

He squinted at her. "You're digging for info, aren't you?"

She dragged her finger along the counter. "Maybe."

He smiled. "It's okay. I like how you all look out for each other."

"You know how family is."

"Not really. I was an only child."

She nodded. "Saffie is too. I worry that she's missing out by not having siblings. She hasn't stopped talking about Kaley since dinner. I'd ask about a play date, but I'm sure a thirteen-year-old doesn't want to hang out with an eight-year-old."

"I don't know. Kaley really took to all of you, and she's enamored of the whole witch thing. Maybe we could do some kind of cookout next weekend."

"Or you and Kaley could come to Saturday dinner again."

He nodded. Getting to know Pandora included getting to know her family, something that could only help strengthen their relationship. "That would be great. We're in. Thank you."

"You're welcome. Now about those flowers... You don't want roses. I mean, they're okay for accent flowers, but Pandora loves big, bright, slightly wild arrangements. I'll put something together."

"I appreciate the help."

She nodded. "You're going to need it with that one. She hasn't dated much."

He stuck his hands in his pockets. "She told me about Ren."

Marigold went to one of the glass-front refrigerators lining the workspace of the shop. "That whole thing was incredibly hard on her. And none of us really knew how to help her. She blamed herself."

"Still does, from what she told me."

Marigold brought bunches of flowers back to the craft table and started arranging them. "We've all told her it wasn't her fault. Charisma even took a series of grief-therapy classes when she was working on her counseling degree to find ways to help. Pandora can't seem to let go of it."

He leaned against the counter, admiring Marigold's deft touch. He'd never really thought of flower arranging as an art until now. "Do you think the accident has anything to do with her magic not working right?"

"No. It was never right. But the accident sure didn't help. She was more reluctant than ever to attempt even the smallest magic. She did her training along with the rest of us, but all her learning was on paper. She knows her spells, knows her potions, all of it. But it's all book smarts. When it came to practice, she'd just flat out refuse. After a while, it was just understood that her gifts were broken." She added some greenery, then turned the bouquet so he could see it better. "There. What do you think?"

That Pandora was good at hiding how hurt she was. His heart ached for her and what she'd endured. "Impressive. And much prettier than a bunch of one-color roses. How much is this masterpiece going to cost?"

"Twenty bucks."

He narrowed his eyes at her. "I may not buy flowers a lot, but I know that has to be a lot more than twenty bucks."

She wrapped them in plastic and paper. "Family discount."

He held out the cash. "That's very kind, but I'm not family."

She took his money, then handed over the flowers. "Play your cards right, and you could be."

He accepted the flowers, unsure what to say in response. He didn't want Pandora's sisters to think poorly of him, but Marigold had to know he and Pandora were only at the beginning of their relationship. There was no guarantee of anything more at this point. Including him staying in town.

She laughed. "I know you're being cautious in case things don't work out between you two, but you'll see."

"Are you a mind reader?"

"No, that's not where my talents lie." She popped her hip to the side. "But you're a man. And all men think pretty much along the same lines, so it's not that hard to guess what's going on in that handsome head of yours." She pointed at him, her expression shifting to one of stark seriousness. "But you'd better not be playing with Pandora's heart."

"I'm not. We're taking it slow. Getting to know each other."

"Good." Marigold crossed her arms and a sudden, inexplicable breeze zipped through the shop, rustling leaves and bending petals. "Because you do not want to get on our bad side."

His brows lifted. Was that magic? There was no other explanation for it. "Noted. And thank you."

He took the bouquet and went home. Marigold's words stuck in his head while he got dressed. He had no intention of hurting Pandora, but he knew that if she fell for him but he didn't fall for her and he decided not to stay in Nocturne Falls, that's exactly what would happen.

And what if the reverse came true? He knotted his tie. If he fell for her and she ultimately rejected him, he'd be hurt. But so would Kaley.

All three of them had so much to lose. He'd manage. He'd been hurt before and gotten past it. But Pandora... He sighed. Pandora would be once again a witch without working magic. How badly would that hurt her?

And then there was Kaley. She was a kid and

very vulnerable. He knew how excited she got every time Lila made any kind of contact.

What would she do if he had to tell her Pandora wasn't going to be in their lives anymore? And not just because they were moving back to North Carolina.

As much as he wanted this evening to be light and fun and carefree, he had to talk to Pandora about this. Protecting Kaley was his priority.

He shrugged on his suit jacket and checked himself in the mirror. He hadn't worn this suit since his annual review. Three knocks rang out from downstairs. He looked at his watch. Pandora was right on time. He grabbed his wallet and went to answer the door.

He opened it, and his jaw dropped. Her little black dress and sky-high heels, combined with her gorgeous red hair and creamy skin, took his breath away. She was easily the most beautiful woman he'd ever had the honor of knowing. And he was about to be seen in public with her. He licked his lips and reminded himself this was just the start of the evening.

"Did you really go to work like that? Because if you did, you must have sold everything."

She laughed, and he decided that was a sound he'd be happy to hear every day. "I had a jacket on. And different shoes."

"I really like the ones you're wearing now." His

gaze traveled down her shapely legs to her black patent leather, open-toed heels. They were the kind of shoes he'd love to see her wear all by themselves. His gaze lingered on them as the thought filled him with heat. Her toenails were painted a hot, juicy pink. Like ripe berries.

She cleared her throat. "Are you going to put any on?"

"Any what?"

She pointed at his feet. "Shoes."

He looked down. Just socks. "Yes. Come in. I have something for you anyway."

She slipped past, letting him get a whiff of her delicious perfume.

"Damn, you clean up well."

She turned as he shut the door. "You, too. I'm impressed with the tie. Does that mean we're going somewhere fancy?"

"I don't know how fancy it is, but we're going to the Poisoned Apple. Is that okay?"

"That's great. It's like a pub-bistro sort of place. Not sure the tie is totally necessary, though."

He shrugged and put his hands on her hips. Keeping his hands off her wasn't part of the equation anymore. "I didn't put the tie on for the place, I put it on for you. Because you're worth the effort."

Her smile turned shy. "That's really sweet." She stretched her arms up and wrapped them around his neck. "I think that deserves a kiss."

"I can start wearing a tie every day."

She snickered. "That won't be necessary."

"I like you at this height." He wrapped her closer. "Lip level."

She kissed him with a kind of languid pressure that made it clear she was going to take her time and do it right. Her irresistible warmth felt like the sun on his skin. It traveled through him all the way down to his toes.

She backed him against the door and pressed herself harder into him, her kiss becoming more insistent, more demanding. Little noises vibrated out of her throat as her hands threaded through his hair.

He lifted one hand to cup the back of her neck, braced himself against the door and shifted his stance so that she was planted between his legs.

She somehow got closer. There wasn't a hair's breadth of space between them. She scrapped her teeth down his neck, sending a shiver of pleasure into his bones. A teasing breath of air spiraled around them and rush of wind spilled over his skin.

"We're, uh…never going to make it to…" He was coiled like a spring and on the verge of shifting, although the pull wasn't quite as strong as it had been before. But her roaming hands were making it impossible to think.

She leaned away to see him, their bodies

remaining in contact from the hips down. Her lids were heavy with need. "Dinner?"

He nodded. "That."

She took a step back and tugged her dress into place. "You're the one who put on a suit and tie."

"That was all because of a tie?"

She wiped the edge of her mouth with a fingertip. "More the suit, really. Not that you don't look hot in your jeans and T-shirts, but there's just something about a man in a suit."

"Apparently." He took a breath and shook himself. "I forgot why we even came into the house."

"Shoes."

"Be right back." He jogged upstairs, happy for the excuse to burn off some of the energy coursing through him. He glanced at his bed and thought about what they could do instead of dinner, but that wasn't the evening he had planned. It also wasn't on either of their agendas until they knew they could risk being bonded.

He put his shoes on and went back downstairs.

"Ready to go?"

"Not quite. Hang on." He went into the kitchen and grabbed the flowers he'd bought her. He'd stuck them in a vase with some water to keep them fresh. He carried them behind his back, brandishing them with a flourish when he entered the foyer. "For you."

Her eyes widened in happy surprise. "More flowers? You're spoiling me."

"Good."

"Those are beautiful." She took the bouquet, bending her face to inhale the fragrance. "I love them. They're so me."

"They should be. Your sister fixed them up."

"Yes, but you went to get them."

"That I did. You want me to put them back in the water until we get home from dinner?"

"Absolutely." She handed them over. "I want them to look this good when I take them home."

"Your cat won't bother them, will she?" he asked as he went to the kitchen to return them to the vase.

Pandora laughed and called after him, "It's cute you think she could actually jump onto a counter."

Cole came back and opened the front door. "How's the diet coming, by the way?"

"Daily protests ensue."

"Maybe you should just let her be fat."

"Trust me, it would be easier."

He shut the door after they were both on the porch, then locked it. "You look way too nice to ride in my pickup."

"So do you, but who cares? It's clean inside."

He stuck out his elbow. "In that case, your chariot awaits."

They were only a few minutes late for their

reservation, but being late because Pandora had wanted to make out was just fine with Cole.

The hostess led them to a booth in the back corner. The high sides gave them a lot of privacy, which was what he'd asked for when he'd made the reservation. Dark wood paneling, deep green paint and burgundy leather made the Poisoned Apple feel like a private club despite the relatively full dining room.

Light from the small oil lamp in the center of the table gave Pandora a soft glow and put sparks in her eyes.

"So far so good?" he asked.

"Perfect. I love this place."

"You come here a lot?"

"I bring clients here for lunch maybe once a week, but we usually sit over on the bar side. I haven't been here for dinner in a long time." She looked around. "I forgot how cozy it is."

"Wine?"

"How many ways can I say yes?"

When the server came over, he ordered a bottle of pinot noir. He kept up the small talk until they'd ordered their meals and were halfway through their first glass of wine.

"Pandora, I need to talk to you about something."

"That sounds serious."

"It is. It's about Kaley."

She leaned in. "Is something wrong?"

"No, nothing like that. I'm just concerned that if things don't go well between us, she's the one who will end up getting hurt the most. After everything with her mother..." He shook his head. "She really likes you. And if I have to be the one to tell her that you're not going to be around anymore, she's going to hate me for a long time."

"So you want me to tell her? If that happens?"

He looked up at her. How could a woman be so beautiful and kind and funny? It was unfair. "I want us to tell her together. No matter what happens between us, I have to protect her."

Pandora smiled a little sadly. "That's really sweet. You're full of sweet tonight."

He matched her smile. "Kaley's my life, you know? I have to put her first."

"I get it. And yes, we'll tell her together." She reached across the table and laced her fingers with his. "But maybe what we tell her won't be bad news."

He smiled. "Maybe not."

And in that moment, he could imagine himself in this life, with this woman. What he'd do for work didn't matter as much as what his heart needed. Love. Companionship. Intimacy. It had been a long time since he'd paid attention to his own wants and desires. Being a father made those sorts of things seem...selfish. But Pandora was good for Kaley too. She was damn good for both of them.

Still, he couldn't help but wonder... "What if I wasn't a familiar?"

She tipped her head. "Then I don't think you'd have ended up in this town."

"But if I wasn't. Do you think you'd still feel the same...attraction to me?"

"Yes. You're so very much my kind of guy." She closed her eyes and shivered. "As much as someone who doesn't date has a kind of guy." She took a sip of wine before continuing. "Look, since we're laying things out, I like you a lot. And yes, I really like what you do for my magic, but I've lived my entire life with broken gifts. I was prepared to live the rest of it that way too. For me, my magic working is just a bonus of being around you. It's not *the* reason."

She swallowed and lifted her chin a little higher. "I'm falling for you, Cole. I know I am. It's not something I can stop. Nor do I want to. I know the risks. All of them. But I'm still willing to give it a shot. I just wish..."

She looked away.

"What?"

She sighed. "That you weren't so unsure about sticking around in Nocturne Falls. Couldn't you give it a year? What would be so bad about making a life here? This place is perfect for Kaley."

He thought about going back to North Carolina and his teaching job. About the stability it offered. About how far away it was from Pandora. About how dull life would be without her. He squeezed her hand. "I don't make rash decisions. I measure everything out, weigh both sides and see what makes the most sense."

Her face fell.

"Choosing to stay here doesn't make the most sense."

"I understand," she whispered.

"Do you? Because I don't. But you're right."

She looked at him, brow furrowed. "I am? About what?"

"About this place being the best for Kaley. It's not going to be easy to find work, I know that, but—"

She sucked in a breath. "Are you saying you're going to stay?"

"I'm saying I'm falling for you too. And I don't want to go back to a life that doesn't have you in it. If things don't work out between us, then it is what it is, but right now, yes, I'm saying we're going to stay."

Pandora let out a little shriek, then quickly covered her mouth with her hand. "Oh, Cole. That's wonderful. And, you know, that means that my magic should keep working, which means I really could be Kaley's mentor."

"I can't think of anything she'd like more."

"I want to tell her when we pick her up. But you have to be serious about staying."

"I am. I swear it."

She shook her head. "I can't believe it."

"Well, after your sister threatened me in the flower shop today—"

"She did what?"

Cole filled Pandora in. Their meals arrived, and they spent the rest of the evening telling each other stories about their jobs and talking about the future and dreaming out loud. It wasn't the sort of thing Cole had ever done, but with Pandora, he was all-in.

As the server cleared their plates, Cole laid his napkin on the table. "What do you say we get three desserts to go, then pick up Kaley from her friend's house and eat them back at my place?"

"I'd love to. In fact, I'll wait to tell her about the mentorship until we're sitting at the table. Then the desserts can be part of our celebration."

"She'll love that." He ordered, paid the check, and twenty minutes later, they had Kaley in the car and were pulling up to the house.

A strange car sat at the curb outside the fence, but Cole didn't pay it much attention. The neighbors were always having people over.

He parked in the driveway. "I forgot to leave the outside porch lights on. Gimme a sec to get them on so you two don't break an ankle."

"We'll be fine," Kaley said.

"You haven't seen Miss Williams' shoes." He turned the engine off. "But really, I just don't want my chocolate cake to end up on the ground."

Pandora shook her head. "It's like you forget who you're with." She snapped her fingers, and the porch lights blazed to life.

"Dude," Kaley crooned. "That is *so* cool."

Cole froze. "Stay in the car. There's someone on the bench."

"Where?" Kaley leaned forward from the back of the crew cab.

The figure stood and stepped into the light.

Cole let out a curse just as Kaley yelled, "Mom!"

16

Pandora's belly twisted into three kinds of knots. "Is that...Lila?"

"Yes," Cole hissed.

Kaley was out of the truck like a shot and running toward the porch.

He shook his head. "I don't know what she's doing here, but I'll deal with it." He reached out and grabbed Pandora's hand. "Please don't leave. You have more right to be here than she does."

Pandora nodded lamely, but that didn't ring true to her. Lila was Kaley's mother, custody or not. And Kaley was clearly happy to see her.

She got out slowly as Cole made his way to the porch. Lila was very pretty. Tall and slim with jet black hair as straight as a sheet and enormous blue eyes. She and Lila couldn't look more different. And Lila's magic probably worked the way it was supposed to, regardless of who was, or wasn't, around.

Pandora hung by the car, listening.

Cole wasn't happy. "Lila, what are you doing here?"

She looked up from hugging Kaley. "I came to see Kaley. After she called me and told me all about the fun she was having, I thought I should come see for myself."

Kaley nodded, staying close to Lila. "I called her. Last night. After the coven meeting."

Lila smiled but bitterness lit her gaze. "A coven meeting. Imagine that. My, my, Cole, you sure have changed."

"I have Pandora to thank for that." He looked to his side like he expected her to be there. When he didn't see her, he glanced back at the car. As soon as he made eye contact, he gave a little jerk of his head as if to say, *Come up here.*

It was just enough to give her the boost of confidence she needed. Cole wanted her, not Lila. That was all that mattered. That, and she was Pandora Williams and she bought and sold this town. No slacker mother was going to intimidate her. No matter how tall or how pretty or how magically capable.

She strode to where Cole was standing, thanking the goddess she'd worn these shoes. They gave her at least four extra inches.

He slipped his arm around her waist, as much as reminding her that Lila was the interloper here, not her. It was like having steel injected into her spine. She didn't need Cole's reassurance to face this woman, but it was damn nice to have. It felt like the seal on the evening they'd just had.

The evening that was not yet over.

Lila smiled at Pandora, but her gaze held enough frost to kill off the last of the summer flowers. "I take it you're Pandora?"

"Yes. And you must be Lila."

Her smile broadened. "Cole talks about me?"

"He told me about his past. You came up."

Kaley took her mother's hand. "Miss Williams is the one who took me to the coven meeting."

"I remember." Lila answered without taking her eyes off Pandora. "I guess that makes us sisters."

A thousand responses flew to the tip of Pandora's tongue, but none of them was polite and none of them would do any good to have Kaley hear. "We're all family under the goddess."

Cole shifted his weight. "Lila, it's late and Kaley has school tomorrow. If you want to see her after that, you can call me."

Lila pursed her lips, but said nothing. Finally, she fabricated a smile, hugged Kaley and walked off the porch and down to her car. She glanced briefly at Pandora as she passed, shifting her gaze quickly to Cole. "I'll talk to you tomorrow, then."

No one moved until her car was a set of taillights disappearing down the street.

Pandora was the first to speak. "I should go home."

"Please don't," Cole said. "Don't let this put a premature end to our evening. Come in and have dessert with us."

"After that? You're sure?"

He nodded. "She doesn't control my life and I certainly don't want her to affect ours."

Pandora smiled. "Good to hear." She lifted the bag. "Okay. Let's eat."

Cole ruffled Kaley's hair as he walked up the porch steps. "Did you know she was coming, Kaley?"

"No. I didn't even think I'd actually get to talk to her when I called last night, but she picked up right away. Wanted to know how I was doing with becoming a witch." Kaley shrugged. "So I told her. Are you mad at me?"

He pushed the door open, then wrapped Kaley in a hug. "Sweetheart, I'm never going to be mad at you for something you have no control over. I'm not happy your mother is here, but that's mostly because I don't want her to upset you. But that's for me to deal with. You don't need to worry about that, okay?"

"Okay."

"Good. Now let's go dig into this dessert."

While Kaley was in the shower the next morning, Cole called her school and spoke to someone in the office to let them know that Lila Aquinos was not approved to pick Kaley up or take her out of school.

He was probably being overly cautious, but it was an error he was willing to make.

Throughout the entire morning of making Kaley breakfast and driving her to school, he couldn't get Lila out of his mind. What the hell was she trying to prove coming here?

Kaley opened the truck door. "See you later, Dad."

"Love you, sweetheart. Have a good day."

"Thanks. Love you too."

She hopped out, and he sat for a moment, watching her find her friends and head in. Lila had no legal grounds to take Kaley away from him, but that did nothing to quell the unease that had settled into his gut the second he'd seen her on the porch.

He drove back to the house and, hoping to shake Lila from his head, tackled the enormous job of clearing out more of his uncle's junk. It worked in a half measure, but then he realized the key to ditching thoughts of Lila was focusing on Pandora.

He replayed the events of the previous night. It

was impossible not to smile thinking about her. And that kiss.

Staying was such a risk, but it felt right. This thing between them was good. Sure, it was early days, but he could imagine the future would be just as bright. And becoming part of Pandora's big family would mean so much for Kaley. Cousins and aunts and a step-grandmother. It could be life-changing for her to have that sort of support group.

He carried out a stack of boxes to the dumpster. Now all he had to do was find a job that would support them. The money from the house would buy them a place to live and give him a cushion if the house in North Carolina didn't sell right away.

Maybe he could talk his dad into moving down after he retired. He couldn't work at the plant forever. And Cole knew that being near Kaley was important to Jack. No, he wouldn't like it, but Jack would come to see that love trumped all.

Cole tossed the boxes into the dumpster, and as they landed with a satisfying thud, he realized what had just gone through his head.

Love.

He wasn't in love with Pandora yet. It was way too early for that. But he was most definitely infatuated with her. And that could turn into love. That *was* how it worked. He shook his head as he headed back inside, a crazy sense of happiness rocking him. His life had done a one-eighty from everything he was used to and yet, he wouldn't want it any other way. Life was good.

He was only one box into the next stack when someone knocked on the door. He wiped his hands on his jeans and went to answer it.

Lila.

He kept the anger from his face. The more civil this could be, the better. "She's already gone to school. I told you to call me."

She smiled sweetly. "I know. And I would have, but I was afraid you'd say no."

His hackles went up. "To what?"

"To talking. Just you and me." She did a flirty thing with her eyes. "You look good."

He ignored her not-so-subtle come-on. "Talk about what?"

She canted her head. "Can I come in?"

He braced himself against the door frame and crossed his arms. "I'm working."

"It won't take long." She did a very familiar pout. "C'mon, Cole. For old times' sake."

"Our old times aren't worth consideration."

She let out a long breath through her nose, slightly deflated. "Please. I won't take long."

He relented and moved out of the way. "Ten minutes."

She walked in. "Thank you."

"Kitchen's this way." He didn't check to see if she was following, just moved. Once in the kitchen, he poured himself another cup of coffee. It would have been polite to offer her some, but it would have been polite of her not to have shown up uninvited. It also would have been polite of her not to sleep with men who weren't her husband. He turned and rested against the counter. "What do you want to talk about?"

"Kaley."

His jaw twitched in anger. He'd known that was what she was here for. At least she'd finally come out and said it. "What about her?"

Lila leaned on the counter opposite him. "I'm not here to take her away from you."

"You couldn't if you tried."

"I know that. But I've been doing a lot of thinking lately. Sort of taking assessment of my life." She stared at the floor. "I know I wasn't a good wife. I'm sorry. I really am. I can't do anything to change that. I also know I wasn't a good mother, but *that* I can work on. If you'll let me."

"In what way?"

"I want to spend more time with Kaley. Try to get to know her. Try to be there for her in whatever way she wants me to be."

"That's a big ask for someone who abandoned that child."

Lila looked toward the backyard. "I know. I don't deserve it." She shifted her gaze back to him.

"But I'm hoping that you'll give me a chance to earn your trust. Kaley needs me right now—"

"You mean because she's becoming a witch? Coming into her powers and all that?"

Lila stared at him with intense curiosity. "You say that like you believe it. Kaley told me you did, and considering you let her go to a coven meeting, I'm guessing it's true, but it's hard for me to imagine after all the years of you doubting me."

He drank his coffee. "Let's just say I've learned a lot in the last few days."

"I'd say." She put her hands on the counter behind her and tipped her head toward her shoulder. "So will you let me spend more time with Kaley? I'm only in town for a couple days, but once you get back to North Carolina, maybe we could set up some kind of once-a-month date."

That sounded a hell of a lot like visitation to him. "Let's say we do that and you get tired of being a mother again. Then what? You disappear and I pick up the pieces? I'm not interested in Kaley getting hurt again."

"You're right. That's fair. We could start slow. One visit at a time, right? No future plans until the current one is met."

She was saying the right things, but she'd always been good at manipulating situations to suit her needs. He stared at her. "I'll have to talk to Kaley."

The Professor Woos The Witch

She nodded. "Okay. I'm good with that."

Like she had a choice. "I have your number. I'll call you tonight."

She smiled and pushed off the counter to walk toward him. "Could I get a cup of that coffee?"

He nodded and moved down the counter a little. "Cups in the cabinet above."

She opened it and took one out. The movement sent a whiff of her perfume toward him. It was the same sweet fragrance she'd always worn. Sometimes he caught it on other women, and it brought her to mind. Not in a happy way, either.

She finished pouring her coffee, then took a big sip. "Mmm, that's the stuff."

It was okay coffee at best, but she was clearly trying to get on his good side.

She rested her cup on the counter, but kept her fingers on the handle. "I really appreciate this, Cole. I know you don't have to do any of this."

He grunted. "I'm doing it for Kaley." Which was why, if she screwed this up even once, he'd do his best to end all contact between the two of them.

"Understood." She looked up at him, her big blue eyes round and liquid. "I've screwed up a lot in my life," she rasped, her voice choked with emotion. "But Kaley is the one good thing I've done. I don't want to lose her completely."

A single tear slipped down her cheek.

"I understand." Cole closed his eyes and took a

breath. He could handle crying females. Some of his students occasionally attempted tears in an effort to get a better grade, but this was Lila, and while he didn't love her anymore, he also didn't wish her ill will. Not while Kaley still wanted her around.

Lila's arms wrapped around him, and her lips pressed against his. "Oh, Cole," she whispered. "We could be a family again."

He jerked back, eyes open. "What the hell are you doing?" He pushed her away, still struggling to grasp that she'd kissed him.

"I thought—you invited me in and—"

"To talk about Kaley." He shook his head, fuming. "I should have known you were up to something."

"I'm not, I swear. I honestly thought..." She gulped back a sob. "I'm sorry." Then she swore softly. "I misread things. That *is* all."

"Get out now. Before I change my mind about letting you see Kaley."

"I'm sorry."

"Now."

She nodded and left. Cole stood in the kitchen until he heard the front door open and close. Then he dug his phone out of his back pocket and sent Pandora a text.

Last night was great. Can't stop thinking about you. If you're not too busy tonight, join us for pizza?

Less than a minute went by before she responded.

Loved last night. Can't stop thinking about you either. Can make it for pizza at 7. Good?

Good, he texted back. Then he tucked the phone away as he walked to the front of the house. He looked beyond the fence. Lila's car was gone.

He'd give Pandora the run down on what happened this evening. Telling your current flame that your ex had kissed you on the mouth was the kind of thing that deserved the courtesy of a face to face. He'd better be able to judge Pandora's reaction then too.

This would be the first test of their new relationship. He hoped she trusted him enough to believe him when he told her nothing else happened. And maybe she'd be a little jealous. He could handle that. Might even be a turn-on. He couldn't remember the last time a woman had been jealous on his behalf.

17

Pandora still had a smile on her face from Cole's invite, which was probably the only reason she hadn't hung up on the house appraiser yet. "You promised me that appraisal this morning. A chance of weather is not a reason *not* to do the appraisal. Ninety percent of the thing is inside!"

"I'll get it done tomorrow. I promise," the woman wheezed. She was a lifelong smoker and had the rasp to prove it.

Pandora pinched the bridge of her nose. "Please. I can't close this house until it's done. If you prevent that from happening and these buyers lose this mortgage rate, I will not be using your services again."

"Understood."

"I hope so. Appraisal. On my desk. First thing tomorrow." Pandora hung up. She loved her job, but there were days when she wanted to strangle people. Maybe now that her magic was working, she could do it without touching them. Like using The Force. She laughed. It was a fun fantasy, but Darth Vader she was not.

She went back to her computer and the listings she was updating. The bell above her door jangled. She turned to greet her new potential clients.

And saw Cole's ex-wife walking through her door, looking hideously perfect in black skinny jeans, ankle boots and an indigo leather jacket. Her make-up was simple, but when you were that beautiful, anything more than a crimson lip was probably overkill.

Maybe the Dark Side wasn't so bad after all. Word was, they had cookies. Pandora stood, glad the day had been cool enough for her high-heeled boots. They weren't last night's stilettos, but they gave her a couple extra inches. "Can I help you?"

"I'm Lila Aquinos. We met last night. At my husband's." She laughed. "Oops! Ex-husband's. You know what I meant."

Yes, Pandora supposed, she did know what Lila meant. "I remember."

Lila put her hands on the back of one of the guest chairs across from Pandora's desk. "I can see why Cole's so taken with you. You're very pretty."

"Thank you." Okay, this had gone from weird to awkward.

"I'm sure you're wondering why I'm here."

Pandora nodded. "You're a regular mind reader."

Lila laughed. "I do make my living reading tarot." She pointed at the chair. "Can we chat for a minute? I know you're busy, but I promise I'll be brief."

"Okay." Pandora agreed more out of curiosity than anything else. She sat down as Lila did the same.

Lila crossed one long leg over the other. Her smile thinned. "I'm sure you've heard all about me from Cole."

"Some."

Lila picked at the seam on her jeans. Her nails were long, purple and filed into soft points. "Enough that you know I wasn't a great wife or mother."

So cheating was not being a great wife and disappearing on your kid was not being a great mother. Pandora could think of better adjectives, but good to know. "I've heard, yes."

Lila sighed and bowed her head and seemed to be trying to get a handle on her emotions. At last, she lifted her head and looked at Pandora again. "I was crappy at both of those jobs. Being young and stupid is no excuse. I hurt Cole—" She put her hand toward the sky. "Thank the goddess he's forgiven me. And I left Kaley with no mother. I take full responsibility for my selfish actions."

Points for that. Not a lot, but some. "That's very adult of you."

"Granted, Cole wasn't entirely blameless in our marriage dissolving, but I'm willing to let the past be the past."

"What do you mean?"

Lila took a breath. "It was...hard. Constantly being told that I was ridiculous for thinking I was a witch? That took its toll. I'm not saying it's what made me stray, but it sure didn't keep me home."

"Why didn't you do something—cast a spell, do a little magic—to show him that it was the truth?"

"You know how it is when you first meet a guy? You keep your cards close to your vest until you feel them out. Make sure they're not like Cole. But with Cole, I fell for him despite that. He was so good with Kaley. And as things progressed..." Lila's bitter laugh filled the office. "His mother made sure I didn't do anything to bring down the ivory tower he'd been raised in."

"Meaning?"

"Cole's mother was a witch. Non-practicing due to some stuff in her past, but she told me straight away that if I used magic around him, or did anything that might show him the truth, she'd report me to the ACW with whatever charges necessary to make sure my powers were stripped. I had to choose the man I loved and the best chance for a father my kid had had so far, or being a witch." She shrugged. "So I didn't practice around him. I think that was part of what drove a wedge between us. Not being able to be yourself around someone you consider family is a difficult thing."

"I can imagine." Pandora was starting to wonder if Cole knew this side of things.

"Anyway," Lila continued. "I got to a place in my life recently where I finally grew up and took assessment of everything I'd done so far, and it wasn't pretty. I was about as big of a screw-up as a person can be."

Pandora's brows shot up. "That's quite an admission."

"It's the truth. It's also why I'm here. I'm never going to be a better wife. Those days are over, no matter how Cole still feels about me, but with Kaley, I can still make a difference."

No matter how Cole still felt about her? What the French did that mean? Pandora tried to ignore that part for the moment. "I'm not sure why you're telling me all this."

"Because I know you've become part of Kaley's life. I appreciate that. She needs a good influence. Especially someone like you."

"Meaning?"

Lila smiled. "A sister witch."

"Ah." Pandora offered a tentative smile in return. For a woman who had very little contact with her daughter, Lila knew a lot about what was going on in Kaley's life. Maybe they talked more than Kaley let on. And maybe most of Kaley's calls to her mother didn't go to voice mail. Especially considering Kaley had also told Pandora her mother was dead.

"Kaley also told me you offered to become her mentor."

Actually, Pandora hadn't gotten around to that last night. With all the excitement of Lila showing up, it just hadn't seemed like the right time. Sure, Pandora had promised to help Kaley get a mentor. But maybe Kaley had wanted her mother to think otherwise.

Lila's smile faltered, and tears rimmed her eyes. "That was very...kind of you." She sniffed. "I'm sorry, I don't mean to cry. I've missed so much of her growing up because of my own foolishness, and now it's cost me this very important part of her life. I'm sure you can imagine what it would be like if you had a daughter and she...and she..." She turned away, hid her face in her hand and let out a hard, shuddering sob.

Pandora bit her lip. She felt for Lila, and that wasn't something she'd expected, but the woman was obviously hurting. *Please let her be sincere and not trying to play games.* "Maybe...we could do it together. I mean, I'd have to talk to Kaley. And Cole."

Lila shook her head, and another small sob

broke from her throat. "No, you've already set everything up and arranged it all. I don't want to barge in and disrupt what you've put in place. I also can't risk making Kaley mad at me."

"It's not like that. We haven't even started yet."

Lila sniffed. "So you'd let me be her mentor, then?" She put her hand to her throat. "I did not expect such generosity. You are amazing." Then she reached out toward Pandora. "The bond of the sister witch is a wonderful thing."

Pandora hadn't exactly offered to let Lila *be* the mentor. But the woman was in a desperate way. And a sister witch. Sort of. They weren't in the same coven. But Pandora didn't want to be the reason things between Kaley and her mother got worse. Kaley could grow to resent Pandora for that. "How about I talk to Kaley about it?"

Lila blinked, and a tentative smile bent her mouth. "You mean it? That would be amazing. I can't thank you enough."

"No promises, now. But I'll bring it up."

Lila shot to her feet. "That's all I can ask for. You're such a good friend to do this. We can be friends, can't we? That would mean so much to Kaley. Especially now that Cole's agreed to let me have time with her. Please say yes."

"I…sure, I guess." Pandora had the feeling she'd been left out of something. "When did Cole agree to that?"

"This morning over coffee. He's such a great guy, isn't he?"

"Yes." Pandora blinked. So Lila and Cole had been together before Lila had come here. Right before Cole had sent her that text.

"Thank you." Lila pressed her hands together in front of her. "I won't take another moment of your time. Blessed be."

"Blessed be," Pandora mumbled.

With that, Lila was gone.

Pandora stared after her as the jangling of bells above the door faded. She replayed the conversation in her head, trying to find the turning points and how they'd gotten to where they'd gotten. But all she could really come up with was that Lila seemed like a woman in pain and Pandora had done what any decent person would do. She'd given a mother a chance to reconnect with her child.

That was all good. Pandora knew that. And yet, she still wasn't entirely sure she hadn't just been manipulated. She felt a little like she had been, but at the same time, felt bad for thinking such a thing about Lila. Either way, there was an unsettled something lurking in the pit of her stomach. She needed to talk to Cole. She picked up the phone to call Cole, then put it back down again.

Some things were better discussed in person.

Cole had finally unearthed the dining room table from the piles of stuff covering it and was underneath it about to haul out another box when three hard raps sounded from the front door. "Just a minute," he called out.

If this was Lila again, he was not letting her in. He got up, brushed his hands off and went to answer it.

"Hey, Pandora. This is a nice surprise."

She brushed past him into the house. "I had a surprise today too, but I can't say it was nice. I'm not sure what it was, really."

He shut the door. "You want to explain? You seem flustered."

"Your wife—sorry, ex-wife—has a way of doing that to me apparently." She paced a few steps down the hall, then turned and came back toward him. "She came to see me at my office today."

"She did what?" Cole was already suspicious of Lila after her visit this morning, but going to see Pandora? That was unnecessary. And an equation that didn't add up. "What the hell did she want?"

Pandora shook her head, her jaw jutting to one side in clear frustration. "I don't know, but I'm pretty sure she got it."

He grabbed her shoulders to hold her in one

spot for a moment. "You're still not making much sense."

She looked up. "The whole conversation was..." She squinted at him. "Did you cut your lip?"

"No, why?"

She circled her finger at his mouth. "You've got something red right there."

He wiped at it, then looked at his hand. He groaned in disgust. "It's lipstick. From Lila. She kissed me."

Pandora jolted back. "She did what?"

He shook his head. "*She* kissed *me*. It was nothing. And it was completely unwanted. She read too deeply into me agreeing to let her come in to talk this morning. That's how Lila is. Turns an inch into a mile." He watched her expression. "Are you mad?"

Pandora crossed her arms. "That she kissed you? Hell yes. I don't like it at all. But I'm mad at her, not you."

Relief poured through him. Pandora really was the woman for him.

She frowned. "We still need to talk. In the course of her visit to me, she told me you had coffee. In fact, she told me all kinds of things. And ultimately, I think I agreed to some things I didn't mean to."

He sighed. "Lila is a master manipulator." He pointed toward the kitchen. "Let's go sit. This is a conversation best had sitting down, I'm sure."

While he made a fresh pot of coffee, Pandora laid out everything that had transpired. He held his comments so as not to break her train of thought. While the coffee brewed, he leaned against the counter and listened. And nodded. And shook his head.

"So that's about it." Pandora looked miserable. He felt for her. Lila had that effect on people.

"You don't have to bring up the mentoring to Kaley at all, you know."

Pandora cut her eyes at him. "So that Lila can do it and make me look bad? This is a lose-lose. I have to."

"Kaley will pick you."

She shook her head. "You think that, but this is her mother we're talking about."

"In name only. You've already showed Kaley more care and attention in the last week than Lila has in years." Behind him, the coffee hissed that it was done.

"But Kaley is *starved* for her mother's attention. I can see it in her. Why else would she have called Lila?"

He brought two cups of coffee and the sugar to the table, then went to the fridge for creamer. "I don't disagree with that. But I don't want Kaley to pick her. I want Kaley to pick you. Can you imagine if Lila disappears on Kaley again while she's supposed to be mentoring her?"

The Professor Woos The Witch

He set the creamer in front of Pandora as she answered. "That kid will be crushed."

"Agreed."

"As much as I don't want Kaley getting hurt, at some point she's going to have to realize her mother is not reliable."

Cole sat down at the table. "She knows that. I think she's just hoping Lila's suddenly going to change."

"Poor kid."

He thought for a moment. "I really hope Kaley didn't say anything to Lila about me being a familiar. I mean, we know she already knew. That's why she married me. But if she knew that I was now aware of my true nature…and that I was embracing it…" He rolled his shoulders as the thought shot tension into his body. "It wouldn't be good."

"I don't think Kaley would have brought it up. I gave her the whole speech in the car on the way to the coven meeting about how that information was not to be shared and how it could put you and your dad in danger. She took it very seriously."

He drank his coffee. "That's good, but you saw how your conversation with Lila went. She has a way of making people tell her things."

"That she does. Fiddlesticks." Pandora rubbed her brow. "You know, I could…no. Never mind."

"What?" He let his coffee cool. "Say it."

She looked up through her lashes while she

stirred her coffee. "I could check in with the ACW. See if there's any reason Lila shouldn't be approved as a mentor. You know, registered complaints, misuse of magic, that sort of thing."

He nodded. "Do it. Please. For Kaley."

She sipped her coffee. "I'm really not mad about the kiss, and I get why you're letting Lila spend time with Kaley—"

"I didn't say it was going to happen, I only said I'd talk to Kaley about it. Which I will tonight. I also said that if Lila screws up once, it's over."

Pandora nodded, her expression tight with reservation. "I just can't shake the sense she's up to something. I've never in my life been so whiplashed by a conversation as the one I had with her today. She even insinuated that you still have feelings for her."

He barked out a harsh laugh. "That woman has a bigger set than most men I know." He sighed. "I wish I could tell her to leave, but if I prevent her from seeing Kaley, I look like the bad guy to my daughter."

Pandora nodded and stared into her coffee. "I don't want you to put yourself in that position. I just hope…" She took a deep breath and looked up at him. "Please tell me she's not going to get in the way of us."

He put his hand on top of hers and gave it a squeeze. "She's not. She might try—"

"I think she already is."

"It's not going to make a difference." He darted forward, scooped her into his arms and settled her on his lap.

She let out a soft whoop and grabbed his shoulders, grinning. "Don't get frisky. I have to go back to work."

"We both do. But right now, listen to me, Pandora. I'm crazy about you. You've opened a whole new world to me. One I'm still not adjusted to, but I'll get there. I'm not about to do anything to change what we have going on. I already said I'd stay, didn't I?"

She nodded. "Yes."

"You want a key to my house? My truck? Want my high school letter jacket? Another one of my feathers? Name it, it's yours."

She laughed. "You had a letter jacket? What sport did you play?"

He scowled at her playfully. "I was a mathlete, thank you very much."

Her mouth bent into an odd line, then she burst out with more laughter. "That makes so much sense."

He clutched at his chest and pretended to be wounded. "Geeks are so under-appreciated."

"Now, now." Her gaze took on a wicked glint as she dipped her head to meet his mouth. "Let me show you how much I appreciate you."

18

The next morning, Pandora caught her mom just as she was unlocking the door to Ever After. "Hey Mom."

Corette turned. "Good morning, darling. On your way to a showing?"

"Nope. I'm on my way here, to talk to you. I do have a showing but not until later. You don't have any brides first thing, do you?" It was a quarter to ten, the same time Corette opened the store every morning.

"I have one at ten thirty. Half an hour enough time? I need to pull dresses for her, so that's the best I can do."

"It's plenty. And I can talk while you get things set up."

"Come on in." Corette pushed the door open.

Pandora walked in and took a breath as her mother locked the door behind them. A faint floral scent always lingered in the air, but beyond that, there was something so fresh and hopeful about her mother's shop. All those wedding dresses on the racks and displayed on the mannequins just waiting for the right bride. Someday... But maybe not any day soon. Not with Lila in town.

Corette flipped the lights on, and the crystal chandeliers and overheads brought the place to life. Fresh flowers, supplied by Marigold's shop, naturally, adorned the front table. Everything was done in soft, flattering pastels, allowing the brides to be front and center.

"I need to turn the sound system on and get the coffee on. Will you keep an eye out for Delaney? She should be by any moment with today's refreshments."

"Sure thing." Delaney Ellingham, recent wife of Hugh Ellingham, who was one of the vampires who'd founded Nocturne Falls, provided the sweets that Corette set out for her customers every day. Pandora smiled. No wonder Ever After was so popular. Who wouldn't want to shop here?

"Thanks. Back in a jiff." Corette disappeared into the offices.

A minute later, easy, romantic jazz filled the store.

A minute after that, Delaney knocked on the front door. She cradled a large pastry box in one arm, the words Delaney's Delectables printed in whimsical script on the top.

Pandora unlocked the door and let her in. "Morning."

"Hey, you're not Corette." She grinned. "How are you?"

"Good, you?"

"Fabulous, thanks. Here are today's goodies."

Pandora took the box. A delicious aroma wafted up at her. "What's in here?"

"Mini coconut cupcakes, lemon petit fours, frosted sugar cookies and white chocolate buttercream truffles."

Pandora stared at the box. "I think I became a diabetic just listening to that. Although I'm a little sad there are no brownies in that mix."

Delaney popped her eyebrows and frowned. "Talk to your mother. She won't allow anything that could stain the dresses. No chocolate, no red velvet, no berries. You get the idea."

"Makes sense." Pandora put the box on the front table.

"I'm glad you're here," Delaney said. "I've been meaning to talk to you. I have a friend who's interested in moving here, but she doesn't have a ton of money. Wait, that doesn't sound right. What I mean is Roxy's not vampire rich. Although with the way her books are selling, who knows? Anyway, she's got plenty of money, but I don't think she wants to blow it all on a house. Is there much on the market in the way of starter homes?"

"Wait, back up. Her books?"

"She's a romance author! Roxy St. James. Isn't that cool?"

"Wow, very. I wonder if Willa knows her. Willa loves romance novels."

"I'll ask Willa next time I see her. I told Roxy this place could be really good for her. If you can't be creative in this town, you just can't be creative."

"I'm sure I can find her something." Pandora pulled a card from her purse. "Give her my info and have her call me. Is she a supernatural, by any chance?"

Delaney took the card. "Nope. Regular old human. But she's fresh out of a divorce and looking for a new start."

"I'm happy to help."

"Thanks." Delaney tucked the card into her purse, then put her hand on the door. "Talk to you soon."

Pandora locked the door behind her just as Corette walked out. "Was that Delaney?"

"Yep, and the box she dropped off is on the table here."

"Thank you." She clasped her hands in front of her. "Now, what can I do for my favorite redhead?"

Pandora took a breath. "Cole's ex-wife showed up two days ago, and every fiber of my witchy being tells me she's up to something."

Corette blinked once, then her eyes narrowed. "Did she come to try to get Cole or Kaley back?"

"No idea. Maybe both. Kaley called her, which she says is the reason she came, but Mom, I don't trust her. She came to see me at my office yesterday right after she paid Cole a visit. And somehow, during the course of that visit to me, she got me to agree to talk to Kaley about her taking my place as Kaley's mentor. Cole and I decided last night that we weren't going to say anything to Kaley until I talked to you about it today."

"What exactly happened?"

Pandora put a hand on her forehead. "I wish I could say. Mom, I've never been so expertly manipulated in my life. I don't trust her, but she hasn't done anything suspicious that I can point to. Yet."

"Trust your instincts, honey. That's something too many women don't do." Corette tipped her head. "How can I help?"

"As the coven secretary, you have access to the ACW's membership files. I want to see if there's ever been a complaint about this woman."

Corette nodded. "If there was, it might be grounds for banning her from becoming anyone's mentor."

"Exactly."

Corette checked her watch. "We've got five minutes. Let's go."

Thirty seconds later, Corette had the ACW website pulled up and had logged onto her account. She clicked through to the membership roster, an area accessible only to those with certain positions in their covens.

"What's her name?"

"Lila Aquinos." Pandora leaned over her mother's shoulder to see better.

Corette typed the name in, hit enter and the processing wheel started to spin. Two seconds later, it retrieved a file marked Aquinos, Lila.

Corette moved the cursor to the file, but didn't click. She shook her head. "This is a violation of the oath of office I took."

"Mom, it's perfectly within your rights to check the file of a witch who's come to town if you think she could be a danger to a member of your coven."

"That's not the violation I'm talking about." She gave Pandora a stern glance. "I have the authority to see the file. You do not."

Pandora straightened. "You're right. And I don't want to get you into any trouble. I'll go wait in the store."

"Thank you. I'll be out shortly."

Pandora walked back into the showroom. She studied the dresses in the window. Pretty beaded confections that would turn some lucky woman into a princess. With a sigh, she went to the front table and snuck a petit four to help pass the time.

The dainty little square of lemony cake and tart icing melted on her tongue. "Oh, wow. Delaney, you have done it again. Of course, that's going to mean an extra ten minutes on the treadmill tomorrow morning."

Corette came out of the office. "What was that dear?"

Pandora swallowed the last bite. "Nothing, just talking to myself."

"Did Charisma suggest that?"

"No, I was just—Mom, what did you find out?"

Corette's mouth narrowed to a thin line. "No report of any kind."

"Not a single complaint?"

"No. Sorry."

Pandora pushed a strand of hair behind one ear. "I guess it's a good thing. Maybe she's not out to create trouble after all."

"Or she just hasn't been caught doing anything yet. A clean report doesn't mean she couldn't be up to something."

"Good point. I'll keep that in mind." Pandora smiled. "Thanks. I should get going and let you get to work too."

Corette smiled. "Happy to help. Have a good day, honey."

"You too, Mom." Pandora left and headed to her showing. Her mother's reminder only confused Pandora more. Was Lila up to something? Or could she really be just a woman who recognized that she'd screwed up and wanted to mend her relationship with her daughter?

If Pandora didn't give her a chance, who would? Maybe it was time to give Lila a few feet of rope. If she hung herself, that wasn't Pandora's problem.

As soon as her showing was over, she texted Cole to let him know she was free like she'd promised him she would the night before.

Come over if you can, he texted back.

On my way.

When she arrived, he was in the driveway pitching stuff into the dumpster. Amazing how sweat and dirt could make a man look so yummy. She waved. "Hey."

"Hey." He didn't smile. "We need to talk."

"That sounds ominous."

He looked around. "Inside."

She followed him into the house, trying not to panic and waiting as patiently as she could until the door was shut. The second it closed, she asked, "What's going on? Is this about Lila? You didn't change your mind about staying, did you?"

He grabbed her shoulders and gave her a firm, fast kiss. "I'm staying, that hasn't changed. But I had a talk with Kaley this morning and—wait, I need to back up. Lila came by last night right after you left."

"You think she was waiting for me to leave?"

"Yes. She said all she wanted was to take a walk around the neighborhood with Kaley. I agreed, but I made Kaley take her phone."

"So you could track her with the GPS app, right? Smart."

He nodded. "That's all they did, too. Just walk. They were gone thirty minutes and then they were back. Lila said good night and left. It seemed like a good start to letting Lila have some time with her."

He wiped his hand over his face, smudging dirt on one cheek. "I talked to Kaley this morning. I tried to play it cool, but she knew I wanted to know what they'd talked about on the walk. She said Lila had asked her if she'd found any *feathers* around lately. Gave Kaley some song and dance about how they're great for making protection amulets for witches who can see auras and she'd make one for Kaley if she found one."

Pandora's jaw fell open, and for a moment, she couldn't form words. "That's BS as far as I know. There's no feather protection amulet for aura-readers. Lila wants to know if there are feathers around because she wants to know if you've shifted. She wants to know that *you know* who you really are."

Cole shifted his weight from one foot to the other. "I did my best not to react to any of it, but I think I failed. I asked Kaley about the phone call that she'd had with her mother, the one that led

Lila to come here. Kaley didn't want to say much about it. So I asked her straight out if she'd told Lila about me being a familiar."

Pandora swallowed. "I think I already know the answer to this."

Cole took a breath. "Kaley told her. She said she thought her mother counted as family."

Pandora's phone chimed with an incoming text. She reached for her purse, then stopped.

"Get it," Cole said. "It could be Kaley reaching out to you."

Pandora grabbed her phone and checked the message. "It's not Kaley, it's my mom."

She tapped the screen to bring up the text.

Dug deeper into Lila's file. Call me.

Pandora glanced at Cole. "I need to talk to my mother. It's about Lila."

He nodded. "You want to go somewhere for lunch? I could stand to get out of this house for an hour."

"Sure."

"Good. I'm going to grab a quick shower and change while you talk to your mom."

"Okay." She started to call Corette back, then hesitated. "Why didn't you call and tell me about this feather business this morning?"

He put his hand on the stair railing. "I knew you were going to talk to your mom and that you had that showing. I didn't want you to be preoccupied with my problems while you were trying to work."

"Our problems." She smiled. "You're my familiar, after all." Just saying the words caused a little charge to zip through her. "Now get showered so we can work this out over lunch."

He grinned. "Yes, ma'am." He saluted and jogged upstairs.

She shook her head as she tapped the button to call her mother, then put the phone to her ear.

"Pandora?"

"Yep. What did you find out?"

Corette sighed. "I looked into the last six years of Lila's records, all the way back to when she was listed as Lila Van Zant. I called the ACW headquarters and spoke to…someone I know there. Someone in charge of the records that aren't computerized because of security reasons."

Top-secret stuff. "And?" Pandora held her breath.

"She's been married and divorced two more times in those six years." Corette's voice held an angry edge. "Both of her ex-husbands were listed on the registry of human familiars."

Pandora let the breath out, but it did nothing to quell the rockslide of emotions sluicing through her. "She's after Cole, not Kaley."

Cole threw on a clean T-shirt and jeans and headed downstairs. Pandora was pacing in the foyer.

"Everything okay?"

"No." She turned to him, her emerald eyes lit with anger and purpose. "Lila's been married and divorced twice in the last six years."

"She should be pretty good at it by now with all that practice," he joked.

Pandora's expression didn't waver. "Both times the guy was a human familiar."

His smile faded. "You know that for sure?"

"Yes, we know it for sure. My mother is the coven secretary. She has access to information most people don't." A muscle in her jaw ticked. "Lila's after you, not Kaley. Or maybe it's both of you. Either way, she's not here to make up for being a lousy mother. I'd say you're on her radar again."

"We need a plan."

"Agreed. But I need to check something first."

"Sure. What?"

"That book in the attic. You mind if I grab it?"

"Be my guest."

Pandora closed her eyes, held her hands out, palms up, in front of her. The air above them wavered, and a second later, the book appeared in her hands.

"Wow. That was impressive." And kind of hot.

"For me, too. But strong emotion can strengthen

a witch's magic, and I'm definitely feeling some right now." She opened the book and ran her finger down the table of contents, found what she was looking for and flipped to that page.

Cole came around to stand next to her so he could see what she was looking at. He took the opportunity to enjoy how good she smelled before focusing on the book. The top of the page read "Cautions."

"There," she said. She pointed to a line about halfway down and read out loud. "The hair, skin, feathers or fur of a human familiar's *animal form* can be used to create a bonding spell."

She looked at him. "Now you know why she wants one of your feathers."

"She's going to force a bond with me. Or try to." It bothered him more that Lila might come between him and Pandora, than that his ex was about to try to force herself on him. "I am sure as hell not going to let that happen."

Pandora nodded. Then she closed the book. "Look, nothing's going to happen until she gets that feather. We have time to figure this out. Let's go have lunch, and tonight, I'll talk with my mom and sisters, and we'll come up with something." She smiled. "I don't want her getting in the way of our time together. Not right now."

"Okay. We can do that." He kissed her forehead, willing to take a breather if she was. "You're amazing, you know that?"

Her smile widened. "Thanks. You're not so bad yourself. Let's go eat."

Twenty minutes later, they were seated in a booth at Howler's. Pandora introduced Cole to Bridget, then when they were alone at the table, she quietly explained that the owner of the establishment was also a werewolf.

"You're kidding me."

"Nope."

He looked at Bridget, who was now behind the bar, and shook his head. Hard to believe werewolves existed, let alone that they could look so...normal. "Get out."

Pandora laughed. "She's pretty, isn't she?"

He turned back to Pandora and let his gaze wander her face. "She's no Pandora Williams."

Pandora blushed. "Bridget is considered one of the great beauties of this town."

"Was that before you moved here?"

She giggled, and the sound pleased him. "Seriously, she is."

"If you say so." He looked at Bridget one more time. "Werewolves, huh? This town is…"

"Nuts?"

"Incredible."

The server came to take their orders. Pandora ordered a salad. He ordered the lunch special, a prime rib sandwich with fries.

As soon as the server left, Pandora pulled out

her phone. "I don't want to be rude, but I need to send a quick text to my mom and sisters about meeting tonight."

"Go ahead. I'll just admire the view."

She looked up at him through her lashes. "You're awfully full of compliments all of a sudden."

"Seeing my ex has brought into full focus just how lucky I am that you want to keep company with me. So I'm trying to up my boyfriend game."

She stuck her tongue into the corner of her mouth. "Is that what you are now? My boyfriend?"

"Too soon?"

She smiled coyly, then went back to her phone. "No."

By the time they were done eating, she'd exchanged a dozen texts with her family and the meeting was confirmed. They drove back to Cole's house in his truck. He threw it into park, hopped out and went around to get her door.

She dug her keys out of her purse. "I have to go back to work."

"I know."

"Listen, there's something you should know…whatever we come up with tonight, it's going to be tricky to execute. We know Lila can read auras, and sometimes, witches who can read auras can tell when people are lying."

"Maybe you shouldn't tell me what you decide to do, then."

She frowned. "We have to. You're an integral part. You're just going to have to be very careful when you speak to Lila."

"I will be." He kissed her. "Whatever you decide, I trust you. So do what you have to do."

She kissed him back. "Oh, I plan to."

19

When Pandora got to Marigold's cottage, Corette was already there, which made sense since they lived so close. Charisma showed up a few minutes later. Saffie said hi to them all, then went back to playing Minecraft on her tablet.

Marigold watched her daughter go down the hall to her room. "She still needs to study for her spelling test, but I figure she's less likely to come out here and overhear something she shouldn't if she's playing that game."

"I appreciate you bending your rules for me." Pandora took a seat at the kitchen table with the rest of her family. Marigold had made coffee and tea and set out a plate of shortbread cookies. "You all know that Cole is a familiar."

"And that his ex is in town," Charisma said. "And that she came to see Cole, then you."

Okay. "How did you know all that?" She reached for a cookie to dunk in her decaf.

Charisma pointed at Marigold. "She told me."

Marigold pointed at Corette. "And Mom told me. She also told me Lila really likes marrying and divorcing human familiars."

Pandora looked at her mother. "Really?"

Corette didn't look the least bit abashed. "Darling, your sisters need to know when one of their own might be facing this sort of dark magic. You don't expect me to keep that a secret, do you?"

"No, you're right. Saves me some time in the explanation too. Here's the latest. Lila, the ex, took Kaley out for a walk. In the course of that walk, she asked Kaley if she'd found any feathers, because one could be used to make a protection amulet for witches who can see auras."

"That's a big fat lie," Charisma said.

Marigold nodded. "I've never heard that."

"Me, either," Corette agreed.

Pandora snorted. "That's what I thought. Especially since I don't think truth matters that much to Lila."

Charisma's brows lifted. "Why do I think this has something to do with Cole's animal form being a raven?"

"Because it does." Pandora took a breath. "Even though I told Kaley not to say anything to anyone about her father being a familiar, she didn't think her mother was included in that. Kaley doesn't know what Cole's animal form is, but the night we were at the coven meeting, Cole practiced shifting, and Kaley found a feather in the house later. I tried to get it from her, but she thought it was cool and insisted on keeping it."

Marigold leaned back, a cookie in one hand. "Do we have any idea what Lila really wants this feather for?"

"Yes." Pandora pulled Gerty's book from her purse, laid it on the table and opened it to the chapter titled "Cautions." Then she turned it so her mother and sisters could read it and pointed out the line about the bonding spell. "I'm sure she plans on using it to force a bond with Cole."

Charisma tapped her delicately manicured index finger on the table. "The ACW needs to know about this."

Corette cleared her throat softly. "I talked to one of my friends there, and they said they need some kind of proof. All we have right now are suspicions and hunches."

Marigold threw her hands up, sending cookie crumbs flying. "We're witches! We're all about suspicions and hunches."

Corette nodded. "I understand that, dear, but the ACW isn't going to strip a witch of her magic just because we say she's up to no good. Let's not forget how the Salem trials began."

"Yeah, I get it." Marigold ate the last half of her cookie. "But we have to do something. We can't let this trollop steal Cole away from Pandy."

"Or," Charisma added, "turn Cole into her personal slave."

"That too," Marigold agreed.

"Exactly." Pandora held up a finger. "Which is why I have a plan."

Marigold smirked. "Is it to sleep with him and get the bonding over with before Lila has a crack at it?"

"Elizabeth Marigold Williams," Corette said.

"Just kidding, Mom," Marigold said as she shook her head to say she really wasn't.

"My immediate plan does not include *that*," Pandora said. "But if you can hold your comments for a moment, I'll tell you."

Charisma and Marigold leaned in, while Corette smiled like she already knew what it was.

Pandora waited a beat for effect. "We're going to set up a sting."

"Ooo," Marigold cooed. "I love it."

"What parts do we play?" Charisma asked.

"Well, about that..." Pandora shrugged. "You guys don't play that big of a part in the actual sting. I was thinking I'd get Sheriff Merrow to do the takedown and—"

"Why can't we help?" Marigold looked miffed.

"Dear," Corette started. "The three of us are not

exactly impartial. We need someone to act as a witness who the ACW will have no reason to question. Sheriff Merrow is perfect. Witches and shifters have always dealt very well with one another."

"What Mom said." Pandora flattened her hand on the table. "*But* I will need you guys at Cole's. You'll have to be ready with a containment spell, because I'm sure she'll try to use magic to get away. You just can't be seen until everything goes down."

Charisma glanced at Marigold, both of their expressions deadly serious but slightly excited. It wasn't often witches got to bring out the big spells. "We can do that."

Corette sipped her tea. "I think I can guess, but what sort of sting do you have in mind, dear?"

"If Kaley agrees to this, because this is her mother we're talking about and I need her to be cool with this, then…" Pandora smiled. "I'm going to give Kaley a safe feather and have her give it to Lila with the story that she found it in the house. Then Cole will tell Lila that she can't visit Kaley that night because she's working on a school project at a friend's house. Which is totally true, by the way. Speaking of what's true and what's not, Charisma, you see auras some. Can you tell if someone's lying?"

Charisma pursed her lips. "Not lying, exactly,

but I can tell when something's off with them. How well can Lila see them? Are you concerned that Cole's aura will tip her off?"

"I don't know. And yes."

Charisma wound a strand of brunette hair around one finger, then quickly let it go like she'd forgotten herself. "Putting a stabilizing spell on his aura probably wouldn't work, either, because Lila could pick up on the magic. I think the best bet is for him to play it as cool as he can."

"Okay, I'll tell him."

Marigold helped herself to another cookie. "When do you think this will all go down?"

"As soon as possible. The longer we wait, the more danger Cole and Kaley are in. Tomorrow, I'm going to talk to the sheriff, then I'm going to Cole's to get the feather—"

"Wait a moment," Corette said. "I thought you weren't using one of his."

"I'm not, but that attic is chock full of Gertrude's supplies. I'm sure there's a substitute feather up there. I just have to find it. Or ask her."

Marigold put her cookie down. "Ask her?"

Pandora laughed. "Didn't I mention Gertrude's ghost is still hanging around in the attic?"

"No," her sisters said in unison.

Pandora looked at her mother. "I guess you don't tell them everything."

Cole met Pandora outside the sheriff station at nine sharp the next morning. She looked gorgeous and dressed for business, as usual, but this morning there was something intoxicatingly powerful about seeing the woman he was crazy about dressed in a sleek black suit, crisp white shirt and glossy black heels. She was clearly here to get something accomplished. The fact that it was on his behalf was not lost on him.

He smiled and wished he could kiss her, but he wasn't sure how'd she feel about it being in public. Further proof they still had a ways to go to get to know each other. "Morning, beautiful."

She smiled back as she came to a stop in front of him. She waited for a moment, then her smile bent into a frown. "No kiss?"

"I wasn't sure how you feel about public displays of affection."

"Tongue is a no-no."

"Got it." He leaned in and planted one on her, brief but definite. "How was that?"

"Perfect. You nervous?"

"It's not every day you meet the big bad wolf."

"Hush," she said. "You can't say that to his face."

"I won't."

"Good. We'd better go in."

He reached for the door, but she put her hand on his arm, stopping him.

"Did I mention his aunt is the receptionist?"

"I don't think so."

"Okay, well, she is. And she's a werewolf too."

"Excellent." This town never stopped being strange. "Ready?"

She nodded, so he opened the door, then followed her in.

The woman behind the reception desk turned from her computer as they walked into the foyer. "Pandora Williams, as I live and breathe. How are you? How's your lovely mother?" Then she leaned to the side to ogle Cole behind Pandora. "And who's that with you?"

Nothing about the woman said werewolf. More like regular bingo player and cruise-aholic.

"We're all good," Pandora answered. "And this is Cole Van Zant. He's meeting the sheriff with me today. Cole, this is Birdie Caruthers." She gave him a pointed look. "The sheriff's wonderful aunt."

Cole stuck his hand out. "Nice to meet you, ma'am."

She shook his hand with both of hers sandwiched around it. "Birdie, please. You are a handsome thing, aren't you?" She narrowed her eyes. "Avian shifter, am I right?"

"Uh…" He hadn't been expecting that.

Birdie laughed, let his hand go and tapped her nose. "Better than a bloodhound."

Pandora looked around like she was checking to see if anyone else had heard. "That's confidential, Birdie." She lowered her voice. "He's a familiar."

Birdie made a face. "I'm no witch but aren't those usually animals?"

"Yes. But sometimes, they're not."

Birdie's eyes widened, and she whistled. "And rare as hen's teeth, am I right?" She mimed zipping her lips and throwing away the key, then winked at Cole. "I won't say a word."

Somehow he doubted that.

The office door adjacent to her desk opened and a man leaned out. "Birdie, have you heard from—" The dark, gruff man in the sheriff's uniform looked at them, then at Birdie and sighed. "Never mind. I can see my nine o'clock appointment is here."

Pandora tipped her head in greeting. "Sheriff."

"Pandora."

"Sheriff Hank Merrow, this is Cole Van Zant."

The sheriff shook Cole's hand. "Call me Hank. Come on in. You two want coffee?"

"I'm good." She looked at Cole.

"I'm fine, thanks."

"Good," Hank muttered. "Birdie's lousy at getting it."

"I heard that, sassmouth," she screeched. "Don't forget I changed your diapers."

Hank grimaced and shut the door. "Make yourselves comfortable."

They sat while Hank went to his desk chair and settled in. He looked like a werewolf. Or what Cole imagined one might look like in human form. Blue eyes, five o'clock shadow at nine A.M., gravelly voice and a slightly predatory gleam in his gaze. It wasn't entirely welcoming, but Cole supposed it suited the man well, considering his occupation.

Hank rested his forearms on the desk. "What can I help you with?"

"This is a supernatural matter," Pandora started.

Hank seemed puzzled. "Witch business?"

"Yes."

"You've always handled that yourselves. What's going on?"

"My ex-wife is what's going on," Cole said.

Hank's brows lifted slightly. "I see."

Pandora explained about Lila and what they suspected she was up to.

The sheriff shook his head. "Not sure what I can do for you." He looked at Cole. "I could add your house to one of the deputies' patrols. Alex Cruz lives in Pandora's neighborhood. He could drive by on his way home."

"I appreciate that," Cole said. "But I don't think Lila's going to be that obvious. And Pandora's got a plan."

"That's really where we need you, Sheriff."

Pandora laid out the strategy to catch Lila in the act. "Ultimately, things will go smoothest with the ACW if there's an impartial witness to this whole operation."

A light came on in Hank's eyes. "And that's where I come in."

"Yes. My sisters and my mother will be there to contain her magic, but I'm sure you can see that us all being related creates a bias. Your impartial word would go a long way towards making sure Lila can't try this again."

Hank seemed to think for a moment. "What will the ACW do to her?"

"The penalty for this sort of violation is usually a five-year suspension from magic."

Hank nodded. "When do you need me?"

She glanced at Cole. "Could be as early as tonight."

Hank scrawled something on a business card. "Text me. I'll be there. And if Marigold needs to drop Saffie off at our house, I know Ivy would be happy to watch her until this matter is settled."

Pandora smiled. "Thank you, I'll tell her. I don't suppose Charlie would mind Saffie's company either."

Hank smiled, shocking Cole. He hadn't thought the man capable of it. "That boy's got himself an awful crush."

The Professor Woos The Witch

Pandora laughed. "I'm pretty sure it's a two-way street."

Then Hank looked at Cole, and his expression went back to sheriff-on-the-job. "You're new in town, so—"

Cole nodded. "New to this whole world, actually."

Pandora put her hand over his. "Cole only recently found out he's not entirely human."

Hank nodded. "That had to be a shock."

"You can say that again."

"Well," Hank continued. "You need anything, you call me. We do our best to take good care of all our citizens, but our supernatural ones especially."

"I appreciate that, but the only thing I'm going to need after this is over is a job."

"What kind of work are you in?"

"College math professor. Algebra and Calculus, mostly."

Hank nodded thoughtfully. "I'll mention it to my wife. She works part time for Delaney Ellingham at the sweet shop, and Delaney's married to Hugh Ellingham."

"One of the town's founders," Pandora supplied.

The name rang a bell for Cole. "She made the desserts that Stanhill brought to dinner."

"That's her," Pandora confirmed.

Hank leaned back. "The Ellinghams run this

town. If there's a job to be had, they'll know about it. Anyway, I'll send word you're looking. Of course, I imagine Corette could do the same with Stanhill, seeing as how he's Hugh's rook."

"Great idea, and one I should have thought of." Pandora stood. "I'll talk to my mother about it. Thank you for all your help. We should let you get back to work."

Hank got to his feet as Cole did the same. He stuck his hand out. "You, your aunt and your sister, who Pandora introduced me to at lunch the other day, are the first werewolves I've met."

Hank smiled again as he shook Cole's hand, but this time it was more amused than overtly joyful. "I can guarantee that's not true. We're just the first ones you're aware of."

20

Back at Cole's, Pandora headed straight for the attic to search Gertrude's things for the key ingredient in their sting, the substitute feather. Cole declined to join her, begging off to get out of his dress clothes and into something suitable for hauling junk out to the dumpster so he could get back to work.

Pandora had a feeling it had more to do with Gertrude than his desire to get the house emptied.

She flipped on the attic light. "Gertrude? I need your help."

A vision in lemon appeared before Pandora. "Hello, dearie!"

"Hi, Gertrude."

The ghost clasped her hands in front of her. "Oh, I do love a visit. You know the stud muffin came to see me."

"I heard. I sent him up here, so you're welcome."

She grinned. "He is a tasty cookie, isn't he? Speaking of, have you had a bite yet?"

Pandora did her best stern face. "Gertrude, that's my familiar you're talking about."

Gertrude put a hand to her mouth and floated back a bit. "Oh my, yes, sorry. No disrespect meant."

"No harm done. And yes, he is a tasty cookie. Now, I need some help."

"Anything, dear, anything. Just name it."

"I'm looking for a very specific ingredient for a spell, and I thought you might have just the thing."

Gertrude hovered up and down, the ghostly equivalent of yes, Pandora imagined. "I'm sure I do. What do you need?"

"A black feather."

Gertrude's smile fell off her face. "What's wrong? The bonding didn't work?"

"It's not what you think. We're not doing *that* until we know each other better and are more sure we're compatible."

Gertrude clucked her tongue. "If you haven't tried bonding the old-fashioned way, then you don't need the feather yet. Trust me, child, nature's way is better, and that's not something I often say when it comes to the craft. Just give it time."

"No, it's not for us." Pandora sighed and gave Gertrude the quickie version of what was going on.

"Oh my, I see. Well, then. A feather." She

floated around the attic, inspecting her shelves and the storehouse of witchly goods contained there. She waved her hand, and a box drifted toward Pandora. "See if those will do."

Pandora plucked the box out of the air and opened it. It was filled with black feathers. "These are perfect. I just need one." She selected one and returned the box to the shelf it had come from. "Where did you get all of those?"

Gertrude's smile held sadness. "They were Ulysses'."

"Are you sure using the feather of another familiar won't backfire? Especially one that's related?"

"Doesn't work that way. At best, she might be able to bond herself to Ulysses, but seeing as he's long gone..." Gertrude sighed and lifted a lacy handkerchief to her eyes.

"You still miss him, huh?"

"I do."

"I hope this isn't too personal a question, but why didn't he end up a ghost like you?"

Gertrude shrugged. "I guess because I had unfinished business here. And once that's done, I'll be with him again. I hope." She hovered lower as she nodded. "He was the great love of my life." She sniffed, then her smile brightened. "You'll see. That man downstairs will be yours."

"Maybe."

"No maybes. He is meant for you, just as you're meant for him. I saw it when you two were up here together the other day."

"I do really like him."

"You love him. You just won't admit it yet. You young people are so scared to be in love these days." She did a little twirl. "In my day, you found a fella, you knew it was right and you acted on it. None of this pussyfooting around." She flopped her hand in the air and fluttered her lashes. "None of this *I like him, I adore him, he's so nice* business."

Pandora laughed.

Gertrude stuck her tongue out and made a rude noise. "Enough. Love is love. You know it when you feel it."

Pandora shrugged. "Maybe I haven't felt it."

"Liar. If you don't love him, why are you doing all this to protect him? Out of the goodness of your heart?"

"Maybe." Pandora was getting mad now. "You don't know what I'm feeling."

"Yes, I do." Gertrude waggled her finger. "I know what he's feeling too." She grinned. "I can't leave the attic, but I can hear him singing love songs in the shower."

Pandora blinked. "He sings love songs in the shower?"

"Not well, but it's very endearing." Gertrude floated closer. "He's got it bad for you."

THE PROFESSOR WOOS THE WITCH

Pandora stroked her fingers down the silky feather. "He did agree to stay. But how do we know if what we're feeling is real and not just a product of the connection between a witch and a familiar?"

Gertrude shook her head. "It's a good thing the two of you are so pretty, because you're both tremendously dumb."

Pandora crossed her arms. "That's not very nice."

Gertrude sighed. "Do you think the connection you're feeling is somehow fake? That it's somehow been manufactured because of who you are? Those feelings are real! If Cole fell in love with you because you were a witch, he'd be in love with your sisters and your mother too. Think, girl. That's not how it works. Those feelings are there *because* you're meant to be together. If you weren't, you'd feel nothing."

Pandora felt like a lightbulb had gone off over her head. "So..."

"*Yes*," Gertrude hissed. "Get out of your own way and just be in love already."

"You say that like it's so easy to do."

"Because it is. Taxes are hard. Raising kids is hard. Learning to drive a stick shift, that's hard. But love?" She did a slow twirl mid-air. "Love is easy."

"I can't just blurt it out."

"Sure you can. Unless you're just pretending at

all this. Are you pretending or do you love him?"

Pandora fell silent and searched her heart. The truth. She did love Cole. "I don't think I have the courage to tell him I love him."

"You already did. And I'm sure he feels the same way." Gertrude looked past Pandora and smiled. "Isn't that right, cookie?"

Pandora turned to see Cole standing in the attic doorway. She shivered. Either Gertrude had just passed through her or it was the cold panic of the realization that Cole had heard the tail end of that conversation. "H-how long have you been standing there?"

"Long enough." His expression looked…funny.

She wished she was a ghost. She twisted to face the conniving apparition. "Gertrude, you tricked me into—" Gertrude was gone.

Pandora stayed where she was. She stared at the feather in her hand. It was easier to have her back to Cole while she dealt with this mortification.

Of course, he didn't stay where he was. His arms wrapped around her and pulled her against his chest. "She's right, you know."

"About what?" She couldn't look at him. Couldn't bear to see rejection in his eyes.

"I love you too."

She stiffened. "Are you just saying that to make me feel better?"

"Yes. But also because it's true." He laughed.

The sound came out shaky. "It's also frightening as hell."

She smiled and turned to look at him. "That's the truth." But his admission allowed her to catch her breath. "So we're in love."

"Seems that way. You all right with that?"

She nodded, and a slow smile bent her mouth. "I am. Still completely freaked out by how fast this is happening, but I guess Gertrude is right. If our feelings are there, why deny them?"

"Agreed." He kissed her. "I still think we should take things slowly. I want you to be completely comfortable before we do any…"

"Bonding?"

He nodded.

"Me, too. Thank you." She held up the feather. "Now we just need to talk to Kaley and make sure she understands the plan."

"She'll be home at three fifteen."

"Good. That gives me a couple of hours to get some work done." And to get used to the idea that she and Cole were in love. She kissed him back. "See you then."

It wasn't until after four that Pandora was able to return to Cole's. She stood with him in the foyer. "I meant to be here sooner, but I had to run comps for a new client, then email them, then they had questions. You know how it is."

"I sure do. Work happens. I get it." He slipped his arm around her waist and kissed her cheek. The comfortableness of his affection was sweet. "Kaley's in the kitchen. You ready?"

"I guess." She bit her lip.

"What's wrong?"

"I'm just nervous Kaley won't go for our plan. What if this doesn't work?"

"We've been through this. It's going to be fine. We'll make her understand. She's thirteen. She needs to recognize what her mother is really capable of."

Pandora let out a little sigh. "Okay, let's do this."

Kaley was at the table eating apple slices and Nutella and texting. She looked up from her phone. "Hi, Miss Williams."

"Hi, Kaley. Is that what you get for an afternoon snack? Man, all I got as a kid was lizard tails and eye of newt. That's what witches eat, you know."

Kaley laughed. "That's totally gross and totally not true." She held up her plate. "Want one?"

"No, thanks, I'm good." Pandora took a seat at the table while Cole leaned on the counter. "How was school?"

Kaley munched a bite of apple. "Good. You know, school is school."

Pandora nodded. "Talked to your mom lately?"

Kaley held up her phone. "She texted me this morning to say have a good day."

Pandora nodded again. Enough beating around the bush. "Your dad told me that you mentioned his being a familiar to her."

Kaley's happy expression disappeared. "I thought it would be okay because she's family."

Pandora made sure to keep her voice soft and kind. "It's something your mom already knew, but she probably didn't know that your dad knew that about himself."

"So I still shouldn't have told her?"

"Well... Based on some other things I've learned, I think your mom could be out to hurt you or your dad."

Kaley glanced at Cole. He nodded. She looked back at Pandora. "What kind of things have you found out?"

"For one, you told your dad that she asked if you'd found any feathers."

Kaley shrugged. "So? She wants to make me an amulet. I think that's cool."

"It would be, if that's really what she wanted to do. But neither my mother nor my sisters or I have ever heard of a feather amulet for those who see auras."

Kaley sat back, eyes clouded with suspicion. "You think she's lying to me? Why?"

"Yes, she's lying," Cole said. "It's because she knows I understand who I am. She wants that feather so she can use it to cast a spell on me. Not a good spell, either."

Kaley crossed her arms. "Of course you'd say that. You hate her."

"I don't hate her." A muscle in Cole's jaw jumped. "I just know what she's capable of and honey, you need to too. Lila's needs come before anyone else's, Kaley. Yours included, unfortunately."

Pandora could feel the mood going south. "Kaley, there is proof in the American Witch Council records that your mother was married and divorced to two other human familiars. We think she's back for another attempt to get your father to bond with her."

"I don't know what that means."

Cole straightened. "It means that I would be permanently attached to her, even though I'm in love with Pandora."

Kaley's eyes got wide. She glanced at Pandora.

Pandora nodded. "I feel the same way about your dad. We're meant to be together, Kaley. Our spirits recognize each other as one half of a whole being. When I'm around your dad, my magic works perfectly. And it never worked right in my life until he showed up."

"And," Cole went on, "I finally know and accept who I am."

Kaley seemed to take that all in. "I still don't get the feather thing."

Pandora looked up at Cole. "Show her."

"I don't think—"

"She's your daughter and a fledging witch. She needs to fully understand."

He nodded and took a breath. "Don't freak out, Kaley." Then he stepped to the center of the room and shifted into his bird form. He stretched out his wings and flew onto the back of the empty kitchen chair.

"Holy crap," Kaley whispered. She looked at Pandora. "Is that seriously my father or did you do that to him?"

"That's your dad." Pandora reached out and stroked one of his wings. "Human familiars have the ability to shift into an animal form. When your dad and I are bonded, I'll be able to see through his eyes when he's a raven and we'll be able to communicate telepathically."

He cocked his head and cawed at Kaley.

She just sat there. "Dude. That is so cool."

Pandora smiled. "I think you can change back now, Cole."

He hopped off the chair, and a second after he landed on the floor, Cole stood before them again. "The feather she wants is one of mine."

Kaley shook her head. "I swear, I won't give it to her."

"Actually," Pandora said, "we want you to do just that."

"You do?"

Pandora pulled the substitute feather from her purse. "Yes. But this is the feather we want you to give her instead."

Kaley took the feather, turning it over in her fingers. "Is this some kind of magic thing? Like, is it poison or something?"

"Nope. Just a feather."

"Then why do want me to give it to her instead of the one I found in the hall?"

Cole answered. "Because that one is mine and it does have magical properties, right, Pandora?"

She nodded. "Right. We can't have the real feather fall into your mother's hands, Kaley."

"Because of the spell she wants to cast," Kaley said.

"Exactly." Pandora nodded.

Kaley stared at the feather. "But if I give her this feather and she thinks it's the real one, won't she still perform the spell?"

"Maybe," Pandora says. "We're going to wait and see."

"And if she does?" Kaley looked up at Pandora like the realization of what was being planned had just struck her. "What then?"

"Then...there will be repercussions. A witch

forcing a familiar to bond with her is a punishable offense."

Kaley's brow furrowed and she frowned. "So I'd be setting her up. Getting her in trouble. That's not cool. She's my mother and I know she's not like a model person or whatever, but she's still my mom."

Kaley slapped the feather onto the table and stood up. "I'm out of here."

She stormed off toward her room and Pandora was about to say something but Cole raised his hand. "Let her go."

Pandora took a breath. "I guess I should have seen that coming."

"She's a kid. She's not going to see this as black and white as we do."

"Of course. But we still need to figure out a new plan."

"Agreed. Any ideas?"

"More coffee?"

He smiled. "I can do that."

But before the pot had finished brewing, Kaley came back downstairs. She still didn't look happy and possibly like she'd been crying a little. "I'll help."

Cole looked at her hard. "I'm happy to hear that, but what changed?"

Kaley stared toward the backyard. "I Facetimed Mom. She asked me about the feather again right away. When I asked her to tell me more about the amulet, her aura went all gray and hazy."

Pandora shook her head. "I don't know what that means."

Kaley shifted to stare at the table, her lower lids rimmed with liquid. "It means she was lying. Big time lying."

She sniffed. "Tell me again what happens if she gets the right feather and does this spell you think she's going to try?"

"Miss Williams thinks she'll force me to bond with her." Cole came and stood next to Kaley. "And I don't want to be enslaved to her for the rest of my life. Or be separated from Miss Williams, either."

Kaley rubbed at her nose. "Both those options are pretty crappy."

"They are," Pandora agreed. "And I can pretty much guarantee that if your mom casts this spell, the next thing that's going to happen is you and your father will be moving out of Nocturne Falls. There's no way your mother will stay here where so many people will know what she's done."

"Is that true, Dad? We wouldn't be able to stay here? Even if we wanted to?"

"I think so." Cole looked at Pandora.

She shook her head. "If a bonded familiar isn't near the witch he's bonded to, it can cause him incredible pain and mental distress."

Kaley took a deep breath. "I don't want to move. I don't want you and my dad not to be together either. And I definitely don't want my dad in pain." A wobbly half-smile curved her mouth. "I like you, Miss Williams. My mom is…my mom, but you're a really nice person and a very cool witch."

"Thank you, Kaley. I like you a lot, too."

A single glossy tear tracked down Kaley's cheek. "I'd rather be like you than like my mother. I'm not a kid anymore. I know she's not a good person. It just hurts, you know?"

Pandora's heart broke for the girl. She reached out and grabbed Kaley's hand. "Oh, honey, I know it does. My dad wasn't so hot either."

Kaley let out a shuddering breath. "Do you promise my mom won't get hurt?"

"I promise to do my best to prevent that, but if she tries to hurt your dad, I'm going to protect him first. Can you understand that?"

Kaley nodded and sighed. "Yeah, I understand. Just tell me what to do."

21

One text from Kaley. *I found a feather.* That's all it had taken for Lila to show up again, looking to spend time with her daughter. They'd gone to get ice cream, during which Kaley had turned over the substitute feather as planned.

Now, a day later, Kaley was at Pandora's for safe keeping. She'd sent Lila a text saying she couldn't hang out because she was doing witch stuff with Pandora until eight o'clock.

Which meant Lila knew Cole would be alone in the house until then.

And so the waiting began.

Cole knew she'd show. It was just a matter of when.

Sheriff Merrow, Corette, Marigold and Charisma were all in the backyard where they could see into the house through the windows. The sliders onto the porch were unlocked. He just hoped they made it into the house before Lila cast whatever spell she was planning to use on him. Fake feather or not, he didn't want to be on the receiving end of Lila's magic.

He glanced toward the backyard. It was still light out, but he couldn't see any of them in the obscene overgrowth. Or maybe they were using magic to conceal themselves. But wouldn't Lila sense that?

If only he'd been raised to understand more about witches and magic and familiars. Corette had assured him that their magic would work no matter the distance and that they could immobilize Lila from their hiding spots. Marigold had added that he would be perfectly safe.

But he felt like a fish in a bowl with a cat on the prowl. He glanced skyward. For a second, he wished Gertrude could access any part of the house, but that would be more of a curse than a blessing.

He passed the time by working. Another day of clearing junk out and the remodeling could begin. There were floors to refinish, walls to paint, light fixtures to change. The stairway to refurbish with wrought iron. Bathrooms to gut and rebuild. The kitchen cabinets and countertops needed to be ordered, too, since he and Pandora still hadn't gotten around to that. Maybe tomorrow.

And there was the outside. Painting, repairs, landscaping… He chuckled at how much remained to be done. But it was work worth doing.

The house would be something special when it was complete. Hell, it was something special now. He stood in the foyer and looked around at the grand space with a pang of regret that he wouldn't get to enjoy it after the work was complete. It was the most amazing place he'd ever lived.

Seemed fitting that he'd met Pandora here, seeing as how she was the most amazing woman he'd ever known.

And she loved him.

His smile was unstoppable. Thinking about her did that to him. With a lightness in his heart that overrode the worry about the events yet to come, he dug into the task of sorting through the last remaining boxes.

He lost himself in the work—and thoughts of Pandora—until a knock on the door brought him back to reality. The sound was a jolt to his system, reminding him of what the real task was: facing down Lila and eliminating the threat she posed to his and Kaley's life once and for all.

Prepared for whatever happened next, he steeled himself and opened the door.

Corette and Sheriff Merrow stood on the other side. Merrow made a face. "We would have come up to the sliders, but it's a jungle back there. Didn't want to drag Corette through the thicket just to reach the back porch steps."

"I understand. Did you need something then?"

"Just wanted to let you know I sent my girls home." Corette looked at her watch. "It's ten to eight. I don't think Lila is coming tonight. She believes Kaley's supposed to be home at eight. Lila won't want to do this with her daughter around."

Cole looked at his watch just be sure. "I didn't know it was that late already."

Merrow nodded. "Call me when you set this up again. Corette, I'll wait for you in the car."

"Thank you, Sheriff." Cole sighed.

Merrow left with a short wave.

"Disappointed?" Corette asked.

"Yes. I wanted to get this over and done with."

"Us too."

"What do you think it means that she didn't show?" He'd been so sure of it. Could he and Pandora have been that wrong?

Corette thought for a moment. "Maybe she couldn't get everything together that she needed for the spell."

"Or maybe she really is making an amulet for Kaley."

Corette's impeccable brows lifted. "My darling boy, there is no feather amulet that is of particular use or power to a witch who can read auras. That's rubbish. Whatever your ex is up to, I can assure you it's no good."

"I know. I just...I don't know."

"You were hoping that Lila wasn't who she was. But she is. I'm sorry."

He nodded. "Me too."

Corette patted his arm. "You want me to have the sheriff take me by Pandora's so I can collect Kaley? I can give her an update on the no-show."

"Don't worry about it. I'll text Pandora. And Kaley's sleeping over. It was part of the deal. She's been dying to spend the night ever since she met Pandora." He smiled. "I made her promise not to be cranky about getting up in the morning."

Corette nodded. "It'll be good practice for Pandora too."

"Practice? For what?"

Corette's smile turned sly. "Motherhood."

"Concentrate on the air around the pencil, not on the pencil itself." Pandora stood a few feet away from Kaley so the kid didn't feel crowded. Learning to control your gifts was hard work. Pandora had had the added pressure of having gifts that had never worked right. She understood the frustration.

Kaley sighed. "I can't do it."

The Professor Woos The Witch

Pandora gave her a reassuring smile. "You absolutely can. Don't get discouraged. You did it once."

"That was a fluke."

"No, it wasn't. Look how easily you grasped calling fire. Now try again." Pandora moved closer to Kaley. "With focus this time. If you want to master your powers, this is what it takes. Practice and patience."

"So *bossy*." But Kaley was grinning. "Okay, here goes." She stared at the pencil on the kitchen table, and her smile drifted away into a sea of concentration.

The pencil trembled.

"Very good," Pandora whispered. "Move the air, not the object. Think light thoughts."

The pencil lifted off the table and hovered a few inches above it. Then it went a few inches higher.

Kaley whooped, and the pencil fell back to the table. "I did it!"

Pandora swooped in to hug her. "I'm so proud of you!"

Kaley hugged back. Hard. Then her slim frame started to shake.

Pandora pulled back to look at Kaley. She was crying. "Hey, what's wrong? Don't cry."

Kaley wiped at her face. "I'm just happy." She sniffed. "And a little sad."

"Why, honey?" Pandora brushed the hair out of Kaley's face.

"You're so nice to me. And you've only just met me. And my mom's known me for years and..." Kaley shrugged. "You've been a better mom in a week than she's been all my life."

Pandora held Kaley's face in her hands as she fought back tears of her own. "Your dad's not the only one I've fallen in love with."

"You mean me?"

"Yes, silly girl, I mean you. And Pumpkin's crazy about you."

"That's because I have beef jerky."

They both looked at Kaley's backpack. Pumpkin was currently curled up on top of it. Snoring. "There might be some truth in that," Pandora said.

Kaley laughed and rubbed at her eyes. "I hope that Lila doesn't hurt my dad."

"She won't. We won't let that happen. I promise."

Pandora's phone chimed. She grabbed it, hoping there was news at last. She read the text. "Speaking of your dad, he wants to know if you're in bed yet."

Kaley rolled her eyes. "It's only nine thirty."

"Go brush your teeth and put your nightgown on."

Kaley made a face. "A nightgown? Really?"

"Whatever you wear to bed. Go get ready. Or I'll

turn you into a catnip mouse and let Pumpkin torture you."

Kaley snorted. "Could you do that?"

"No. Remember, animate to inanimate is a high-level skill. I could turn you into a real mouse, though."

Kaley shrieked. "Ew!"

Pandora flicked her fingers, and the hall light came on. "Teeth. Now."

Kaley held up her hands. "Going."

Pandora grinned as she took her phone to the couch to text Cole back. *She's brushing her teeth now. How'd it go with Lila?*

She never showed.

What? You think she saw the sheriff and knew the gig was up?

Not sure. Your mother thinks she didn't have the spell ready.

Could be. But Pandora didn't like that the loose end of Lila remained untied.

How'd it go with Kaley?

Great. Taught her how to shoot lasers out of her eyes and how to turn straw into gold.

O_o

Just kidding. She practiced levitating a pencil.

So much better. Wish you were here.

Ditto.

Maybe the next sleepover should be you and me.

A shiver of wicked anticipation rippled through

Pandora. She bit her lip. Before she could answer, he texted again.

When the time is right of course. How about lunch tomorrow?

That might be a little soon for a sleepover.

Haha. I meant for actual lunch. Mummy's?

It's a date.

See you at noon. Love you.

She grinned and then texted words she'd only ever sent to her sisters and mother. *Love you too.*

22

At eleven forty-five the next day, Cole found himself wandering on Main Street. He stopped in front of a store called Illusions. The windows were full of sparkly things, but also watches, and he'd always had a weak spot for a good-looking chronograph.

He'd left the house early to get to Mummy's in time to snag a table before the lunch crowd descended, but as he'd parked, he'd gotten a text from Pandora telling him she'd had an eager seller call about listing their house.

He'd told her to take her time, but she insisted she'd meet him at twelve thirty, no later. Truth was, he loved how successful she was, how she was very clearly her own woman with her own life. It was incredibly sexy to have a woman like that want *you*.

Because if there was anything Cole knew about

Pandora, it was that a woman of her caliber could have any man she wanted.

Being with her was an honor and a privilege. With that in mind, he slipped into the jewelry store. There were two women behind the counters waiting on a smattering of customers. He had no purpose in mind other than killing time, but the thought of buying Pandora a little something had merit. *If* he found something that seemed like her.

He worked his way around the store until he came to a display case of engagement rings. He paused there, lost in the idea of putting that sort of ring on his sexy redhead's finger.

"Can I help you?"

He looked up. A pretty blonde woman smiled at him, her aqua eyes bright. "Just looking."

She nodded, then canted her head and, with a coy look in her eyes, said, "You wouldn't be looking if you didn't have a reason."

He laughed. "True."

"What's her name?"

"Pandora."

"Pandora Williams?"

He nodded. "I guess everyone in town knows her, huh?"

"Yes, but she's also a really good friend of mine. Her cat and my cat are brother and sister."

"Pumpkin?"

"Yep. Jasper's back there in my office right now."

"Is he also…" Cole puffed his cheeks up.

"Fat? No. Jasper's a lean, mean, sleeping machine." She laughed and offered her hand. "I'm Willa Iscove. You must be Cole."

He shook her hand. "If you know who I am, that must mean Pandora's mentioned me. I hope it was good."

Willa's smile kinked. "Yes and no. No at first, yes lately."

"Yeah, I had some things to learn."

"She mentioned some of that." Willa leaned in. "Are you looking for an engagement ring for her?"

He hesitated. "Not yet. But I can see that day coming."

Willa clasped her hands in front of her. "That's awesome. She's the best. She deserves to be happy."

"I agree." He looked at the rings one last time. "I wouldn't mind getting her a little present, though. I'm meeting her for lunch in a bit. Any ideas?"

"Come with me."

He followed her to a new case.

She pulled out a sterling silver pendant in the shape of an antique key decorated with little vines. It hung from a delicate chain. "Considering that she's a realtor, I thought this could be appropriate.

Could also be the key to your heart." She held it out. "What do you think?"

Seeing that the Pilcher Manor was also part of their story, he loved it. "It's perfect. How much? And do you gift wrap?"

"I'll give you the friends and family discount since this is for Pandy. And I'd be happy to wrap it for you. So long as you promise to come back to me when it's time to do some ring shopping."

He pulled out his credit card. "Deal."

She took the card and the pendant. "Be right back."

A few minutes later, she handed him his card with his receipt and the wrapped box. "We should all go out to dinner sometime, you and Pandora and me and my fiancé, Nick."

"Sounds great. I'll tell her. Thanks again." He tucked the gift in his jacket pocket and headed back to Mummy's. He couldn't wait to see Pandora's face when she opened it.

Mummy's was busy, but he put his name in for a table and sat on one of the benches outside. It was a great Southern fall day. Crisp enough to wear a light jacket, but the air held no bite. He tipped his face into the sun and let his mind wander back to his favorite subject. Pandora.

What would it be like to be married to her?

Nothing like life with Lila, that was for sure.

But that thought took him down a different

path. He was unhappy that things with Lila were still unsettled. He understood that she wanted time with Kaley, but whatever else was going on needed to be dealt with. Maybe she wasn't planning anything nefarious, but the not knowing was like waiting for the other shoe to drop.

Could he force the issue? Somehow push her into making a move? At least that way, he and Pandora would know what was going on. He got his phone out and sent Lila a text, crafting it so that she'd answer right away. He knew her well enough to know what buttons to push.

Thought about what you had to say and you were right. We should talk about our future.

If that didn't get an instant response, something was wrong.

Ten minutes later, with the no response, he had the sour feeling that there really was something wrong.

Then his phone rang. But it was Kaley. A jolt of panic shot through him. "Everything okay, sweetheart?"

"No, not really." Her voice was hushed and he realized she probably wasn't supposed to be on her phone at school. "Dad, I can't find the feather."

"I thought you gave it to your mom?"

"I did. I can't find the *real* one."

Oh. Crap. "Where was it?"

"My backpack. And now it's not there."

Was it possible Lila has sensed something was off with the substitute feather? Could she have riffled through Kaley's backpack and found the real one when they'd been out for ice cream? This was not good. But he also didn't want Kaley panicking when there was nothing she could do about it. "I'm sure it's no big deal. Don't worry about it, okay?"

"You're sure? I'm worried. What if Mom has it?"

"Yes, I'm sure. It's probably still in your backpack somewhere. Get back to class. It's fine."

She sighed. "I'm totally sorry."

"I know, but it's no big deal. Love you."

"Love you. Bye."

"Bye." He hung up and shot Pandora a fast text about the feather. Hopefully they could figure this out, but better she know now in case there was something she could do about it. He tucked the phone in his pocket and went back to waiting. He wanted to see Pandora more than ever now. Just being around her made everything better.

The hostess came out and yelled, "Cole, party of two."

He stood up and looked around. No Pandora yet. He waved to get the hostess's attention. "Move me back on the list, my date's not here yet."

She nodded and went back inside.

He checked the time. Twelve thirty-two. And no sign of Pandora.

The sour feeling returned.

Pandora arrived at the address the seller had given her. It was an older home on the outskirts of town and not in great shape. Well, the woman *had* said she'd just inherited the home and wanted it sold as quickly as possible.

This wasn't an area Pandora knew well, but she could sell anything. The key was under the welcome mat like the seller had told her. Pandora went inside to look around and wait for the seller to arrive.

The house was empty and a damp, musty smell hung in the air. It would need work—and a good airing out—to make it saleable, but nothing like the Pilcher Manor. A full paint job inside and new carpet would go a long way here. The kitchen was outdated, but few sellers in this kind of situation wanted to shell out the cash for a remodel. Maybe she could list it as a fixer-upper.

She turned, studying the space. Or maybe she could make the seller a cash offer, get it for a really good as-is price, and then she and Cole could rehab it and flip it.

Hmm. That would be interesting. Nocturne Falls had been around a long time before the Ellinghams had taken over, and the houses that remained from those early days were at best considered vintage.

She and Cole could definitely make a business

of it. In fact, she might be able to talk to the Ellinghams about buying up a bunch of them for a reduced price. She made a mental note to talk to Stanhill about getting an appointment with Hugh. Although, if it was a financial deal, that would mean meeting with Sebastian Ellingham, too.

Her lip curled at the thought. Sebastian was a notorious grump who kept an iron fist on the Ellingham finances. If it benefitted the town and meant increased business, though, he'd have no reason not to agree to the deal.

Didn't mean he couldn't find one, just that one wouldn't be obvious.

She also needed to talk to Hugh about getting Cole in to interview at Harmswood. She still thought Kaley ought to be going there too. Especially now that she and Cole were staying in Nocturne Falls.

Her to-do list got longer with every passing minute.

Back to the work at hand. Almost twelve fifteen and the seller hadn't shown up yet. She wasn't happy about being late to her lunch with Cole, but he'd been really understanding about it. He was pretty awesome like that. Still, another couple minutes and she'd text him again. She pulled out her tape measure and note pad and went to work measuring the bedrooms.

While she was finishing up the master, she

heard the front door open and close. "In the bedroom," she called out.

She walked into the hall to meet the woman she'd spoke to on the phone.

And straight into Lila.

Her heart jolted, and the bitter taste of foreboding coated her tongue. Every nerve in her body went on alert. "What are you doing here?" But she already knew, didn't she? She'd been set up.

Lila's smile was as pleasant as a crocodile's. "Meeting you."

"No, I'm meeting Hildie Martin." The woman on the phone had had a very distinct Southern accent and sounded about seventy years old.

Lila put her hand to her chest and grinned. Then a new voice came out of her mouth. "I am Hildie Martin."

The voice was an exact match. Pandora's belly went colder still. No one knew where she was. "How did you get a key to this house?"

Lila laughed. "The human men in this town are very gullible. All it took was a little story to the local locksmith and a pinch of magic. Anyway, it was the easiest thing."

Pandora's dread turned to anger. Lila needed to be put in her place. Nocturne Falls was Pandora's town, and the people in it were good people. They didn't deserve to be conned by this side show. "What do you want?"

Lila shrugged one shoulder. "Just to talk."

Pandora dropped her tape measure and note pad into her purse without taking her eyes off Lila. "So talk."

Lila's purse buzzed—her phone no doubt—but she ignored it. "Cole and I are going to be getting back together. I thought you should hear it from me first. I'll let Kaley know you won't be around anymore. Don't worry, I won't make you look bad. I appreciate that you've been so kind to her."

"What the hell are you talking about?"

Lila sighed. "Come on, Pandora. This can't really come as a surprise to you. I can't help that he's never fallen out of love with me."

"You're out of your mind, you know that? He's not in love with you. He's in love with me."

Lila's eyes took on a dangerous glint. "Maybe this will help you understand." She reached into her purse, pulled out a compact and opened it.

How makeup was going to help, Pandora had no idea.

Then Pandora saw that what was in the compact wasn't makeup, but sooty, gray ashes.

Her witch instincts kicked in as Lila puckered up and blew the ashes out of the compact. The tangled threads of her magic reached out to Pandora.

She threw her hands up and cast a spell to freeze Lila in place. It worked. The bits of ash stilled in the air like gray snow. Lila's face was suspended in a mask of anger and superiority.

"Not so full of it now, are you?" But Pandora was at a loss for how this was going to come to a good end. She could already feel the strain of holding the spell. She hadn't successfully cast a spell this large in...well, forever. And she didn't have Cole here to strengthen her magic. Her fingers began to tingle with fatigue. If she was going to grab her phone and try to call for help, she'd better do it now.

She just didn't think she could hold a spell this heavy with one hand. But she had to try. She inched one hand toward her purse.

Lila's right eyelid twitched.

Bother. The door to the master bedroom was a few feet away. Maybe she could hold the spell long enough to get in there and shut the door.

"Let...me...go," Lila mumbled.

"Sure. That sounds like a good idea." Sweat trickled down the back of Pandora's neck. Actually, talking made it easier. Maybe because then Lila wasn't fighting the spell so much. She shuffled back toward the master bedroom door. "What were you trying to cast on me anyway?"

"Bonding...spell."

"And here we thought you were prepping that for Cole." Pandora thought about that for a moment as her fingers went numb. She made a little more progress toward the door. "So you were going to bond to whatever's in me that works with Cole's familiar spirit?"

"Yes," Lila hissed.

"I have to say, we did not see that coming." Wait until she told her family. And Gertrude. Pandora's wrists throbbed with pain, and she started to feel sick to her stomach. At best she had another thirty seconds in her. Maybe twenty. Time to make her move. "Well, wish I could say it was nice talking to you, but you're an awful human being, a really crappy witch and a real turd of a mother."

The freezing spell dissolved. Pandora leaped into the master bedroom as Lila reared back to cast the ashes forward again. Pandora got the door shut and locked just in time.

Lila howled in frustration.

Pandora collapsed against the door, panting and feeling faint. She flexed her fingers, trying to get the feeling back. She knew she needed to call for help, but if her fingers weren't working, that was going to make using her phone tricky. Why hadn't she set up voice command dialing? If she lived through this, she was doing that first thing.

On the other side, Lila muttered the words of a new spell. Based on the few words Pandora could make out, Lila was trying to funnel the ashes under the door.

Pandora took a few deep breaths of ash- and magic-free air while she could and went for her phone. "You really need to give up, Lila. Those ashes aren't going to do a thing."

Lila kept chanting the spell in a voice too quiet for Pandora to make out.

She brought her phone to life and saw a text message from Cole that caused new panic to rise within her.

Lila might have the real feather by accident.

Nausea made liquid pool in Pandora's mouth. If that was true, she was in serious danger. She swallowed against the panic clawing her throat.

Magic might once again take the man she loved.

Hell no. She was not about to let that happen twice. Not without a fight.

A thin curl of ash wormed beneath the door.

Pandora held her breath, screwed up her courage and prepared to do battle.

23

Cole's fear turned to anger when he saw Pandora's Mercedes parked outside the old house. "Stay here," he said to Corette.

"I think not."

They both jumped out of his truck at the same time. Cole tried the front door, but it was locked. He threw his shoulder against it, driven by the burning need to save the woman he loved. The frame splintered, and the door gave way.

He raced into the house. "Pandora!"

"Cole!" The voice was muffled, but definitely Pandora's.

As he skidded to a stop in the small living room, he could see clearly down the hall.

Lila stood in front of a closed door, hands outstretched, focused intently on whatever she was mumbling.

Corette thrust her hands out and yelled something.

Lila jerked like a rag doll and hit the rear wall. She got to her feet, scowling. "Stay out of this, witch."

"Not when my daughter's in the balance." Corette closed one fist and pulled it toward her.

Lila was dragged in their direction, nails raking down the hall. "Let go of me."

Corette yanked forward again until Lila was out of the hall. She held Lila in place and turned to Cole. "Get Pandora."

He didn't need to be told twice. He ran down the hall and opened the only closed door.

Pandora was crumpled against the wall, phone in one hand. Her skin was pale and she was trembling. She lifted the phone a few inches off the floor. "I tried to call."

He pulled her into his arms and lifted her, holding her close to his chest. "I'm here now."

"Yes, you are." She slumped against him.

"Are you okay? Are you hurt?"

"Nope. I'm pretty good. Just magically hungover." She exhaled a long breath. "How'd you find me?"

"Your mother. Something about a locating spell."

Pandora let out a weak laugh. "The witchy version of your GPS app."

"Apparently." He carried her into the living room.

Lila was now sprawled on the floor.

Cole's brows shot up, and he looked at Corette. "Is she..."

"No, she's not dead." Corette smiled. "Sleeping Beauty spell. She'll be out for twenty-four hours. Sheriff Merrow's on his way, and I've also called our local ACW rep."

"Nicely done." The Williams women were not to be messed with. "You should know that Kaley thinks she might have accidentally given Lila the real feather."

"That's all right. It might even be better. Those ashes will become evidence, and if they're fully potent, that will only make our case stronger." Corette brushed the hair off Pandora's forehead. "How are you, my darling?"

"Good. Tired. Wore myself out holding a freeze spell for longer than I thought possible." She yawned. "Wow. Really tired."

Corette took Pandora's hand and patted the back of it. "It's a testimony to how powerful a witch you really are that you were able to hold that spell at all when your gifts have gone unpracticed all these years. You'll probably feel drained for a day or two, but this is a good start to regaining your power."

"So a couple days of rest are all she needs?" Cole asked.

"Yes." Corette put her hand on Cole's arm. "Take her home. I'll keep you posted on how things go."

He hesitated. "I feel like I should stay with you until the sheriff gets here."

"Take my daughter home. I'll be fine." She shook her head at Lila. "That one's not going to be causing anyone any more trouble for a long time. Stanhill and I will take care of bringing Pandora's car back."

The mention of Stanhill reminded Cole that he was supposed to talk to the man about getting in to see the Ellinghams about work, but there'd be time for that later. "I'll need her keys to get into her house. Do you have a set of her car keys?"

Corette smiled knowingly. "I don't need keys to start a car."

He snorted. "I guess you don't. See you later. And thank you."

"Thank you for taking care of my daughter."

Cole got Pandora into his truck and belted in, then drove through town to Pandora's house. By the time they arrived, she was out cold. He found her keys in her purse and opened the house. Pumpkin greeted him with a loud meow and a head butt to the leg. "I'll feed you as soon as I get your mother into bed."

He brought Pandora in and laid her on her bed. Her shoes came off easily, but her suit jacket took a little more work. He drew the quilt over her, then pulled the shades to darken the room, finally closing the door most of the way.

Pumpkin meowed endlessly as he walked into the kitchen. "Okay, I get it, you're hungry." He dug around until he found a can of food and a plate.

Pumpkin fell on the food like she was starving. He shook his head and checked the time. Kaley would be out of school soon. He didn't want to leave Pandora, but he didn't have a choice. And Lila was being handled. He scrawled a quick note and put it on Pandora's nightstand in case she awoke, then jumped in his truck to go pick Kaley up.

When they got back to Pandora's, she was still sleeping.

Kaley peered in through the cracked bedroom door and whispered, "Is she going to be okay, Dad?"

"She's going to be fine." He put his hand on Kaley's shoulder. "You want a snack? I'm sure she won't mind us rooting through her kitchen for edibles."

Kaley shrugged. "Sure."

"Okay, come on." He shut the door and gave Kaley a squeeze. He knew she was upset. She'd been in a funk since he'd explained what had happened on the ride back to Pandora's. "Hey, I know you think this is your fault. It isn't."

"I'm the one who let Lila have the real feather."

"We don't know that. And you didn't let her have it. If she got the real one, it was because she went through your stuff."

"I guess." Kaley took a seat at the kitchen counter while Cole rummaged through the fridge and cabinets. She sighed a few times, then finally spoke. "I don't want to see Lila anymore."

Cole turned, a box of mac and cheese in his hand. "Because of what she did?"

"Yes, that. But everything else too. She would have hurt Miss Williams. And you." Kaley picked at her fingernail polish, frowning. "She's not a good person. And she's not a good mother."

"You're sure about this?" Cole thought he'd be happier about the decision, but he hurt for Kaley. Realizing the unsavory truth about a parent was a scar she was going to carry the rest of her life.

Kaley nodded.

"Okay." A moment of silence passed between them. He broke it by rattling the box of pasta. "Mac and cheese?"

"Sure." She put her earbuds in and tuned out.

He said a silent thanks to Pandora for stocking the kid-friendly staple. He dug around some more for the tools to make it with, then got cooking.

As he dumped the pasta into boiling water, Kaley pulled her earbuds out. "Are you going to marry Miss Williams?"

He was glad he was faced away from her. He blinked hard. "Um—"

"Because I'd be okay with it if you did."

He smiled as he gave the pasta a stir. "Thank you for that." He turned. "Any other thoughts on the subject?"

"If she makes you happy, you should marry her. You've been alone a long time."

"I haven't been alone. I've had my Kaley-did."

She made a face like she was tolerating the endearment. "You know what I mean. I know boys have needs."

No chance to hide his face this time. "Needs? What exactly are they teaching you in that school?"

"Dad, I'm not a baby. I know about kissing and *sex*. I'll probably be getting my period like any day."

He groaned and covered his face with his hand. "I wish you were four again. Four was a good age."

She laughed. "Yeah, well, I'm not."

He looked up. "Have you kissed a boy?"

"*No.*" She made a shy face. "But there is a winter dance coming up. I was thinking Miss Williams could take me to get a dress."

"Does that mean you have a date?" A date. His little girl *on a date*. The world was coming to an end.

"No, but there's a boy who might ask me." She sat back. "If he's lucky, I'll say yes."

The Professor Woos The Witch

Cole stifled a laugh. "That's my girl."

She gave him a long look. "You didn't answer my question."

"About?"

"Are you going to ask Miss Williams to marry you?"

"Maybe. Eventually."

She crossed her arms. "Women don't like men who can't make up their minds."

He stared at her. "Where is all this coming from?"

She shrugged. "I like having her around. It's nice having another girl to talk to. And Lila's never going to be a real mother to me, so…"

His gut knotted. Was that what this was about? Having a mother? The hiss of water hitting the stove got his attention. He spun around and knocked the heat back as he lifted the pan to keep it from boiling over a second time. He checked the clock. The pasta had cooked long enough anyway.

He drained it, added the packet of sauce and stirred. He could very easily see himself married to Pandora. He also couldn't imagine himself with any other woman.

What if they tried bonding and it didn't take? Did it matter? That wouldn't change the way she felt about him, would it? He spooned the mac and cheese into two bowls and put one on the counter for Kaley. "Food's ready."

"Okay, in a sec." She was on the floor with Pumpkin, swinging a fuzzy toy on a stick and laughing as the cat swatted at it.

He wanted Kaley to be happy. Hell, he wanted that for himself. But asking didn't mean Pandora would say yes. Truth was, all this worry and concern could be for nothing if Pandora wasn't ready.

Kaley put the toy down and came to eat. He took his bowl and sat in the chair next to her. "Look, about Miss Williams and what we were talking about, she and I still need to get to know each other, but we're committed to each other. And if things go the way I think they will, then yes, I will ask her."

Kaley nodded and took a bite, smiling while she chewed. "Cool. I can live with that answer."

He picked up his fork. So could he.

Pandora woke with a start. She sat upright, heart pounding, trying to determine where she was. The space was pitch black. She blinked to get her eyes to adjust, then impatiently snapped her fingers. The lights flared on.

Her own bedroom. That's where she was.

"Hey, what's with the lights?"

She turned to see Cole's lanky form sprawled in

the dainty toile club chair she'd artfully angled in the far corner. "What are you doing here? What time is it?"

"Keeping an eye on you." He squinted at his watch. "It's nearly three in the morning. How do you feel?"

She rolled her shoulders. "Not too bad. A little tired. Maybe a little achy. Why? Should I feel worse?"

"I have no idea. Do you remember what happened?"

She thought for a moment, and it all came back to her. The old house. Lila. The ashes. Cole and her mother. She nodded. "I fought Lila, used a considerable amount of magic and passed out right after you and my mother showed up."

He nodded as he shifted in the chair. "Then I brought you back here."

"Who's watching Kaley?"

"We are. She's asleep in your guest room. Which reminds me, Lila didn't have the real feather. Kaley found it stuck between the pages of her biology textbook."

"That's good to know. At least Lila's spell wouldn't have worked." Pandora looked around. No sign of her cat anywhere. Panic tickled her spine. "Where's Pumpkin? You didn't let her out, did you? She's not an outside cat."

A half smile bent his mouth. "She's also asleep

in the guest room. On the bed with Kaley, actually."

Pandora's brows lifted. "My cat is sleeping with someone else?"

Cole pursed his mouth. "Kaley might have slipped her some mac and cheese."

Pandora rolled her eyes. "Food traitor. Not surprising."

He held his hands up. "I did tell Kaley she was on a diet, but—"

"Oh, Kaley knew that already. I'm not mad. But eating all those carbs has probably set her diet back to square one."

Cole snorted. "Because she was making such progress."

"Yeah, I know." Pandora lifted up the covers. "I'm wearing a tank top and underwear." She put the quilt down and gave Cole the eye. "You want to explain that?"

"Your mother undressed you when she and Stanhill came over to give me the update on Lila."

So Cole hadn't seen her naked yet. That was good. She relaxed. "Which is?"

"With Sheriff Merrow's assistance, Lila was transported to the nearest ACW headquarters in Alpharetta. They have samples of the ash and your mother's statement of events. I have to give one, and so do you, when you feel up to it. Then they'll deal with her."

She nodded. "That chapter is pretty much closed, then."

He stood and stretched. "Yes. Thankfully. You'll be happy to know I spoke with Stanhill, and he's going to talk to the Ellinghams about work for me. Maybe a teaching position at Harmswood Academy. He also gave me the number for admissions so I can get Kaley enrolled whenever she's ready."

"She's ready now, isn't she? How'd Kaley take it?"

"Yes. She was thrilled. Getting to go to school with witches and whatever other supernaturals go there? She practically danced around the room."

"No, I meant about what happened with Lila. You did tell her, didn't you?"

"I did." He moved to sit on the edge of the bed. "It was a big reality check for her. She doesn't want to see Lila anymore."

"She said that?" Poor kid.

He nodded. "She's over her dream of Lila ever being a real mother." He smiled, thinking of some of the other things Kaley had said. He took Pandora's hand. "Kaley wants you to take her dress shopping for the winter formal."

Pandora let out a happy sigh. "She does? That's so cool. I would love to. I love that kid."

"She'll be happy to hear that. She loves you too." He brought her hand to his mouth and kissed it. "I'm so glad you're okay. If anything had happened to you today..." He closed his eyes for a moment.

"You saved my life. Thank you. I'm so glad you're such a smart man. It's very sexy, you know, all those brains."

He grinned as he let her hand go to take something out of his shirt pocket. He held out a wrapped box. "I was going to give this to you at lunch."

Smiling, she took the gift. It was too big to be a ring, *not* that she was expecting one at this stage in their relationship. She unwrapped the box and saw the store name on it. "You went to Illusions?"

He nodded. "I met Willa. She helped me pick this out."

"Isn't she great? She's fae. Did you see her pointed ears?"

"No, I did not. But then, I wasn't really focused on her."

Pandora couldn't wait to tell Willa everything that had happened. She took the lid off the box and let out a soft gasp. Inside lay a gorgeously decorated silver key. A key. How perfect. "Oh, I love it, Cole. It's so pretty."

"Very fitting, right? Since it's a key and you're a realtor and we're working on the house together." He gently cleared his throat. "Plus, it's the, you know, key to my heart."

She laughed. "Took a lot for you to get that out, didn't it? I know sappy's not your style. You're practical and you like a plan."

"What I like is you. I *love* you." He stared at his hands for a moment, then lifted his head. Determination shone in his eyes. "There was something else Kaley wanted me to ask you."

She lifted the pendant free and fastened the chain around her neck. "What's that?"

"She wanted me to ask you to marry me."

Pandora's mouth opened, but she didn't say anything. She hadn't anticipated *that*.

"I told her I would." He took Pandora's hand again. "When the time is right."

She still couldn't bring herself to say a word.

"I know we have a lot of getting to know each other to do, but I thought you should know what my plan is. In case you wanted out before things got serious." He looked at her with clear expectations of an answer.

She shook her head. "I don't want out." Ever. She was so in love with this man her insides felt like they were doing their own kind of magic. She needed him in a way she'd never experienced before. "Brace yourself, because here comes some sap. You make me whole. I know part of that is because you're a familiar and I'm a broken witch, but whatever, it's what I feel. I cannot imagine being without you."

"I feel the same way. I never thought I'd find a woman I'd consider spending the rest of my life with after everything that happened with Lila. Now I can't picture a future where we're not together."

Her heart felt about to burst. "I can already tell you what my answer will be."

He smiled back. "When I ask, it's not going to be in the middle of the night with you recovering from battling my ex. It's going to be special. It's going to be something memorable and amazing."

She nodded. "I like the sound of that, but I have to tell you that in light of everything that happened today and the fact that I could have lost you forever, I'm done waiting. It's time."

"Time for what? Are you saying you want me to ask right now?"

"No." She tugged him closer with the kind of wild urgency coursing through her. "I'm saying it's time to see just how *bonded* we can get."

"Oh." His eyes widened. "*Oh*."

"Uh huh." She snapped her fingers, and the lights went out.

24

Habit woke Cole before dawn. Pandora lay beside him, fast asleep, her back to him, her hand curled in front of her mouth like she'd just heard something shocking. He leaned down and kissed the silky, freckled curve of her shoulder and inhaled her warm perfume.

She smelled of fabric softener from the sheets, her floral perfume and *him*. He smiled as some sort of deep-seated possessiveness overtook him. His woman. His witch.

And someday, his *wife*.

The thought broadened his smile. He was ridiculously in love and didn't care who knew it. Whether or not they had bonded last night, he wasn't sure. But they'd definitely given it the old college try. How Pandora had had the energy to *bond* after everything she'd been through yesterday, he had no idea.

He slipped quietly out of bed, threw on his clothes and shut her door, then went into the kitchen.

Pumpkin was already there and looked on the verge of a serious bout of meowing. He gave her a scratch on the head to pre-empt it. "I'm going to feed you first, how about that?"

He found her food, filled a bowl and set it in front of her before the crying begin. Pumpkin buried her face in it, happy and occupied.

Cole turned his attention to coffee next. Kaley didn't need to be up just yet, but he'd have to take her home soon so she could get ready for school. He'd make her breakfast there, too. There was no way to do that quietly, and he wanted Pandora to rest.

While the coffee was brewing, he took the pad of paper by the phone and a pen and wrote Pandora a note. He didn't want her thinking he'd just abandoned her. He scribbled everything he needed to say, folded it in half and went back to her bedroom.

She hadn't moved, which just reinforced his thinking that she needed to rest and recover. He put the note on her nightstand under her phone, then went back to the kitchen.

Kaley trudged in as he was pouring himself a cup of coffee. She blinked at him, her eyes still thick with sleep.

"You don't look awake," he said softly.

"M'not." She stretched. "Miss Williams still sleeping?"

"Yes, and we need to be quiet so she can stay that way. When you feel up to it, gather your stuff and we'll go back to our house. You can leave on the pajamas you borrowed from Miss Williams. We'll shower and eat at home. Okay?"

She nodded, yawned, and shambled back toward the guest room.

He wasn't sure anything he'd said had registered through the haze of sleep, but a few minutes later she was back, flip-flops on, backpack in hand. She crouched down to pet Pumpkin. "Morning, kitty."

"You ready?"

Kaley looked up at him and nodded. "Is Miss Williams going to be okay?"

"Yes. She just needs to rest. I'm going to come back and check on her this afternoon."

Kaley stood and hugged her backpack to her chest. She looked younger than her thirteen years, and a wave of nostalgia swept through Cole. He wrapped her in his arms and kissed the top of her head. "I love you, Kaley-did."

"Love you too, Daddy."

By the time he'd dropped her off at school, he had a pretty solid list of what he hoped to accomplish that day. Corette had texted him to say she'd swung by Pandora's and she was still sleeping, so he figured he could finally finish the last of the clean-out downstairs before he went back to check on Pandora himself. The more uninterrupted sleep she got, the better.

As he pulled into his driveway, his phone rang. He checked the number, thinking it was Pandora, but it wasn't one he recognized. The area code was Georgia, though. "Hello?"

"Cole? This is Stanhill. Sorry for the early call, but you didn't strike me as a man who sleeps in."

"No, I'm definitely not that. What can I do for you?" Cole hadn't expected to hear from the man so soon, but it was encouraging.

"Actually, it's what I can do for you. I mentioned to Hugh about your teaching qualifications, and he and his brother Sebastian would like to meet with you. Are you available today?"

"Sure." Wow, that was fast. "What time?"

"An hour from now. I'll text you the address. Will that be enough time?"

"Absolutely."

"Very good. Sending the address now."

"Thank you."

Stanhill chuckled. "You don't have the job yet, son. And if you want to thank anyone, thank Corette. There's no denying a Williams woman when she wants something."

"I've noticed."

"I'm sure you have. As much as Pandora wants you here, so does Corette. Right here where you can make her daughter happy. And possibly provide her with grandchildren."

"I'll make a note of that. And I'll be sure to let her know how much I appreciate her strong-arming you into getting me this interview."

"Now you've got it." Stanhill laughed as he signed off.

Cole checked the text with the address. He brought up his GPS to check the driving time. Twenty minutes. More than enough time to shower and get on the road.

His drive took him to an enormous iron and stone gate. Worked into the iron over the entrance were the words Harmswood Academy. The school for supernaturals. The place his daughter could be attending very soon.

What would it be like to teach here? If things went well, he'd soon know. He stopped before the gate and a guard came out of the security building.

Cole rolled his window down.

"Can I help you, sir?" the man asked.

"Cole Van Zant. I have an appointment."

The man checked a list on a tablet, then nodded and tapped the screen. The gate began to swing open. He nodded at Cole. "Have a good day."

"You too." Cole drove through.

The campus was amazing. Set in the hills, the woods alongside the drive eventually gave way to several large stone buildings and a few smaller ones. Most were three stories. The main building was four. This was the most impressive private school he'd ever seen.

He followed the signs for visitors, parked in the lot and walked in with a manila envelope containing his resume tucked under one arm. The place was swathed in dark wood and tapestries. Marble tiles provided flooring while shelves of books and framed maps lined the walls. In the center of the space sat an ornate globe about the size of a compact car. Very Old World. Very old money.

The reception area was just beyond the foyer. A woman with pointed ears greeted him. "Good morning. Welcome to Harmswood. How may I help you?"

"I'm Cole Van Zant. I have an appointment with Hugh and Sebastian Ellingham."

"Of course." She stood. "Right this way."

She led him down a broad hall. Oil portraits of the board members decorated one side. Many of them were decidedly not human. He tried not to stare. The receptionist turned into a small alcove with two doors. She knocked on the right one.

A voice called out, "Enter."

She opened the door. "Mr. Ellingham, Mr.

The Professor Woos The Witch

Ellingham. Mr. Van Zant is here." Both of the Ellinghams stood. She stepped out of the way to let Cole into the large conference room, then closed the door.

And left him alone in a room with two vampires.

It was impossible not to feel some level of discomfort.

One of the men stuck his hand out and smiled. "Hugh Ellingham." He gestured to the other man. "This is my brother Sebastian. Good of you to join us on such short notice."

"Thanks." Cole shook the man's hand. It wasn't cold like he'd imagined. "I appreciate the opportunity."

"You don't even know what it is yet," Sebastian said as he sat behind the table.

Hugh took the chair at the head of the table, so Cole took the one across from Sebastian. "True," Cole said. "But whatever it is, I still appreciate the opportunity and your time." That might have been a little bit of a suck-up, but it was true.

And they were vampires. Best to stay on their good sides.

Hugh clasped his hands and rested them on the table while Sebastian continued to stare at Cole like he was trying to map the veins in his body. Not the most calming of thoughts. Hugh cleared his throat. "We've checked up on you. Your resume is impressive, and your colleagues speak highly of you."

"You spoke to my colleagues?" He hadn't yet told the college he wasn't planning to return.

Hugh held up a hand. "Discreetly, I promise."

That was something. Cole laid his envelope on the table. "I assumed this was about a possible teaching position, so I brought my resume."

"It is about a teaching position. And we'd be happy to add the resume to your file, but you graduated with honors from M.I.T. a semester ahead of your fellow students. I don't know what other recommendation we'd need."

That information was available in his online bio. Not the part about being a semester ahead, though. "You did your homework."

Sebastian nodded. "We're very thorough."

"Are you looking for a math teacher, then?"

"We are," Hugh answered. "Specifically for Advanced Placement classes. Algebra and calculus. As the school is expanding, we're trying to broaden our curriculum. And as you can imagine, it's not always easy to find qualified teachers who are also supernaturals. We need teachers who are both skilled in their professions and sympathetic to the particular needs of our students."

Hugh paused. "I should mention, you'll need to meet with the board of trustees and the dean as well, but it's merely a formality. They're all in agreement that you'd be an excellent addition to the school's faculty."

"Thank you. I appreciate that."

Sebastian glanced at his brother. "And seeing as how we control the school's finances, they also weren't inclined to be anything but in agreement."

Cole thought for a moment before he spoke. "You understand that I'm fairly new to being a supernatural, let alone knowing that supernaturals exist. I hope that's not going to be a problem."

Hugh smiled. "We know. And from what we've been told, you've adapted extraordinarily well. It's not an area of concern for us. As long as it's not an area of concern for you."

"No," Cole said. "It's not. But I am still learning."

"That's a healthy place to be in," Hugh said. "I understand you're interested in enrolling your daughter here."

"I am. What is the tuition? I'm afraid I don't know much about the school."

"That's all right. We keep a low profile outside of the supernatural community. Tuition for students requiring room and board is twenty thousand a school year. For students not requiring room and board, it's ten thousand. However, for the children of our faculty, all fees are waived."

"That's a nice perk."

"We believe in taking care of those who take

care of our students. And I assure you, we're an excellent school. We run all grades from kindergarten through twelfth, and our students have been accepted into every college you can think of. I believe you'll find our offer very competitive." Hugh looked at his brother.

Sebastian opened a leather portfolio and took out a sheet of paper and slid it across the table to Cole. "It's a fairly standard deal."

Cole picked it up and read it. The highlights were paid vacations, holidays *and* summers, full insurance including dental, and a non-disclosure agreement, which, considering the nature of those working at and attending the school, seemed fair. The only thing that gave him pause was the figure at the bottom. It was thirty-five percent more than his college salary.

He looked up at the brothers, then turned the sheet around and pointed to the sum. "This number here. This is the salary?"

Hugh glared at Sebastian. "I told you that was too low." He shifted his gaze to Cole. "We're prepared to offer another ten thousand a year, as well as—Sebastian, the other agreement?"

Sebastian made a growly sigh, took a second sheet of paper from the portfolio and added it to the table. "If you sign a five-year contract, there's a seventy-five-thousand-dollar signing bonus."

Cole stared at the contract, unable to react. The

amount of money they were offering him was life-changing for him and Kaley. In so many ways.

He thought about what it would mean for him and Pandora. With a calmness that surprised him, he picked up the five-year contract and skimmed it. There was a lot Cole didn't know about this school, but what he did know was he was being offered the opportunity of a lifetime.

After a moment, Hugh said, "I can arrange for a complete tour of the school tomorrow as well as arrange the meeting with the dean and the board of trustees and some of the teaching staff so that you can have a more complete idea of who'd you'd be working with and what the school is like. I understand this is a big decision. Do you have any questions I could answer now?"

Cole put the contract down. "Just one. Do you have a pen?"

Pandora stepped out of a hot shower feeling almost a hundred percent better. She could probably sleep more, but she didn't really want to. What she wanted was to catch up with her mother and Cole and see what had transpired since she'd passed out.

Well, she remembered *one* thing. Last night.

With Cole. She grinned as she dressed. That wasn't something she'd ever forget.

Her phone rang. She grabbed it, checked the caller ID and smiled harder. "Hello, *lover*."

Cole laughed. "I guess I didn't wake you."

"Nope. Just got out of the shower."

"How are you feeling?"

"Pretty good. A little tired still, but better. And starving actually."

"Perfect. I happen to have two of Mummy's cheesesteaks with fries in my truck right now. Should I bring them over?"

A whiff of grilled meat and spices filled her senses. Was this what being bonded did? Her mouth watered. "You got hot peppers on them, didn't you?"

"Is there another way to eat cheesesteaks? Still, good guess."

"It wasn't a guess. I could smell them. I think that means we're bonded."

"Wow. Really? That's…amazing."

"I know, right?" Her stomach growled. "Did you get gravy for the fries?"

"Does two plus two equal four?"

"Yes, it does! Bring them over right now. How did you know?" She gasped. "Did you sense my hunger because we're bonded? Do you think us being bonded means that you can now anticipate all my needs? If so, I approve."

He laughed. "I just thought you'd be hungry. I'll be there in five minutes. And I'll be happy to attend to whatever *other* needs you might have."

"Feed me first then we'll talk."

Ten minutes later, they were elbow-deep in greasy, delicious cheesesteaks and fries smothered in gravy. Cole smiled at her and pointed at a spot on his face. "You have a little something right here."

She wiped a napkin over her mouth. "Better?"

He nodded, then eyed her plate. "You weren't fooling about being hungry."

"I went full Pumpkin on that cheesesteak, didn't I? I was starving."

"You did miss dinner last night. And breakfast this morning." He ate a fry. "You should go to bed early tonight."

She leaned back in her chair and twirled a fry between her fingers. "Is that a come-on?"

He laughed. "As much as I would like it be, no. You need your rest. And Kaley and I probably need to talk a little more about everything that happened. It's going to take her a while to get past what Lila did."

Pandora nodded. "With you for a dad, she's going to be fine."

"I'm sure that's true. But we still need to talk about it." He cleared his throat. "Speaking of talking about things, I have good news and I have bad news."

She put the fry down. This wasn't good. Well, the good news was, but what if the bad news was worse? She nodded, her mood completely shifted. "Bad news first." That was the way to do it. Get that out of the way.

"Okay." His face went solemn. "I'm not giving you the listing on the house."

"You're not?" She thought about it, then nodded. He needed the money. She got that. She took a breath. "All right. I can accept that. So what's the good news?"

An enormous smile erupted across his face. "The reason I'm not giving you the listing. I'm not selling the house. Because Kaley and I need a place to live."

She squinted at him, not fully understanding. "I can find you a more affordable place. And a family who won't care about Gertrude in the attic."

He shook his head. "I don't want a cheaper place. I want that place. Gertrude and all." He reached out and took her hands. "I want a place where our kids can grow up. If we have kids. A place that means something to both of us. The history of us includes that house. I don't want another family living there. Especially since I'm going to be here a long, long time."

"You are?" The lightness of her mood started to return. "For sure?"

He leaned over and kissed her. "For sure. I

The Professor Woos The Witch

signed a five-year contract this morning to teach at Harmswood Academy."

Her mouth dropped open. "You're kidding me."

"Nope."

She got up to sit on his lap and throw her arms around him. "That's amazing. I'm so happy. Thank you." She kissed his face, then his mouth.

After a long moment, she pulled back. "I love you."

"I love you too. I'm just sorry I couldn't make your dream come true."

She frowned at him. "What are you talking about?"

"There's no white picket fence around Pilcher Manor."

She grinned. "Wrought iron is just fine."

"Good." He stood, picking her up in his arms as he did. "And now, you should probably be resting. We still have to remodel that house, you know."

"I can't rest. I'm too excited!" She wrapped her arms around his neck. Her life had suddenly gotten amazing.

"Oh, my apologies. Did I say you should be resting?" His eyes darkened with a wicked glint. "I meant *bonding*."

The End

Want to be up to date on all books & release dates by Kristen Painter? Sign-up for my newsletter on my website, www.kristenpainter.com. No spam, just news (sales, freebies, and releases.)

If you loved the book and want to help the series grow, tell a friend about the book and take time to leave a review!

Other Books by Kristen Painter

URBAN FANTASY

The House of Comarré series:
Forbidden Blood
Blood Rights
Flesh and Blood
Bad Blood
Out For Blood
Last Blood

Crescent City series:
House of the Rising Sun
City of Eternal Night
Garden of Dreams and Desires

PARANORMAL ROMANCE

Nocturne Falls series
The Vampire's Mail Order Bride
The Werewolf Meets His Match
The Gargoyle Gets His Girl
The Professor Woos The Witch
The Witch's Halloween Hero – short story
The Werewolf's Christmas Wish – short story
The Vampire's Fake Fiancée

Sin City Collectors series
Queen of Hearts
Dead Man's Hand
Double or Nothing

STAND-ALONE BOOKS

Dark Kiss of the Reaper
Heart of Fire
All Fired Up

Nothing is completed without an amazing team.

Many thanks to:

Cover design: Janet Holmes
Interior formatting: Author E.M.S
Editor: Joyce Lamb
Copyedits/proofs: Marlene Engel

About the Author

Kristen Painter likes to balance her obsessions with shoes and cats by making the lives of her characters miserable and surprising her readers with interesting twists. She currently writes paranormal romance and award-winning urban fantasy. The former college English teacher can often be found all over social media where she loves to interact with readers. Visit her web site to learn more.

www.kristenpainter.com

Printed in Poland
by Amazon Fulfillment
Poland Sp. z o.o., Wrocław